Time was

Melinda pulled Chad from the submerged vehicle and swam upward. She gasped for air as her head splashed above the lake's surface, then saw that Chad was floating facedown next to her.

How long had they been trapped in the car? One minute, two minutes? Melinda couldn't be sure—every second had seemed endless. She wondered if the gunmen who had forced the car off the road were watching them now.

Grasping Chad by the shoulder, she swam ashore and dragged him onto the beach until he was lying flat on his back, his arms above his head. Was he breathing?

Don't die, she pleaded silently. *Please don't die!*

Melinda began pressing the heels of her hands against Chad's chest, just under his rib cage. *Good air in, bad air out,* she repeated to herself.

It didn't seem to be working. . . .

Dear Reader,

Do you want something more in your romance books?

Then welcome to the world of HARLEQUIN INTRIGUE!

You have chosen a story that interweaves the dynamics of a contemporary sophisticated romance with the surprising twists and turns of a puzzler. Mystery and suspense are the elements that provide "something more." We like to call it a *challenge*. And the romance you will find in a HARLEQUIN INTRIGUE is what has made Harlequin a household name—both nationally and internationally—for almost forty years.

We promise to bring you two exciting INTRIGUE novels every month and to uphold our standards of the highest quality. Our wish is that you will have many hours of pleasurable reading. We look forward to your comments with great interest.

Reva Kindser and Marmie Charndoff,
Editors

RANSOM IN JADE

FRAN EARLEY

Harlequin Books

TORONTO • NEW YORK • LONDON
AMSTERDAM • PARIS • SYDNEY • HAMBURG
STOCKHOLM • ATHENS • TOKYO • MILAN

Harlequin Intrigue edition published July 1987

ISBN 0-373-22069-3

Chapter One

"¡*Cuidado!* Be Careful!" the boat boy shouted, brusquely waving aside Melinda Harding's offer to help him wrestle the twin-hulled sailboat down the embankment and onto the wind-rippled blue waters of the lake. "I do it myself, señorita. This is tricky business—very tricky indeed." He planted a scrawny shoulder against the left hull and, huffing and puffing and muttering curses under his breath, shoved until his tanned cheeks darkened in frustration and strain.

It was no use. The catamaran was of a mind to remain ashore this cool October morning.

The boy straightened up and gave the boat a baleful stare, silently but nonetheless eloquently consigning it to eternal damnation for embarrassing him in front of his customer.

Melinda stepped back from the catamaran and crammed her hands into the midriff pockets of her hooded gray sweatshirt as if to signal that she had no intention of intruding upon his responsibilities. "I think it's stuck on a rock," she ventured, speaking softly in colloquial Spanish. Her pale green eyes sparkled in gentle amusement, and her soft, full lips quivered in a benign smile. *Don't laugh,* she told herself. *He's trying very hard and the last thing you want to do is hurt his feelings.*

"Impossible," the boat boy snorted. "It is just stubborn, like my cousin's mule."

Moving forward to the bow of the starboard hull, half hidden from the lad's view, Melinda kicked aside an imaginary stone. "There," she called out, tossing her head to dislodge the long, silken tangle of reddish-brown hair that had blown across her eyes. "Why don't you try it now?"

Again, the boy bent his back to the port stern, squinting in fearsome concentration as he struggled mightily to move the sixteen-foot fiberglass sailboat.

Seeing her chance, Melinda leaned down and put her own shoulder to the stern on her side. She shoved as hard as she could, the supple muscles of her trim legs flexing below the frayed hems of her cutoff jeans. The catamaran slid forward, a few inches, a foot, two feet.

Together, Melinda and her young assistant gave a final push and the boat glided out onto the water, sending a cold chop sloshing against the grimy khaki pant legs bunched up around the boy's knees. Stoically ignoring the chill, he watched Melinda splash through the water, scramble aboard the catamaran and tug at the halyard to raise the red, yellow and orange striped mainsail. "I told you I do it myself, señorita," he announced proudly.

"I never had the slightest doubt," Melinda said, securing the halyard to a cleat at the base of the aluminum mast. Nimbly sliding back across the canvas trampoline stretched between the hulls, she positioned herself at the tiller and hoisted the jib.

"*Tenga mucho cuidado,*" the boy cautioned her.

"Don't worry, I'll be careful—I promise!"

The wrinkled expression on the lad's face mirrored his doubt. He was perhaps twelve years old, thirteen at the most, and already a willing victim of the machismo that shaped the lives of so many Latin American males. Melinda knew exactly what he was thinking: sailing a boat, even a toy such as this, was man's work, not a thing to be undertaken by a woman, especially not by a slip of a woman wearing nothing but a baggy sweatshirt, skimpy cutoffs and flimsy thongs.

Melinda settled back on the trampoline. *I have news for you, child. I was sailing bigger boats than this on Long Island Sound long before you were born.*

Lowering the stabilizing daggerboards and hinged rudders into the water, she swept the tiller back and forth to nudge the catamaran into the onshore breeze. As mainsail and jib began to fill, she tugged at the rope securing the boom until she could feel the starboard hull lift clear of the water. Kicking off her thongs and locking her feet under one of the web straps that ran the length of the deck, Melinda leaned backward out over the water on the high side to counterbalance the force of the wind.

For the first time in years, she felt wholly at peace. And why not, she reflected. After only nine years in the United States Foreign Service she was well on her way up the ladder. She'd paid her dues—two tours of duty in little backwater consulates in Argentina, then three years in the teeming concrete jungles of São Paulo, Brazil. Now back to Washington and bigger and better things, maybe even someday an ambassadorship.

Someday...

First, though, a stopover here in the Guatemalan Highlands for a much-needed vacation. At least that's what she'd told the personnel people. But it was more than that. It was a visit she *had* to make, a thing she *had* to do, to clear her conscience after all these years.

Glancing up at the bits of dark blue yarn that fluttered from the mast stays to indicate wind direction, Melinda eased off on the sheet. The starboard hull slapped back down onto the surface of the lake and the craft began to slow.

No daredevil racing today. It had been years since she'd done any serious sailing and she was out of practice. Besides, it was much too pleasant sprawled on the trampoline looking up at the fleecy clouds drifting across the blue sky, thinking of everything and nothing, just relaxing.

In the parallel lines of her wake, the clean white half circle of the Hotel Del Lago grew smaller and smaller. She could still make out the royal-blue balcony of her fourth-floor room, but just barely. A hundred yards or so south of the hotel, she could see a battered old launch set out from one of the public docks for its regular morning run across the lake to the Indian village of Santiago Atitlán.

It was late in the season in this part of the world, and less than a third of the one hundred rooms in the lakefront hotel were occupied. Even during the height of the summer, tourist traffic was seldom heavy. Long years of domestic upheaval and guerrilla warfare, now mercifully grinding to an end, had left their mark on the land.

The catamaran, which had been drifting aimlessly in the warming sun of midmorning, began to heel sharply as the breeze picked up, puffing out the sails. Grabbing at one of the trampoline straps to steady herself, Melinda reached out and loosened the sheet, causing the sail to luff as the unsecured aluminum boom swung loosely in weathervane fashion.

Let's just park here for a while in the middle of the lake and soak up some sun, she decided. *I can't even start to do what I have to do for a few days.*

She looked around. The nearest boat was the launch and it was a quarter mile away, its track taking it well clear of her.

Why not?

Lying flat on the trampoline, Melinda wriggled out of her sweatshirt, then quickly turned over on the canvas and unhooked her bra. Using the balled-up sweatshirt as a cushion, she closed her eyes to enjoy the caress of the autumn sun on her bare back.

Just like Cannes, she thought, another smile forming on her pink-glossed lips.

Cannes. The summer she graduated from Sarah Lawrence College, she'd spent ten days in Cannes with Tony Germaine. And ten days had been quite enough to convince her she'd been right her junior year at Sarah Lawrence: Tony wasn't the man for her.

Looking back, it all seemed so childish...wearing Tony's class ring on a gold chain around her neck; making love under a blanket on a moonlit beach; and afterward strolling hand in hand along the shore, pretending they had a future together when they both knew it wasn't meant to be.

Tony was gone now, lost in a scuba-diving accident in the Caribbean. Poor Tony. Such a sweet man: sweet and teddy-bear lovable, but also immature and utterly undependable. For all his money, he had been an anachronism, a naive playboy in a demanding world that no longer tolerated playboys. Definitely *not* the man for her.

But, then, was there such a man? Interesting question. Interesting and probably unanswerable. Meanwhile...

It was going to be nice to live in the States again. She'd made friends in South America, but now she was looking forward to renewing old acquaintances. Her college roommates, for example. She'd kept in touch with Stefanie Travers over the years, and through Stefanie had kept up on the career of Ellen Stuart.

Ellen. Timid, baby-faced Ellen whom everyone said would turn out to be the perfect wife, mother and homebody. Twice divorced, she was now vice-president of a Fortune 500 company in Chicago, with a reputation as a very shrewd, hard-as-nails businesswoman.

You just couldn't tell about people, could you?

And Stefanie. They'd shared apartments for three years, but Melinda never really had known *what* to make of her friend. Stefanie's story was pure soap opera. *She* liked playboys, so she'd married Tony and the wedding had been the most dazzling social event of the season in New York. Then things turned sour. Stefanie's stockbroker father went bankrupt in a scandal that rocked Wall Street, and he committed suicide. Tony's New York ad agency fell on hard times, and two years later he lost his life skin-diving off the coast of Belize. Stefanie had had to pick up the pieces and start anew. And she'd apparently done quite well for herself, too, as an art dealer and importer.

She had even written to ask Melinda to leave government service and come to work for her. "There's a lot of interest in Latin American art," she had pointed out. "You have contacts there and I have contacts here. We could make a *fortune*, Lindy."

"I'll think about it," Melinda had written back.

She hadn't, though. Never seriously.

Half asleep, Melinda squirmed about to find a more comfortable position on the trampoline. As she moved, two things happened. The coiled end of the mainsheet—the line controlling movement of the boom—snagged in the lacing at the edge of the trampoline. At that moment, with the boom locked in position, a gust of wind came up and the catamaran heeled, its starboard hull rising up off the water a full three feet.

Startled, Melinda pushed herself up from the trampoline, bumping the tiller and causing the boat to jibe at a right angle to the wind. The boom whipped out and thudded against her shoulders, near the base of her neck, throwing her off balance.

She grabbed at the aluminum spar for support. Her weight, coupled with the force of the gust and the locked position of the boom, was enough to send the boat flipping over onto one side.

She heard a sharp cracking noise, and the next thing she knew she was in the water, thrashing about under a sopping wet blanket of red, yellow and orange Dacron that seemed to be doing its best to drag her deeper down into the water.

Momentarily disoriented, she tried to move her legs to swim out from under the sail. She couldn't move.

I'm paralyzed, she thought as icy fingers of fear clutched at her.

MAYBE SHE'S ONE OF THEM, Chad Young mused as he leaned in across the open-sided deckhouse of the launch and trained his binoculars on the woman stretched out on the catamaran, which lay dead in the water a hundred yards astern. Planting his elbows on the roof of the deckhouse to steady himself, he adjusted the knurled focusing ring of the glasses.

Maybe, maybe not.

Chad studied the woman, his gaze taking in everything from the lustrous tumble of auburn hair that fluttered lightly on the breeze to the well-turned ankles tucked securely under the canvas strap that ran the length of the deck. But mostly it lingered on the tanned bare back and the sensuous curve of the hips pressed against the faded blue fabric of her cutoff jeans.

He grinned. The lady obviously didn't have anything to hide. Not in *that* outfit. Nice. Very nice.

He lowered the glasses and let them dangle from the leather strap around his neck. Taking a small notebook from the pocket of his faded blue chambray shirt, he flipped through it.

What was her name? Hammond? Hardy? No, it was Harding—Melinda Harding. He'd seen her check in the night before, several hours after the others had arrived on a Turismo bus from Guatemala City. She'd driven up in a rented Nissan, and she'd had only a couple of pieces of luggage. As far as he knew, she'd made no effort to contact any of the others. But he couldn't be sure.

Again, Chad raised the binoculars. She was a fairly small woman. He guessed she was about five four, maybe five five, and no more than one hundred and twenty well-distributed pounds. And pretty—very pretty, with wide-set, sparkling eyes and a turned-up nose and clear, soft skin that exuded a crisp coolness.

So what, Chad thought, the index finger of his right hand straying from the binoculars to stroke the tiny curved scar that blended into the sandy hairs of his right eyebrow. The small ones could be just as deadly as their burly, muscle-bound pals. Ever since that night a year before in Veracruz when a sweet young thing had pulled a flick knife from her handbag and had come within an ace of blinding him, he could attest to *that*.

He stared at the image in his binoculars. Small or not, this Melinda Harding kept herself in shape. She was pretty, yes—but certainly not in a fragile way. She came across as a woman who knew how to handle herself.

Chad grunted at the thought. So had that dizzy broad in Veracruz, he remembered. But there was a big difference: up close, Veracruz had had a hard look about her, a tightness around the corners of her mouth and a steely glint of meanness in her eyes that should have given fair warning. Not so Melinda Harding. He'd never gotten close to her, but he sensed a warmth and sensitivity he'd seldom encountered in a woman.

Cut it out, he scolded himself. *You've misread that gut instinct of yours too often. You're lucky you're still alive!*

He looked longingly at the smooth bare back, the cute little bottom, the graceful legs that flowed like works of art out from under the frayed legs of her cutoffs. *Could* she be one of them?

Maybe. But, then, what was she doing with a diplomatic passport?

Better find out, damn it! That's what they pay you for, isn't it? You're supposed to lie and cheat and play both ends against the middle and do whatever else you have to do—whether it's sweet-talking the ladies, or buddying up to guys who'd just as soon cut your throat as look at you. Trouble is, after so long you don't want to trust anybody, not if you want to go on living.

Chad decided he'd have to find some way to strike up a conversation with this Melinda Harding. He'd buy her a drink, get her to talk. The direct approach: sometimes it was the only way. He was running out of time. He had to get back to the States in a few days. The big man was losing patience, had told him if he didn't score soon he could damn well haul his carcass home and turn the job over to somebody who'd get results—somebody whose gut instinct served him more efficiently.

Oh, well, he'd *still* buy Melinda Harding a drink. Even if he didn't learn a damn thing, it might be a pleasant experience. He *needed* something pleasant in his life for a change.

He continued to study her, turning slowly and keeping the glasses trained on her as the launch chugged along, putting distance between itself and the catamaran. He guessed that she was about thirty, give or take a year or two. The night before, when he saw her check in at Del Lago, he'd have said thirty-five, but that was because she looked tired and just a bit bedraggled. She must have driven up from Guatemala City right after her plane landed, and these mountain roads were rough on the nerves, especially in the dark.

Now, though, she looked younger. Younger and innocent. Not *too* innocent, though...

Chad reached across the roof of the deckhouse for his rucksack and shoved the binoculars and notebook inside, using a wadded-up blue nylon windbreaker to cushion the glasses from the snub-nosed, blue steel revolver nestled at the bottom of the bag. Easing himself back along the side of the launch, he swung down into the open rear cockpit and deposited his rucksack on the planked seat, alongside a netted bundle of pineapple. He had the cockpit to himself.

The other passengers, a black-frocked German priest, five Indian women and a pair of traveling salesmen wearing shiny, ill-fitting dark suits, were lounging inside the deckhouse, along with two deckhands and the captain.

"¡Señor!"

Chad glanced forward. The captain, a plump young man with a droopy black mustache, was turned about on his perch, poking a stubby forefinger at the dark squall line that had suddenly blotted out the volcanic hills on the horizon.

"You are going to get very, very wet if you stay out there," the skipper said in Spanish, raising his voice to make himself heard above the rumble of the engine.

The other passengers were looking in Chad's direction, smiling toothily and motioning to him to come inside.

"Whatever's right," he said with a shrug, gathering up his rucksack.

As he stepped down into the deckhouse, he looked back at the catamaran, just in time to see the squall line flip it over on its side, hard, as a sheet of wind-driven rain pelted the sails.

"Come about!" he shouted in Spanish, pointing to the capsized sailboat. "And make it fast! That lady's in trouble!"

EVERYTHING WAS a cold, bubbly blur that exploded with a mighty splash, followed by the muffled creaks and groans of the damaged rigging as the sail dragged Melinda below the surface. The Dacron fabric had ripped, and, peering upward through the opening, she could see that the catamaran had gone all the way over in the water and its mast now was pointed straight down toward the bottom of the lake.

Don't panic, she told herself. *You've capsized before. It's no big deal. You know what to do.*

Pushing at the wet sail, she tried to kick free.

Her legs wouldn't budge.

I can't be paralyzed, she thought. *The boom knocked the breath out of me, but that was all.*

She wriggled and tugged, reached down with her hands and yanked at her knees. *Move,* she screamed inwardly as the need for air began squeezing at her lungs.

And then, dimly through the roily water, she saw that her ankles were still locked under the trampoline's hiking strap.

Dummy, she berated herself, feeling foolish as fear gave way to embarrassment. Forcing herself to remain calm, she worked her ankles free of the wet webbing and twisted about in the water to thrust for the surface.

At that moment, something hard and heavy—something *alive*—bumped at her shoulders and she felt a new wave of panic close in upon her.

There's nothing else here, she quickly told herself. *Just me and a stupid little boat that flipped over because I let myself get careless. It happens. Catamarans are always capsizing unless you watch what you're doing.*

Something, or someone, grabbed at her hair and she felt herself being yanked through the water amid a blinding flurry of bubbles. Instinctively, she opened her mouth to cry out and at once began swallowing water, choking, flailing her arms in an attempt to break free of whatever it was that had seized her.

One of her hands brushed a rough, swiftly moving surface, and fear of the unknown sent a shock wave coursing through her. She'd heard about the freshwater bull sharks in some of the larger Central American lakes, but here? Surely not here.

She groped out again with both hands, trying to break the invisible grip on her long, auburn hair. Just as her fingers closed around a thick, powerful wrist, her head bobbed up above the rain-pelted surface of the lake. Blinking, coughing, gasping for air, she pulled free and twisted around to find herself staring into the bluest, most piercing eyes she'd ever seen. They were cobalt eyes that seemed to burn right through her...eyes wholly out of place in a face that was clean-cut and smilingly innocent. The eyes, she thought, were almost the eyes of a devil...almost, not quite. They were eyes that saw everything, were quick to assess and equally quick to challenge...eyes that in a lifetime not all that much longer than hers had perhaps seen too much.

"The Olympic tryouts are over for today," her rescuer said with an easy chuckle, gently brushing the hair from her cheeks.

"Not very funny," Melinda gasped, shaking her head to clear the fuzziness from her brain.

The eyes didn't change, but the tone of voice did. It became huskily solemn. "Sorry. Are you all right?"

"I...think so," she sputtered as she trod water. "Where'd you come from?"

With a quick movement of his head he indicated the area behind her right shoulder. Fifty feet on the other side of the capsized catamaran, barely visible in the downpour, the launch from Panajachel was standing to, its engine idling, passengers and crew watching anxiously.

"The Good Ship Lollipop over there. We saw you flip and we figured you might need help." There was a flicker of uncertainty in his eyes. "You *are* all right? No broken bones, no concussion?"

"I said I'm fine." Melinda turned on her back and kicked her feet to swim out away from the overturned boat. As she looked down along the length of her slender body, she realized she'd lost her bra in her struggle to free herself. Her cheeks turned pink, she stopped swimming and resumed treading water, her arms folded clumsily across her chest just under the surface.

"Have you got a cramp?" he asked, swimming in close with a single kick of his legs, ready to reach out for her.

"No cramp—problems," Melinda said quickly, avoiding his eyes. "I'd appreciate it if you'd look around and see if you can find a gray sweatshirt."

He glanced at her quizzically, cocking his right eyebrow. It was then that she noticed the scar . . . a tiny, curving white scar that was shaped almost like a question mark.

He *had* seen too many things, she thought.

There was a twinkle of sudden recognition in those blue eyes and he quickly dipped down beneath the surface.

This is ludicrous, Melinda thought. If only he'd go away and leave me alone. I'm perfectly capable of turning the boat upright and sailing back to Panajachel. But as long as he's here, I can't do much of anything.

There was a splash of water behind her and she turned to see him floating there, his lips curled in a grin of amusement.

"I'm afraid your sweatshirt has gone to a watery grave."

"I don't find that very amusing, Mr. . . . ."

"Young. Chad Young." He reached out to shake hands, but Melinda primly kept her arms folded across her chest.

"Mr. Young, if you'll be good enough to help me turn the boat over, I'll get back to Panajachel on my own."

"It can be a bit difficult sailing while you're using both arms to cover up."

Again, Melinda felt herself blush.

Noticing her discomfiture, Chad shrugged and began squirming about in the water. She couldn't see what he was doing, but a minute later he was thrusting a soggy ball of blue chambray at her. "Allow me, Miss Harding. I'll make do with a T-shirt."

Melinda blinked at him, her eyes narrowing in suspicion as she accepted the shirt. "How'd you know my name?"

"I asked the desk clerk at Del Lago. I told him the lady in Room 311 looked like someone I'd very much like to know. He was very helpful. These *Ladinos* are dyed-in-the-wool romantics."

Melinda wasn't at all sure she liked the idea of someone snooping around for information about her. He seemed to sense her displeasure, and he promptly moved to make amends.

"I'm a travel agent, and I'm working with some people down here putting together package tours. You're one of a handful of Americans I've seen at the hotel, so I was planning to invite you to have a drink with me later today. I wanted to ask you what you like and don't like about the place. You know, product testing."

Melinda hesitated, her frown softening, and then, turning her back to him, she began wriggling into his shirt. "This is awfully embarrassing," she murmured, fumbling with the buttons. "I appreciate you helping me out."

"The least I can do." He ducked beneath the surface of the water, but came up almost immediately. "You missed a button."

Suppressing a smile, Melinda's fingers searched out the empty buttonhole and forced the button through the slit in the wet fabric. "All right?"

Chad took another look, then bobbed back up. "All right. You know something? You look good in a wet shirt."

"I'd better see about the boat," Melinda sighed. She swam toward the nearest of the two hulls and made a quick inspection of it and the sail that lay stretched across the water. Crawling onto the hull, she reached across the bottom of the trampoline, got a firm grip on the second hull and started pulling.

"Let me give you a hand," Chad said, taking up a position alongside her.

With his added weight, the catamaran swung up onto the side of one hull, hesitated a second and then splashed upright, its sail drooping limply around the aluminum boom.

As if responding to a signal, wind and rain slackened and the sky began to clear.

"I don't think you're going anywhere else in this today," Chad said. "Check out the mast."

Melinda looked up at the aluminum spar that towered above them, holding the soggy mainsail aloft. About two-thirds of the way up, the mast was dented sharply and was angled to one side.

Chad shook his head. "The least bit of wind and it'll double over on you. It must have slammed into the water pretty hard."

"Oh, great!" Melinda groaned, remembering the boat boy who'd been so worried when she'd set out alone. "I just can't leave this thing here in the middle of the lake."

"Hang on. I'll have a word with the skipper."

Chad swam to the waiting launch and, clinging to the side of the boat, spoke with the captain. Without taking his eyes off Melinda, the latter removed his straw sombrero and scratched his head as he considered the problem. Finally, his bland face crinkled in a smile of inspiration and, giving his mustache a twirl, he rattled off instructions to Chad.

A minute later Chad was back at Melinda's side.

"The captain suggests we tow you into Santiago. You can phone Panajachel and have them come over with a new mast. No sweat." He winked, and again the question-mark scar made its presence obvious. "You can probably even charge it on your American Express card—provided, that is, that you haven't left home without it."

Ten minutes later, she was sitting on the afterdeck of the launch watching the disabled catamaran scoot along in their wake at the end of a stout line. The squall had moved on and the skies had cleared.

Melinda discreetly studied the man perched upon the stern rail alongside her as they dried themselves in the welcome warmth of the sun. Chad Young was in his mid-thirties, with an unruly mop of sandy hair that was a perfect match for his look of naive innocence. He was good-looking enough in a robust, outdoorsy sort of way, with a square jaw and blunt features chiseled upon a wide, open face. There were tiny wrinkles around the corners of his mouth and eyes, and

Melinda found herself wondering if those wrinkles were the result of laughter or pain, or both. He was not a big man, not by any means; she doubted he was more than four or five inches taller than she, and she was a very medium five four. But the clingingly wet T-shirt he wore revealed the barrel chest and flat stomach and taut, sinewy muscles of a man who could be quite physical when the occasion demanded.

Knotting the tail of the borrowed shirt around her waist, Melinda turned her gaze forward. In the distance, she could see the brush-speckled promontory that jutted out into the lake from the sheltered harbor of Santiago. Above and to the left of the village loomed the volcanoes called Tolimán and Atitlán.

"Is this your first visit to Guatemala, Mr. Young?"

"Yes and no."

She glanced at him. "Yes and no?"

He laughed. "Yes, it's my first visit. And no, don't call me 'Mr. Young.' The name's Chad. After all, once a man gives a woman the shirt off his back, they ought to be on a first-name basis. Don't you agree, Melinda?"

She smiled. "I suppose. Anyway, thanks again for coming to my rescue, Chad. And especially thanks for the shirt. I'll give it back to you in Santiago. I'm sure I can pick up something to wear at one of the stalls in the market...oh, damn!"

"What's the matter?"

"I left my purse at the hotel. I didn't think I'd need any money out on the lake."

"No problem." He hopped down from the stern rail and reached for the rucksack on the deck by Melinda's feet. Unstrapping it, he brought out a billfold and took out two fifty-quetzal notes, equivalent to about forty American dollars. "Here," he said, stuffing the money into her shirt pocket. His knuckles brushed against the curved firmness of one breast, and he withdrew his hand quickly, as if afraid he'd offended her. "Pay me back later."

"Usted es muy amable," she murmured, pushing the notes down into the depths of her pocket where they'd be safe. His touch had been accidental, she knew, but for some reason she found herself strangely disconcerted.

Watching as he put his billfold back into the rucksack, she caught sight of a pistol poking out from under a windbreaker.

Chad quickly strapped shut the bag and dropped it at his feet. "Sorry," he apologized, "you've lost me. I don't speak Spanish all that well."

"I said 'You're very kind.'" She hesitated. "May I ask you something?"

"Ask away."

"Why do you have a gun in that bag?"

The piercing blue eyes looked away from her, and Melinda sensed a guarded alertness. "It's just an antique I picked up the other day in Guatemala City. I should have left it in my room."

She wanted him to be aware she knew he was lying to her. "Snub-nosed Smith & Wesson revolvers are hardly museum pieces. What's more, governments in this part of the world take a dim view of foreign visitors who carry weapons. You could get into serious trouble, Mr. Young."

The innocent look returned. "I thought we were friends!"

"My friends don't pack guns. Are you *really* a travel agent?"

He chuckled. "Actually, I came down here to start a revolution. I'm an agent provocateur—can't you tell?"

"I'm serious, Mr. Young."

"So am I, Miss Harding. I'm just as serious as I can be." He pretended to grab for her. "You know, I think I'll throw you back. I didn't realize I'd be in for a lecture on how not to be an ugly American."

Melinda shifted to avoid his grasp, then realized he was joking. *Maybe, just maybe, he has a logical explanation for the gun,* she conceded to herself. "If you have any sense, you'll think about what I said, Mr.—"

"Chad."

"Chad." She raised up and looked over the top of the deckhouse. They'd entered the harbor and the village of Santiago lay before them, a scattering of whitewashed stucco buildings nestled on a hillside, their tile roofs a flamingo pink against the lush greenery. Several narrow, rickety wooden docks extended out into the harbor from the muddy shoreline, and it was toward one of these docks that the launch was heading.

Chad gathered up his rucksack and slung it over his right shoulder. "I'll walk you to the village and you can buy yourself something to wear. Wait for me, and we'll ride back together."

The launch swung about and one of the deckhands clambered up onto the stern rail, next to where Chad was sitting, and paid out the line attached to the catamaran to keep the towed craft from banging into the larger boat. Leaping up onto the dock, he secured the line to a piling well clear of the launch.

The skipper cut the engine and came out of the deckhouse. Melinda smiled at him and pointed at the catamaran. "Will it be all right there until the hotel can send someone over to fix it?" she asked in English.

The man looked at her blankly, then glanced at Chad for translation.

"Better ask him in Spanish," Chad suggested. "I don't think he speaks English."

Danger signals flashed in Melinda's brain. Out on the lake, she remembered, Chad had swum back to the launch and had engaged the skipper in a rapid-fire conversation. And yet he had told her that he didn't speak Spanish very well. Why had he lied to her?

As she repeated her question in Spanish, she watched Chad out of the corner of her eye. She was sure he knew exactly what she was saying.

"Sí, sí, señorita," the captain assured her, nodding affably and explaining that the people who ran the boat concession were relatives of his. In fact, he suggested, it would be much easier if he simply towed the catamaran back to Panajachel.

"Muchas gracias," said Melinda with a nod of agreement.

Chad stepped up onto the dock, which consisted of two narrow planks laid side by side between the pilings, then reached down and helped her disembark. "Ever been to Santiago before?" he asked as he led her down the dock, toward shore.

"Never."

He pointed up the hillside. "There's a cobblestone street that starts halfway up the slope. You'll find a whole bunch of stalls where they sell native dresses and the like."

At the foot of the dock, he jumped down from the boat and again turned to help her. The barefoot Melinda eyed the muddy shore with distaste.

Laughing aloud, Chad swept her into his arms and carried her away toward the hill and the beginning of the cobblestone street.

"Hey!" she squealed. "Put me down!"

He squeezed her, as a child would squeeze a prized doll, and kept going. "No way, lady. You've just had a bath and I want to make sure you keep those pink toes of yours clean until we can get better acquainted."

"People are staring!"

"They'd be staring even harder if I hadn't loaned you my shirt. So, shut up and enjoy it. I don't do this for everyone."

Chad broke into a trot, and Melinda settled back in his embrace and closed her eyes, feeling like a child again.

He didn't stop until he was well onto the cobblestone street, in front of a stall halfway into the block. The booth was separated from its neighbors by a network of taut ropes from which hung a colorful assortment of handwoven tablecloths, blankets and serapes.

"One size fits all," Chad announced, carefully setting her down on her feet on the swept sidewalk outside the stall. He pointed to an elaborately embroidered, poncho-style long cotton blouse hanging from one of the ropes. "That red *camisa* would look great on you." Chad nodded to the frail Indian woman hurrying out from the back of the stall and pointed first to the red blouse and then to Melinda's bare feet. "Better buy some sandals, too," he said. "I'd hate for you to cut yourself on a piece of broken glass."

Melinda made her purchases, then ducked behind a hanging blanket at the rear of the stall and took off the shirt Chad had loaned her. She pulled the *camisa* over her head and shoulders, then slipped on the leather *huaraches* he'd suggested she buy.

Stepping out from behind the blanket, she saw Chad wave off a man who'd been standing on the corner of the street leading to the plaza. The man, a heavyset Hispanic several years older than Chad, ducked around the corner and out of sight.

"Am I keeping you from something?" Melinda inquired, handing over the still-damp shirt she'd borrowed.

Chad set down his rucksack and put on the shirt, leaving it loose and unbuttoned. The tail was badly wrinkled where Melinda, without thinking, had knotted it around her waist while still on the launch. "Nothing that can't wait," he replied.

"I DO NOT LIKE IT, my friend," Gil Ramirez grumbled, staring moodily at his untouched bottle of Gallo beer. "This Melinda Harding arrives on the scene within hours of the others. Further, my sources say she is an old school chum of one of them. A bit too much coincidence, eh? I do not believe in coincidence.''

Chad slid his chair around to where he could keep an eye on the swinging doors of the tavern. He hoped Melinda wouldn't decide to look inside and see him. He'd already made a couple of slips dealing with her. He had no desire to complicate things.

Leaning back in the chair, he laced his fingers behind his neck and half closed his eyes. ''I'll take care of my end, amigo. You worry about taking care of yours.'' He paused, then asked, ''Any luck on that other matter?''

Ramirez shook his head. He was a big, darkly handsome man, a full head taller than Chad, and even sitting at the table in this dreary little saloon his bearing was erect, almost aristocratic. ''None. I checked out every lead I had on this side of the lake, and I narrowed them down to two. Both proved worthless. Neither man remembered anything unusual the night in question.''

''You suppose a few quetzales might help them remember?''

His companion shrugged. ''Perhaps. Do you want to come along with me and try?''

Chad glanced at his watch. It was almost noon. He'd told Melinda to meet him at noon at the end of the street, and she'd be wondering what had happened to him if he wasn't there.

He leaned forward and started to get up, then changed his mind. He had a better idea. If they missed the noon boat, it would allow more time to do what had to be done.

''You handle it.'' He reached into his rucksack and brought out his billfold. Peeling off several hundred-quetzal notes, he shoved them across the table to Ramirez.

Ramirez frowned, his pride wounded. ''That is not necessary, my friend. I have my own resources.''

''I know it's not necessary, amigo, but my people want results and they're willing to pay. Besides, I fed the boss this cock-and-bull story about having to shell out *mordida* every step of the way. He's going to wonder about me if I come back with too much cash.''

Ramirez's dark brown eyes twinkled. ''Ah, *mordida*— 'the bite.' I am not sure which is worse: bribery as an art form, or the illusion you have of us as greedy, grasping fellows, little better than your gangsters.''

''Correction,'' Chad said, unconsciously fingering the scar above his right eyebrow. ''I have no illusions. I lost them all a long time ago.''

''Pity,'' Ramirez clucked. ''Illusions sometimes make life so much more interesting. Now about your new lady friend: what do you want me to do?''

''DID YOU HOLD UP ANY BANKS this morning?'' Melinda asked as the Range Rover bounced along the up-and-down dirt track that linked a seemingly endless succession of sleepy little lakeside villages named for the Apostles. They'd already put San Pedro behind them and they still had San Juan, San Pablo, San Marcos and heaven only knew where else to go.

''Not a one,'' Chad replied.

''Did you take any potshots at little old ladies or children on tricycles? Maybe at a stray dog or two?''

''I considered it, but none of them got close enough.''

''Hmmm. I'll bet you fought a duel. That was it, wasn't it? A duel. Ten paces, gentlemen, and then turn and . . .''

''Okay!'' he protested. ''I get the point. You don't like guns.''

She glanced at him. ''How'd you ever guess?''

It was almost four o'clock and they'd been riding in the four-wheel-drive Range Rover for two hours, doubling back from time to time as they encountered one washout after another. Chad had really turned on the charm. She had the most gorgeous green eyes. That *camisa* was made for her. Was she staying long in Guatemala? Lovely country, wasn't it? Under other circumstances, it might have been fun. He was thoughtful, intelligent, gentlemanly—a perfect escort. He also was an out-and-out liar. She knew it, and he *knew* she knew it.

"I'll take it back," he said as the Range Rover rattled down the main street of San Pedro.

"Take *what* back?"

"The pistol. It really isn't an antique. The markings on it say it was made in 1982. And it's no good for target practice. Barrel's too short to hit the broad side of a barn."

"Just make sure the barn doesn't shoot back."

"Touché!"

By the time they'd reached the hotel and Chad had paid off the driver, the sun was sinking behind the volcanoes to the west.

"Can I buy you a drink?" he asked cheerfully as they walked into the lobby of Del Lago.

Melinda shook her head. "Thanks anyway. I want to change and then go see about the boat."

"Afterward, maybe?"

"'Fraid not. I need a good night's sleep. I'm bushed."

"Whatever you say, Melinda." Before she realized what he was doing, he leaned over and gave her a peck on the cheek. "If you change your mind, I'll be in the bar."

And then he was gone.

She thought about him as she rode up on the elevator to the fourth floor. What a strange man, such a blend of contradictions. He was both brash and a little bit shy. He was an accomplished actor capable of turning the charm on or off at will. He wanted to be thought of as thick-skinned, but, down deep where it counted, she was sure he was quite sensitive.

Strange. Very strange.

Entering her room, she drew the drapes, then stripped off her clothes and dropped them on the bed. Retrieving her carry-on bag, she opened it to look for fresh undies.

Suddenly, she stopped and slowly and carefully began patting the items packed into the bag.

She turned and got her purse and garment bag, and repeated the operation.

Everything was there, all right. But nothing was the way she'd left it.

She'd lived out of a suitcase for much of her life and she knew how to pack: skirts and blouses and everything else folded in precise order of anticipated need, cosmetics arranged so she could find them quickly, passport and airline ticket tucked away in separate compartments of her black leather travel wallet.

They'd been moved. Everything had been shuffled about. She could tell.

Why would anyone want to search her room, she wondered. And why would they want her to know it?

Chapter Two

Melinda was standing on the balcony, a white terry-cloth robe belted loosely at her waist, when the wake-up call came at six. She hurried in to answer the phone, thanked the desk clerk and then stepped back outside to gaze again at the volcanic peaks that stabbed into the gray haze of the horizon beyond the lake.

The highlands held a special enchantment for her. It wasn't the town. Panajachel was unabashedly touristy, with its curio stalls and summer bungalows, its scruffy little open-air cafés and block-paved streets, its bands of long-haired flower children who'd come south chasing threadbare dreams. No, not the town but the setting: the lofty mountains and forests, the incense-clouded mix of pagan ritual and Christian tradition found even on church steps, the sacrificial altars hidden among the pines where ashes and chicken blood and splashes of cheap rum gave silent testimony that the past lived side by side with the present.

Melinda could almost see the ghosts of Mayan kings who once ruled these mountains, leading their subjects to new, fertile surroundings every few years, building terraced monuments to their gods and leaving behind cleared fields made barren by slash-and-burn farming. She could feel the clanking specters of steel-armored conquistadors who'd come from across the sea with cross and sword to save the

Indians from themselves. For two thousand years, the history of the land had been that of scheming villains and hesitant heroes, but mostly of a stoic common folk who'd survived war and famine, floods, earthquakes, volcanic eruptions and all the other destructive whims of nature, not to mention sickness and salvation—most of all salvation.

The kings and the conquistadors were gone now. There still were a few villains, even fewer heroes, but mostly it was the common folk who tilled the soil and tended the flocks and handed down from one generation to another a legacy of quiet endurance. Almost everywhere else Melinda had traveled, the past was a shadowy backdrop to the present; here, the past reigned supreme.

She lowered her gaze from the horizon to the narrow beach just outside the protective high walls of the hotel. Chad was walking near the water's edge with another man, and they were engaged in animated conversation. The second man, whose dark features were screwed up in an angry scowl, was taller than Chad and he carried himself with a military bearing that hardly fit with the shabby denims he wore. He looked very much like the man whom Melinda had seen Chad wave to the day before. All their gesticulating suggested they were speaking Spanish.

Melinda watched them for several minutes as they strolled along the shore, pausing now and then to examine what appeared to be a map carried by the second man.

Could Chad's companion be a guide of some sort, she wondered. If Chad really was a travel agent, he might well want to hire a guide to show him around.

Or would he? As a consular officer, Melinda had frequently dealt with travel agents—and this wasn't how travel agents worked. Travel agents usually traveled in groups, relying on host countries to arrange such details as guides. Surely Guatemala's Tourist Commission would seek out a more even-tempered and presentable guide than the character she saw talking to Chad.

Another of life's little mysteries.

Melinda went back inside, sliding shut the screen door behind her. She showered quickly, then, wrapping herself in a fluffy white towel, poked through her bags for an appropriate outfit for the outing she'd planned for the day.

She didn't have a lot of choice. Most of her belongings had been shipped ahead to Washington and she had with her only a much-traveled green plaid garment bag and a small, canvas carryon she'd picked up in São Paulo. Still, she had enough clothes to see her through and settled on a short-sleeved khaki bush jacket, jeans and sturdy chukka boots.

On the way to the dining room, overlooking the pool at the rear of the hotel, she stopped off at the porter's desk and asked if the porter could help her find a guide—someone who wouldn't mind spending the afternoon tramping through the hills with her.

Not to worry, the porter assured her. His nephew was free that day and knew these hills intimately. Did she wish to see anything in particular?

Melinda shook her head quickly. "No, nothing in particular," she said. She just wanted to look at some of the countryside.

The porter reached for his telephone. *"A su servicio."* He nodded amiably. If the señorita would care to have breakfast, he would arrange things instantly if not sooner.

Rewarding him with a smile, Melinda headed for the dining room. It was still early and only a handful of guests had come down for breakfast. One of those guests—alone now—was Chad. He waved to her from a window table and she walked across the room to join him.

Chad inspected her hiking outfit as he got up and held out a chair for her. "I take it you're not planning on swimming today?"

"Hardly," Melinda laughed as she sat down. "But I didn't plan on swimming yesterday, either. It just happened." She glanced at the menu, then put it aside. "How about you?"

He shrugged. "I thought I'd just take it easy and maybe spend the day looking around, getting a feel for the place."

"Did you hire a guide? I saw you from my balcony. You were having quite a discussion with somebody on the beach."

Chad shrugged. "It was just a fellow hustling souvenirs."

"Ah. ¿Compró algunos?" Melinda said quickly.

"No, I—" He broke off and stared at her blankly. "What did you say?"

"I asked you if you bought any."

"Sorry. As I told you, I don't speak Spanish very well. In answer to your question, I sent him on his way. I'm traveling light this trip—no room for junk."

"Just guns, huh?"

He reached down to the floor by his feet and brought up his rucksack. Unstrapping it, he held the bag open for her to see. "I took your advice and left it in my room. Satisfied?"

The waitress came and Melinda ordered coffee, orange juice and toast. When the girl was gone, Melinda leaned forward on her elbows, resting her chin in the heels of her hands, and studied her companion. He still had that easygoing, boyish look, but he had something else, too, beneath the surface: a steely kind of toughness that said he was a man who meant business. "The travel agency business must be fascinating. I have some friends in your line and they're always on the go, checking out new places."

"You have to keep on top of things," Chad allowed.

"Just where is your agency?"

"New York."

"Oh? I wonder if you know Will and Judy Norton."

"New York is a big place."

"Surely you've heard of Norton's Wanderlust."

Chad frowned, as if searching his memory. "It doesn't ring a bell."

"You *must* have heard of the Nortons. They're very active in your trade group—the American Society of Travel Agents, or whatever they call it. Their place is on Thirty-fourth, near Lexington."

"We may have met. Probably have, in fact. I just can't quite place them."

Don't bother trying, Melinda thought. *Will and Judy Norton don't exist, and neither does Norton's Wanderlust. Just who are you, Chad Young? Could it be that you don't exist, either?* "Well, should you happen to run into them be sure to say 'hi' for me and tell them I'll be in touch one of these days."

"I'll make a point of it." Chad seemed relieved the talk of fictitious acquaintances had run its course. To make sure of it, he attempted to change the subject. "Have you worked for the State Department long?"

Melinda eyed him questioningly over the rim of her coffee cup. "How'd you know I was with the State Department?"

Chad's grin became sheepish. "The desk clerk mentioned it when I struck up a conversation with him last night. I informed him that the good-looking redhead in 311 had nearly drowned. Next thing I knew he was telling me you had a diplomatic passport."

Another lie, Melinda thought. She hadn't once taken her diplomatic passport out of her purse since she went through Guatemalan immigration two days earlier at La Aurora Airport. There was no way the hotel could know she was in the United States Foreign Service. And no way Chad Young could know, either.

Unless he'd had someone search her room.

"You need your eyes examined, Mr. Young," she said evenly, wondering what to make of him. "My hair is auburn—not red."

"It's red when the sun hits it just right. Incidentally, I thought we'd progressed to a first-name basis. Are you ticked off at me for some reason?"

Why should I be, Melinda thought. *All you've done is tell me one lie after another since the moment we met.*

Finishing her coffee, she took her billfold from a side pocket of her bush jacket and withdrew a one hundred-quetzal note. "I almost forgot," she said, sliding the note across the table to him. "This is the money I borrowed in Santiago."

Pursing his lips thoughtfully, Chad examined the note. "This covers the principal, but what about the interest?"

"Interest?"

He pocketed the money. "Sure. You don't think I dove into the water to rescue you out of the goodness of my heart, do you?"

Was he joking, she wondered. Surely, he . . .

"I'm serious," he said with a deadpan face. "I expect to be compensated for my trouble."

He wasn't joking, she decided. Glaring at him from across the table, she reopened her billfold. "All right, Mr. Young, how much?"

Chad settled back in his chair, rubbing his hands together. "Let's see . . . there was a good three or four minutes spent fishing you out from under that sail, another six or seven minutes helping you turn the boat upright again, and then there was all that discomfort of sitting on the stern rail in a soaking wet T-shirt and pants. It all comes to . . ."

Melinda pushed back her chair and stood up. "I'm well aware chivalry is dead, Mr. Young. Just tell me how much."

"One dinner," he announced, a suppressed smile quivering at the corners of his lips.

Melinda studied him and her frown melted. Could she ever be sure how to take this man? She doubted it. "It's a deal," she said. "One dinner on me. It's the least the rescuee can do."

He shrugged. "I'll flip you for it, if you like. And then after dinner..." He let his words trail off.

"After dinner, *what*?" Perhaps he was more serious than she thought.

"Some people I met are throwing a party. They insisted I bring you along. How about it?"

"Just what sort of party is it?"

"A get-together for the artsy-craftsy crowd. The people hosting it are named Patterson. They're an American couple who have a gallery here in town. You know the type: well-heeled, semiretired expatriates who live abroad for the tax breaks, but who don't want to cut too many strings. How about it?"

Melinda hesitated. "I don't know. I didn't bring too many clothes this trip. I wouldn't want to embarrass you."

Chad reached out for her hand and squeezed it. "The only way you could possibly embarrass me is by *not* coming, Melinda. Besides, I already said we'd be there."

"We?"

"We—you and me, the two of us. Especially you."

Melinda was mystified. "Why especially me?"

"They've got a surprise planned for you."

"YOUNG," MUSED HER FRIEND at the Passport Agency. "Did you say 'Shad Young'?"

"It's *Chad* Young, Peg," Melinda corrected her, raising her voice to make herself understood through the static on the overseas line. "*C* as in Charles, *H* as in Henry, *A* as in—"

"Oh, *Chad*! Do you have anything else to go on, Lindy? An address, date of birth—anything like that?"

"He may be connected with a travel agency in New York, but I can't swear to it. I don't know his date of birth, but he's about thirty-five or so. He's about five nine, medium build, sandy hair and dark blue eyes." The bluest eyes she'd ever seen, in fact, but no need to add *that*. "Oh, yes...he has a little scar over his right eyebrow."

"Pardon me for asking, but is this official business?" Peg inquired in a bemused tone, obviously aware of the answer before she asked the question.

"Hardly," Melinda admitted. "I'm just curious."

"I see. This is apt to take some time, but as long as I've got you on the phone let me check the hot sheet. Hang on."

Peg was back on the line in a minute. "Nothing," she said. "At least your friend isn't using a stolen passport."

"I didn't think he was," Melinda said quickly. "I just thought you might be able to tell me something about him."

"Wait a minute, Lindy, there's one other list I want to check." There was a long pause. "No luck. We have a man named Mark Cronin on our advisory list. He's a helicopter pilot who's been missing in your neck of the woods for three months now, but he's obviously not the same man. Cronin is forty-five years old and six feet one. The description you gave me isn't even close."

"Where's he from?" Melinda asked.

"Cronin? New York, I think. Hold on another sec...there, I've got the computer file called up. Mark Cronin is a former army flier who'd been working as a charter pilot in Central America—hauling geologists in and out of backwoods landing strips. He was last heard from on a flight from Petén to Guatemala City, carrying some seismic equipment in for repair."

Melinda closed her eyes and summoned up a mental image of the last Guatemalan map she'd studied. Petén was a region of tropical jungles, rivers and low hills, and lay north and east of the highlands—far off any direct course between Panajachel and the capital. "What was he doing in this part of the country?" she asked.

"The file I have up on my screen doesn't say. I assume he was off course and crashed into one of those big mountains. In any case, this isn't your man."

"No," Melinda agreed, "it isn't. Well, see what you can find out about Chad Young. I'll call you back."

JORGE REMOVED HIS DARK GLASSES and, glancing back furtively over his shoulder, frowned. "You have a jealous husband, señora?" he inquired, obviously ill at ease.

"I do not have a husband," Melinda assured her guide, bringing the rented Nissan Sunny to a halt at a stop sign and looking up at the rearview mirror. A late-model black Toyota had been following them for almost a mile, ever since they had left the hotel, turning wherever Melinda had turned and always hanging back, keeping its distance. "I do not have a husband," she repeated, "jealous or otherwise. Therefore, it's señorita, not señora."

She started to turn left, onto the road that would take them to the narrow, winding highway connecting Panajachel and Sololá. Midway through the turn, she jammed on the brakes and swung right, toward the main part of town.

"A boyfriend, perhaps?" Jorge prodded her.

The black Toyota had turned right, too.

"No boyfriend," she said between tight lips, keeping an eye on the rearview mirror.

Jorge wasn't satisfied. "Possibly you have a brother who takes umbrage when you are seen, unchaperoned, in the company of a handsome man." Melinda couldn't be certain, but she thought she saw his eyelashes flutter when he spoke the words *handsome man*.

"I don't have a brother!" she said sharply. "I don't have a brother, a boyfriend, *or* a husband. All I know is that some yo-yo is following us and I don't like it."

The road forked and she turned off to the right, then swung into a narrow street separating blocks of stuccoed houses. The Nissan scraped bottom as it bounced across the gutter.

"Señorita!" Jorge yelped, grabbing at the dashboard to steady himself. "This is a—"

"I know, a one-way street. Well, I'm only going one way."

"But the police! They..."

"I'd like nothing better than to run into a policeman about now. Where do I find one?"

"The office of the *Policía Nacional* is up the next street, to your right, señorita. But it is also one way."

"Great," Melinda said, dropping down into a lower gear as she swung onto the street indicated. She saw that the black Toyota was still behind her.

Tires squealing, she straightened out, sent the Nissan rattling over some speed bumps without slowing, and then executed a skidding U-turn in front of the police station.

"Wait here," she ordered Jorge. "If that creep gets close, check his license number."

She marched into the police station—a large, single room with rows of benches lining the poster-bedecked walls. A portly, blue-uniformed officer was seated at a rickety desk at the front of the room, sipping a bottled Coke and reading a newspaper.

"A man is following me," Melinda announced, stepping up to the desk. "Please do something about it."

The police officer took a last swig of his Coke, then turned and slipped the bottle into the yellow wooden case on the floor behind the desk. Wiping his lips with thumb and forefinger, he rose ponderously to his feet.

"Where are you from, señorita? No—let me guess. Argentina. Argentina or Chile, no? I am very good with accents."

"Where I'm from has nothing to do with why I'm here. I don't like being followed."

The police officer frowned. "This man—he had molested you? He had said something offensive perhaps?"

"No. He's never come any closer than a block or so."

"Aha! Then how he has bothered you, señorita?"

"He's following me, and I have no idea what he wants."

The police officer shook his head. "Panajachel is very small and has very few streets. He is probably going to the same place you are, but neither of you knows it, eh?"

"Oh, never mind!" Melinda sighed, turning on her heel and heading for the door.

"Señorita!"

She glanced back over her shoulder. The officer was looking out the window at her parked Nissan.

"Señorita, it is against the regulations to park on the street in front of the police station. I do not wish to give you a ticket, so would you please move your car?"

"Gladly!" Melinda snorted.

GIL RAMIREZ WAS LAUGHING when he hung up the phone. He was laughing so hard his dark eyes sparkled with tears and he had to massage his ribs to ease the ache. "Poor Carlos! He was beside himself. It is one thing to look foolish, but another thing to be *made* to look foolish by a beautiful woman."

Chad zipped up his ocher-and-brown splotched coveralls and hooked the ammunition belt around his waist. "I told you, amigo: this is a bright girl we're dealing with and she's no pushover. I just wish the hell I knew which side she's on."

Ramirez tried to stop laughing, but made a miserable job of it. "What you say is true," he admitted, "but until we find out, we shall have to continue to consider her an enemy. I only hope it is not necessary to take, ah, extreme measures with her."

"I'll handle her," Chad said quickly, wondering why he was suddenly feeling so protective about Melinda Harding. He sat down on the edge of the cot and began lacing up his high-topped boots. "Tell me, what did she do to Carlos?"

"Well, to begin with she spotted him before they were out of sight of the hotel—"

"She was *supposed* to," Chad cut in. "If you'll recall, the idea was to let her know she was being watched—the same as when we had her room searched. It just makes sense to keep her off balance until we learn how the hell she figures in this."

"True, but she did not care for the idea. She drove to the Panajachel police station and sought to file a complaint against Carlos."

"And what did the police do?"

"Nothing," Ramirez replied, shaking his head. "These country bumpkins have no idea what is going on in their own backyard."

"And Carlos? Did he stay on her tail?"

The laughter bubbled over again, and Ramirez sank into a chair behind the desk. "He followed her out of Panajachel and she led him a merry chase, up through the hills above Patzún. She had someone in the car with her—probably that idiot guide she hired at the hotel—and he was petrified, my friend, absolutely petrified. Over hill and through dale they went, sending up vast clouds of dust in their wake. At a wide spot in the road, this Melinda Harding braked to a halt and went into a tiny store and bought two bottles of lemon pop."

"Lemon pop?"

"Lemon pop." Ramirez nodded as gravely as his high humor could manage. "Vigorously shaking both bottles, she walked back to Carlos's car and knocked on the window." By now his laughter was so rib-shaking that he had difficulty continuing.

"Go on!" Chad insisted. "Don't keep me dangling!"

"Carlos—this is really outrageous, my friend—opened the window and she pointed both bottles at him and took her thumbs off the tops. Carlos was *drenched* with sticky, eye-stinging pop! I mean, he could not see his hand in front of his face. Our Miss Harding reached in and took his keys out of the ignition and threw them away. And then—you will die at this, my friend—she patted Carlos on the head and said, and I quote, 'Drop dead, buster.' With that, she walked back to her car and drove off.''

Chad shook his head in amazement. "She didn't!"

"Ah, but she did!" Ramirez beamed. "Frankly, I hope she *is* on the other side. A most worthy opponent, if I do say so."

Still chortling, Ramirez got up and went to a closet. He opened the door and brought out two submachine guns, handing one of them to Chad. "Have you ever used one of these, my friend?"

Chad hefted the weapon, then nodded. "An Uzi? Yeah, I'm familiar with them."

"Good." The merriment was gone, and Ramirez was deadly serious. "They may prove useful this afternoon."

SITTING AT THE WHEEL of the Nissan, studying the sign-plastered windows of the store across the road, Melinda cast her mind back ten years. She remembered getting off the bus at Sololá, after a miserably uncomfortable all-day trip from the Mexican frontier. The bus, a rusting green rattletrap with cases of live chickens and rope nets of produce and pottery lashed to its roof, huffed and puffed through the twists and turns of the Inter American Highway, belching black smoke and breaking down several times during the fifty-mile passage from La Mesilla to Huehuetenango. That was in February, and the rainy season had ended three months before. Or at least it was *supposed* to have ended. Trouble was, no one had told the weather gods, and most of the trip was made through a solid sheet of cold, stinging rain that mercifully obscured the passengers' view of the hazards ahead and to either side as the bus careered down one hill and limped up the next.

Then, miracle of miracles, the rain stopped as the vehicle swung off the main highway and barreled downhill toward Sololá. A bright sun burned through the overcast, and in the

distance Melinda and her two roommates could see the blue
waters of Lake Atitlán shimmering in the golden glow of late
afternoon.

They'd gotten off the bus right there at that store, she remembered. They'd gone into the store and bought a half
pound of soft white cheese and a sack of warm corn tortil-
las and three bottles of Orange Crush—canned pop not yet
having made its debut in rural Guatemala. Leaving the store,
they'd set out hiking down the road, hoping to reach the
beach at Panajachel by nightfall.

Melinda turned to her guide. "Isn't there a turnoff part-
way down the hill?" she asked. "You know—some sort of
place where you can stop and look out at the lake?"

"Sí, señorita," nodded Jorge, whose respect for his client
had grown immeasurably since she had ditched the man
following them. "It is not far from here. I show you."

Melinda started the engine and pulled out onto the highway. She drove carefully through Sololá, slowing to a crawl
every few blocks in deference to the bone-jolting *topes*, or
speed bumps, that stretched across the pavement in front of
schools and other public buildings.

It was Thursday morning, and there were few people in
the street. The next day would be different, she knew. The
weekly market was on Friday in Sololá, and it would bring
hundreds of colorfully clad Indians into town to set up shop
in the plaza. Gray-haired, pinch-faced women wrapped in
black shawls would sit cross-legged on blankets spread with
neat stacks of apples, onions, cabbages and other produce,
while their men milled about, cackling about politics and the
price of coffee beans. There would be pitchmen from the
capital: glib young fellows with slicked hair and tight pants,
hawking pots and pans and cheap plastic shoes and Los
Angeles Dodgers T-shirts. Of course, there'd be children
everywhere: round-faced, wide-eyed, and—Melinda knew
from long experience in Latin America—heartbreakingly
adorable.

"You want to come back tomorrow for the market, señorita?" Jorge asked, as if reading her mind. "It is a fine
market, better than Panajachel."

"We'll see," Melinda replied. "First I'd like to look at the
countryside."

The turnoff was farther from Sololá than she remembered. It was at the outside of a wide curve that hugged the
mountainside between the humpbacks of two smaller hills,
and from it they could see the lake in the distance.

Melinda pulled off the road and killed the engine. This
would be the tricky part. She had to find the cave and she
needed Jorge's help. But she didn't want him to know what
she was doing.

Reaching into the glove box, she brought out the Pentax
camera that she'd owned for years and hardly ever used. She
couldn't remember if it still had film in it, but it didn't matter. It would serve the purpose.

"I'd like to take some pictures," she announced, setting
the handbrake and stepping out of the car.

"I know a better place," Jorge spoke up, staying put in
the front passenger seat. "My father-in-law, he has a house
that looks straight out at both of the big volcanoes across
the lake. It would make a fine picture."

"I'm sure it would," Melinda said, "but I like this spot."

Jorge was not one to give up quickly. "My father-in-law,
he also carves wooden masks, which he sends to the capital
to sell. They are fine masks, the very best in all Guatemala."

"I'll remember that when I'm in the market for a mask."

"You would pay three, four times as much in the capital,
señorita. Here there is no middleman, no extra overhead,
eh?"

"Perhaps later," Melinda sighed, looking around for the
path she'd taken that February day ten years before.

This *had* to be the jump-off point she remembered. She
and her two friends had gone down the mountainside a

hundred yards and picnicked in the clearing. That's when they had found the cave.

Slinging the camera over her shoulder by its strap, Melinda pushed aside the brush bordering the turnout and tentatively stepped down onto the hillside.

"Señorita! What are you doing?"

"Exploring."

Jorge got out of the car and hurried over to her. "They are very dangerous, these mountains. There are snakes and wild pigs—and once even a jaguar was seen here."

Jaguar! Melinda looked at him sharply, but Jorge didn't catch the glint of alarm in her eyes.

"Really, señorita, you could get hurt trying to walk along the mountainside. Who would be there to help you?"

"You would, of course, Jorge," Melinda replied sweetly. "I wouldn't dream of roaming around these hills without a real *man* at my side to protect me."

She could see the anguish in the guide's eyes. She knew exactly what he was thinking: *this crazy gringa has boxed me into a corner and I must either come to her aid or else proclaim that I am a coward. Since Jorge Villares de Castillo is not a coward and does not wish to be known as a coward*....

"Watch your step, Jorge," Melinda suggested. "The path is covered with loose stones and very difficult to follow."

With Melinda leading the way, they moved slowly along the mountainside, feeling their way through the thick green brush. Once or twice, she was sure she sensed something fast and slithery moving underfoot, but, biting her lip, she kept her fears to herself. She needed Jorge—at least for the time being.

From time to time she stopped and peered down the slope, hoping to catch sight of The Three Bears she remembered so vividly, but they were nowhere in view.

They came to a clearing, and Melinda sank wearily into a crouching position at the foot of a stunted evergreen and looked around. There was a superb view of the lake and, to keep up the pretense that she was on a photography expedition, she pointed the camera at it and clicked the shutter.

"The view is better from the house of my father-in-law," Jorge grumbled, breathing hard but reluctant to admit he was also tiring.

"It probably is," Melinda admitted.

"My father-in-law, he is home today," Jorge added.

"How nice."

"He is home today and making some wonderful carvings to sell in the capital. Ah, if you could only see his carvings."

"Another time," Melinda said. "I'm afraid I have other things on my mind just now."

"I tell you, señorita, the view from the house of my father-in-law is the greatest view in all Sololá. You can see the length of the lake and even beyond. You can see the farmers tilling their fields on the far shore, the fishermen casting their nets, even the angels in the heavens."

"Keen," Melinda sighed, rising slowly to begin searching another expanse of mountainside.

Jorge made no effort to join her. "It has not always been thus, señorita. At one time, my father-in-law owned a house with no view at all. But that was before they changed the highway."

Melinda stared at him. "Before they what?"

Jorge shrugged philosophically. "The government came and built the new highway and they moved my father-in-law and my mother-in-law and all their children to another plot of land. If they had only known what a magnificent view my father-in-law would have from his new property, they would not have given it to him. No, they would have sold it to someone for a fine hotel."

"When was this?"

Jorge threw up his hands to indicate he couldn't bother to keep track of such trivial details. "Five years, ten years—who knows? A very long time ago."

"Think. Was it *less* than ten years ago?"

Her guide reluctantly considered the question. "Possibly. My wife Rosa was not yet my wife, as I recall."

"When did the two of you get married?"

"Seven years ago. Or was it eight? No, it was seven. Let me see, we have five children, and . . ."

Melinda straightened up and squared her shoulders. "Can you take me to the home of your father-in-law?"

Jorge's fatigue was forgotten. "Ah, the carvings! You will not be disappointed, señorita. For you, a very special price."

"I can hardly wait," she said softly, letting her guide lead her back up the hillside with a renewed spring in his step.

Fifteen minutes later, they were parked outside a tumbledown stone hut hidden among the trees just off the blacktop highway that wound along the mountainside. Beyond the hut was a postage-stamp patch of open land studded with dried corn stalks, and beyond that a small orchard where a scraggly flock of gray and white goats grazed, gnawing at the bark of the tree trunks.

Jorge's father-in-law was sprawled in a hammock at the rear of the hut. Farther down the slope, two women and a half dozen small children were busy hacking away with machetes, clearing the undergrowth for a new plot of terraced cropland.

"Don Felipe is an old man," Jorge explained under his breath as they approached the hammock. "He has sired many children and has had a hard life. The doctor tells him he now must let others do the work in the fields. That woman you see—the younger one—she is my wife. She comes three days a week to help her mother."

Hearing them approach, Don Felipe swatted aside the dog-eared girlie magazine shielding his eyes from the mid day sun and sat up groggily. As he did so, an empty rum bottle tumbled to the ground from the hammock. *"¡Ay!"* he clucked. "Where has the day gone? I lay down but for a moment to rest my aching bones, and already you are here to collect your family. What is the hour, Jorge?"

"It is early yet, Don Felipe. We apologize for disturbing your siesta, but this young lady has expressed a keen interest in viewing your carvings, and therefore I have brought her here to see you. She is from the United States and I told her you would give her a very special price."

Don Felipe eyed Melinda appraisingly, noting particularly her camera and designer jeans. "Ah, a rich young lady from the United States, eh?" he rattled off in Spanish to his nephew. Beaming, he rubbed his hands together and came alive as visions of new wealth appeared before him.

"I am sorry, old man," Melinda said quickly in his language, "but I am not rich, only a poor foreigner who wishes to visit your land."

"La señorita speaks the language, Don Felipe," Jorge announced belatedly.

"Ah," Don Felipe nodded, giving his son-in-law a withering look. "I will bring out some of my better work while you look around." He returned his attention to Melinda, bestowing upon her a wide smile that revealed two black-gapped rows of crooked teeth. "My house is your house."

"You are very kind," Melinda nodded.

"It is nothing." Don Felipe shrugged in all due modesty. "I welcome all North Americans to my humble abode— whether they buy my carvings or not. It matters not that they promise to bring me many new customers, as has my other guest this afternoon."

"Another gringo has been here today?" Melinda asked.

"Sí, señorita. Just before siesta, he came with a friend, a countryman of mine, and walked the length and breadth of my land, admiring its beauty. Before he left, he gave me twenty quetzales—for my time, he said. He, too, spoke our

language beautifully, and he told me he would try to send business my way."

"What did this gringo look like?"

Don Felipe threw out his hands. "He was a young man—about the age of Jorge, I would say—but much more handsome." Don Felipe glanced quickly at Jorge to make sure the insult had not missed its target. "He had fair hair and very dark blue eyes, and he was very quick to smile. I am sure he has broken many hearts."

"I'll bet he has," Melinda muttered. She looked around. "Did you go with him when he walked around your property?"

"I would like to have done so, but I was unable. My legs are not what they once were, and the gringo and his friend moved too swiftly for me—almost as if they were hunters racing after a wild beast."

"Which way did they go when they went off by themselves?"

The old man pointed. "They walked down the hill from that new field where the women are working. An hour later, they came out of the trees on the other side of the orchard."

"Did they find whatever they were looking for?"

"I cannot say, señorita."

With Jorge dogging her steps, Melinda set out on the dirt path leading down to the field that was being cleared. Jorge's wife and her mother, who were rolling boulders into position on a new terrace, eyed them suspiciously, then broke into shy smiles as Melinda greeted them pleasantly in Spanish. She asked them about the route taken by the two men who'd visited the hacienda earlier in the day, and they pointed.

"Señorita!" Jorge shouted, trotting along after her. "Tell me what you are looking for. Perhaps I can help you find it, eh?"

I have no idea, Melinda thought, moving on.

Fifty yards down the slope from where the women and children were building the new terraces, she stopped and pretended to take a photo of the lake.

"You see what I tell you?" Jorge said, more in self-congratulation than anything else. "It is magnificent, eh?"

"It's all right, I suppose," Melinda allowed. "I just wish I had a little different focal point for the foreground."

"Focal point? What is focal point?"

"You know," Melinda said, trying to keep her tone casual. "Something to serve as a center of interest in the photograph."

Jorge seemed dubious. "The lake is not enough? And the two volcanoes?"

"I have plenty of photos of the lake and the volcanoes. I was thinking of something else—something different."

Jorge thoughtfully fingered his black mustache. "If you like, señorita, you may take my photo."

"I already have one of you," Melinda fibbed. "I was thinking of something like a unique rock formation. You don't know of any rock formations around here, do you?"

Jorge shrugged. "There are many rocks on the mountainside. The rocks make it difficult when one wishes to cultivate the land. One must move them, and they are very heavy." Was he thinking of his wife and mother-in-law straining against the boulders that lay in the path of their new gardens, Melinda wondered. Possibly, for he seemed mildly fatigued by the thought.

"Rocks are like clouds," Melinda observed. "Sometimes they take on the shape of people, even animals. Rock formations like that make very nice photos."

"Animals?" Jorge mulled this over. "Down that way—" he pointed along the mountainside "—near the old highway, there is just such a rock formation. It is known as *Los Tres Osos*."

It took a few seconds for the Spanish to sink in. When it did, Melinda had to struggle to keep her excitement from showing.

Los Tres Osos. The Three Bears.

"I would like to see these rocks," she said softly.

"Of course. We will go back to the house and look at Don Felipe's carvings, and then we will get in your car and drive down the road and—"

"I would like to see these rocks now. Can't we walk there from here?"

"Ah, it would be easier to drive, señorita."

"I need the exercise."

"If you say so," Jorge grumbled.

He set out across the mountainside, cautioning Melinda to be careful as they clambered down one side of a ravine and up the other. The timber grew taller, the undergrowth thicker. After a while, he settled down on his haunches at the foot of a tree. "The old road is up there," he announced, with a flick of his head. "*Los Tres Osos* are not far—just over the next rise. You like bears?"

"Not if they come any bigger than Winnie the Pooh," Melinda replied, scrambling up the rise that separated them from *Los Tres Osos.* "I'm quite fond of Pooh Bears."

"Don Felipe can make you a bear mask, if you like. And he will give you a very special price. Only fifty quetzales."

"That's a lot of money," Melinda said absently, grabbing at a clump of bushes for support as she dragged herself up the steep slope. Fifty quetzales probably was more cash than Don Felipe had ever seen in a month, she knew.

"True, señorita, but Don Felipe has many mouths to feed. Of course, you could offer him forty quetzales and he might consent to meet you halfway—say forty-five. After all, you are a special client...."

Melinda wasn't listening. She had reached the top of the rise and was lying there, peering out at The Three Bears she'd first seen ten years before—and at the two men slouched against the base of the towering rock formation, looking over a map and talking. One of them was Chad, the other the man whom Chad had waved away in Santiago and then had strolled with on the beach that very morning. Both were wearing ocher-and-brown splotched coveralls.

Melinda watched quietly, keeping low against the crest of the rise, wondering what the two were doing on the mountainside. Something told her it would not be wise to break in on them and ask, not just now.

After a while, Chad put away the map and the other man pointed down the slope, toward the lake. Chad nodded and the two of them reached down and gathered up their equipment and slung it over their shoulders.

Part of their belongings was concealed within small, military rucksacks made of camouflage material. Melinda had no idea what the kits might contain.

There was no mistaking the other part of their equipment, though. Each was armed with a deadly looking submachine gun.

Chapter Three

"You mentioned something about a surprise," Melinda said as they carried their drinks to a table by the pool to watch the autumn sun dip behind the volcanoes across the lake. "Just what sort of surprise were you talking about?"

Chad grinned at her with that special innocence of his. He was even more a young boy in a man's body this evening, scrubbed and fresh-faced, his sandy hair brushed, and looking comfortably casual and neat in a lightweight khaki suit and open-collared black knit shirt. "Sorry, but I can't tell you that."

"Can't—or won't?"

"Both. The Pattersons didn't let me in on it. They just said to be sure to bring you along. Besides, a surprise wouldn't be a surprise if you knew what was coming."

Drawing her white sweater jacket around the bare shoulders above her strapless white silk sheath, Melinda settled back in her chair and thought about it. She prided herself on her memory for names and faces; she'd met several Pattersons over the years, but none who fit the description Chad had given her. "Did they mention me by name?"

"They did indeed, only they referred to you as 'Lindy,' not Melinda." He took a sip of his rum punch and, making a face, set it aside. "You mind if I call you 'Lindy,' too?"

Melinda nodded absently. She was still trying to place the Pattersons. It was no use. She didn't know them, and she barely knew this man sitting across the table from her. Why were they interested in her?

"I was in their house a few days ago—just after I arrived in Panajachel," Chad said, as if in reply to her unspoken question. "They have a lot of fascinating things to show off. Maybe that's part of the surprise."

Melinda's ponytail, tied back with a white silk bow, danced lightly around her shoulders as she shook her head. "I hardly think so. I'm not an art collector, so there's no point in them trying to impress me." A guilty thought occurred to her as the irony of her remark hit home. In her entire lifetime, she'd managed to collect only one piece of original art—and it was that single piece that had brought her back to the highlands.

Chad winked at her. "You want to know the truth, you'd be unfair competition for anything the Pattersons have on display."

"That's a line if I've ever heard one." She smiled. Of course, it was a line, but a very nice line.

The little-boy look on Chad's face gave way to the intense expression of a grown man with something serious on his mind. "You're a beautiful woman, Lindy. Of course, being an Irishman I'm partial to red hair, anyway."

She laughed. "My hair is auburn, but I won't argue the point." She looked away, avoiding those piercing blue eyes but increasingly mindful of the secrets locked behind them. She had the distinct feeling he wanted to be more open with her but didn't know quite how. "Did you have a busy day?"

"So-so. I just looked around a bit."

"Oh? Did you get up to the Indian market at Sololá?"

"Sure did. Spent the whole afternoon there. Very colorful. I'm going to have to include it in one of my tours."

"Do that," Melinda said, almost adding, *and be sure to point out the market is held on Monday, Tuesday and Fri-*

day—never on Thursday. If you're going to lie, Chad Young or whatever your name is, better check the tourist handbills first!

At one end of the patio, a small marimba band had set up its instruments and had launched into a tinkling rendition of *"Cuando Calienta el Sol."* Chad inclined his head in the direction of the musicians. "Marimbas seem to be very big down here."

Why did she get the distinct impression he suddenly wanted to change the subject? "Marimbas were developed by the Indians of Mesoamerica," she explained patiently. "Tell me, did you buy anything at the market?"

"Just some souvenirs to take back to the kids."

Melinda glanced at him warily. "You have children?"

"No, but my two sisters do."

"Oh." Was that just another fast recovery on his part? "I was in Sololá this afternoon. Funny I didn't see you."

"Sololá's a pretty good-size town."

"Not so big."

"Big enough."

He had an answer for everything, didn't he, she thought. *Or maybe I just haven't come up with the right questions.*

THE PATTERSON HACIENDA was built into a mountainside overlooking the lake, northwest of Panajachel. Chad had pointed to it from the hotel patio, but in the waning light of dusk all Melinda could make out were the rock steps that zigzagged down the slope, from the lower walls of the hacienda to the water's edge.

"They've got a private dock down there at the foot of the steps," Chad had explained. "If I'd thought about it, I could have rented a boat and delivered you to the party in style."

Melinda had laughed at that. "Thanks anyway, but I've had enough time on the water for one vacation."

Now, though, bouncing along in Chad's rented Volkswagen, twisting through one switchback after another on a gravel road hacked out of the mountainside, she wasn't at all sure it might not have been safer to have taken a boat. In some places, the road was only inches wider than the track of the car, and there was no shoulder to speak of—just an abrupt drop into the water on the one side, and the steep, rock-studded slope on the other.

"What if you meet someone coming down the mountain?" Melinda inquired, knuckles white against the dashboard as she avoided looking out at the glistening blue-black emptiness below.

"If you'll notice, there's a turnout every once in a while," Chad pointed out, slowing up to ease the VW through the narrow opening left by a boulder that had tumbled down the mountainside and taken up residence on the inside of the road.

Melinda gritted her teeth as the left rear wheel of the car dipped sharply. "What if you're between turnouts?"

Chad gunned the engine and closed the gap between the edge of the road and the side of the boulder, bringing the right-hand door of the car so close to the boulder that Melinda could have reached out and brushed her hand against it. "One of us would have to back off and let the other pass."

Beyond the next turn, the gravel road leveled off and widened and the car's headlamps picked up stone pillars flanking an open, wrought iron gate. Beyond the gate was an outer courtyard in which were parked a half dozen small vehicles, and on the far side of the courtyard was a tile-roofed breezeway connecting a series of white-stuccoed, colonial-style buildings.

"The living quarters are in that building on the right," Chad pointed out as he maneuvered the Volkswagen into a narrow space between the outer wall and an open Jeep. "Kitchen, dining room and servants' quarters are there on the left. The building in the middle is one huge salon—kind of a miniature museum."

"How'd you happen to meet the Pattersons?" Melinda inquired, wishing she'd chosen something other than white to wear as she squeezed through the narrow opening between the Volkswagen's door and the dusty side of the parked Jeep.

Chad shrugged. "You know how it is when one American abroad runs into another: you start talking, and suddenly it's old home week. I wandered into their gallery in town the day I arrived, and next thing I knew they invited me up here for dinner. When they heard you were at Del Lago, Nicole Patterson phoned and asked me to be sure to bring you along."

Melinda slipped her arm through Chad's and let him lead her across the rough cobblestones to the breezeway. Not only had the white silk sheath been a mistake, but the high-heeled white sling-backs were positively treacherous on the cobblestones. Who was she trying to impress, she wondered, already knowing the answer.

They could hear music and the buzz of cocktail party chatter coming from the brightly lighted center building where the salon was located. A shaggy-haired, white-bearded bear of a man was standing in the open double doorway under the breezeway, squinting out at them.

"Chad, old boy!" a husky voice thundered out into the night. "I *thought* I saw lights coming up the road. We'd about given up on you!" Arms outstretched, he stepped forward and crushed Chad in the traditional Latin embrace as he took a close look at Melinda. "This divine creature has to be Miss Harding!"

Before Melinda could speak, he released Chad and seized her hands, touching her fingertips to his lips and bowing from the waist. "Welcome, welcome!" He promptly launched into a torrent of Spanish in which he announced that Melinda was without a doubt the most splendid exam-

ple of female pulchritude ever to pass through the portals of
Hacienda Patterson, that she was to consider his house her
house, and that he would be cut to the quick should she be
wanting for anything while she was his guest.

"*Muy amable,*" Melinda murmured, amused by the ef-
fusive greeting. You are very kind. You also act very foolish, even for a gringo gone native! "Have we met before,
Mr. Patterson?"

"Please, my dear little girl! The name is Joel. And no, it's
my great misfortune that we have *not* met before." He
straightened up and stepped back, still holding Melinda's
hands, and for the first time she realized how huge he was:
almost three hundred pounds, she guessed, and at least six
foot six. But for the richly embroidered white cotton shirt
that hung loosely outside his black slacks, he might have
been a north woods lumberjack.

"Then how..."

Patterson held up his massive hands to silence her. "Ah,
you're wondering about the surprise we have for you. Alas,
I must keep you in suspense a bit longer. Come meet our
other guests."

Ignoring Chad, he put an arm around Melinda's waist and
guided her through the double door and into the salon. A
dozen other guests stood around sipping champagne and
admiring the Mayan artifacts arranged against the dull white
walls and in groupings of display cases protected by thick
polished glass.

Chad was right, Melinda thought, the salon *was* a miniature museum. Everything, from the smallest grouping of
display cases, to the most elaborate carved stone lintels set
on free-standing mahogany bases, was highlighted by expensive, ceiling-mounted track lighting that showed the
collection to full advantage.

"Do you own all this?" Melinda asked, twirling out of
Patterson's grasp and stepping forward to look around the
room.

He seemed amused by the idea. "Good grief, no, my dear little girl! Most of what you see here is the property of the Guatemalan government. I'm considered something of an authority on Mayan culture of the Late Classic and Post Classic periods. The government graciously allows me temporary custody while I help catalogue these treasures. As recompense, I'm given first crack at contracting out quality reproductions."

"You've lost me already," Melinda confessed. "What do you mean by the 'Late Classic' and 'Post Classic' periods?"

Patterson smiled tolerantly. "I refer to the years between 500 A.D. and the early 1500s when the conquistadors arrived. In my humble opinion, the early sixteenth century was the most interesting time in the Mayan experience, particularly when the dying remnants of those once-proud tribes found themselves up against the Spanish greed for gold."

"Greed is hardly exclusive to any one nationality," Chad spoke up. "The fast-buck artists have been around since biblical times, and they'll always be with us."

Patterson nodded knowingly. "True, old boy. I dare say we could find a few latter-day conquistadors right here in this room if we were to do a bit of research. But such is the flawed nature of the beast. Come, let me get you a glass of bubbly and have you meet our other guests."

The group was a cosmopolitan mixture. One couple had been friends of the Pattersons in Paris, another couple were art collectors from Miami. Several men and women were owners of New York art galleries.

"A pretty tame bunch, if you ask me," Chad observed as their host ambled off to fetch them glasses of champagne. "No surprises there." He glanced quickly around the room. "Maybe Nicole's taking care of that part of the evening. I haven't seen her yet."

"Nicole?"

"Mrs. Patterson."

"Oh."

An arrangement of jade glyphs in a display case caught Melinda's eye and she moved in close to examine the pieces as Chad headed off to mix with the other guests.

Arrayed on a white felt board were nine pieces of rounded jade, each of them about five inches in diameter and an inch thick. There was a sequence to the arrangement, and alongside each of the nine glyphs was a Polaroid color print showing the reverse side of the corresponding glyph. Read from left to right, the jade seemed to tell a story. The first piece depicted a king on a throne, a robe of spotted fur over his shoulders. The next glyph showed the king and another man locked in combat. In the third, the king had slain his enemy and was about to flee. In the fourth glyph, he still wore the jaguar skin robe, but had changed his appearance to that of a quetzal bird. As the story progressed, the king moved into the mountains and took flight. The panorama ended at an empty felt cavity, the size and shape of a missing tenth glyph.

As Melinda stared at the display, intrigued by the mystery of its message, slender arms circled her neck and soft, delicate fingers pressed lightly against her eyes.

"It is very dark ... very, very dark," she heard a woman's voice say. "There are ghosts rattling around everywhere, ready to pounce. Ah, but you fearlessly stand your ground...."

Melinda started to turn, but the fingers remained over her eyes, shutting off her sight.

"You peer into the darkness and you see the evil, yellow eyes of a jungle cat staring out at you. At that moment, you want to turn and run, but you can't. Don't you remember how it was, Melinda Harding? You should. After all...this is your life!"

Melinda pushed aside the fingers and spun around, her face aglow with delight. "Stuffy! Stuffy Travers, is it really you?"

The willowy blonde who stood facing her, a smile on her lips, a devilish twinkle in her eyes, bore scant resemblance to the roommate she remembered. Stefanie had lost weight and her once-long hair now was cut short in pageboy fashion, making her seem younger. She'd acquired style, as well. The old Stefanie had been a college woman of the seventies, more at home in faded jeans than in skirts, in klutzy shoes than in high heels. But this Stefanie Travers who stood before her was sleekly elegant in a sleeveless, red silk shift and golden, open-toed sandals.

"Darling, don't stand there with your mouth open, staring," Stefanie teased. "Say something diplomatic."

Melinda leaned forward and hugged her old friend. "So *you're* the surprise!" She laughed in delight. "What are you doing *here*?"

Stefanie kissed her on the cheek and smiled. "Same thing you are, taking a few days off and enjoying myself hugely. Our hosts are trying to expand their market, so they invited a bunch of us down here to see how their reproductions are made. I decided to take them up on it and kill two birds with one stone. See—" she nodded to a nearby display case "—Lord Quetzal or whatever his name is is back home again, none the worse for wear."

Melinda looked at the case Stefanie had indicated. Leering out at them from behind a golden mask of undisguised hostility was an eight-inch-high statuette of the Mayan god Quetzalcóatl. It was the only artifact in the case and it seemed to be warning all others not to dare to intrude upon its glassed-in solitude.

"One down, one to go," Melinda said with a smile. She stepped back to take another, longer, look at her friend. "Why didn't you answer my last letter? I wrote to you about—" she nodded toward the statuette.

"You know how it is, Lindy—rush, rush, rush, never enough time to get everything done. I tried to call you in São Paulo, but you'd already signed out. The consulate said you

were closing up your apartment and couldn't be reached. I
wanted to tell you that I was coming down here to Guatemala on business, and I could have saved you the trip. I
mean, I could have easily taken care of things. After all,
we'll see each other in the States.''

"It's something I have to do myself." Melinda saw Chad
approaching with another, much older man reluctantly in
tow. She didn't want to bare her soul to a stranger, so she
lowered her voice. "We'll talk about it later." She smiled at
Chad. "There you are. I'd like to have you meet a friend of
mine. Stuffy, this is Chad Young. Chad, Stefanie Travers...pardon me, Stefanie Travers *Germaine*. We roomed
together in college."

"Any friend of Lindy's..." Chad said affably, reaching
out to shake hands.

"We just met," Melinda said quickly. "Yesterday, in
fact."

"Sounds serious," Stefanie teased. "Where's home,
Chad?"

"New York."

"What a coincidence! That's where I'm from—Lindy,
too, for that matter when she's not off at some godfor-
saken outpost doing her thing for the State Department."
Stefanie turned to Chad's companion, a frail, rumpled old
man with half-moon spectacles propped absently atop a
halo-like fringe of silvery hair. "And this is..."

"Professor Juan Lara Saavedra," Chad announced. "Dr.
Lara is on the faculty at the University of San Carlos."

The professor, who seemed ill at ease, nodded at the
mention of his name and bowed stiffly from the waist.
"Enchanted," he murmured coolly, taking Stefanie's hand
and then Melinda's and kissing each of them on the fingertips.

"Dr. Lara does consulting work for the National Museum," Chad explained. "He's helping the Pattersons cat-
alog some recent additions to the collection you see here."

Shifting about nervously, the professor managed a wan smile. "I doubt that these ladies are interested in my musty pursuits."

"On the contrary," Melinda said. "I find archaeology quite fascinating."

"So do I," piped up Stefanie, not to be outdone.

"Actually," the professor said, "I am an anthropologist, not an archaeologist—"

"In other words," Chad explained, "he's more concerned with people than places."

Lara looked mildly pained at this oversimplification, but even so his distant manner faded somewhat. "I am particularly impressed by that Quetzalcóatl there," he said, cocking his head toward the display case where the golden figurine sat in solitary splendor. "If only it could speak, what stories it could tell!"

Melinda and Stefanie exchanged glances.

"It must be quite valuable," Melinda said.

"Indeed it is, my dear lady. Oh, intrinsically it is not worth a great deal of money—it is merely poor-quality gold leaf pressed upon a crude stone carving—but that does not diminish its value. On the contrary, it enhances it."

"How's that?" Stefanie inquired.

The professor's nervousness had disappeared, for he now was in his element, discussing a subject of keen interest to him. "It adds credence to a theory of mine. Some time during the early sixteenth century, when the Mayan civilization had all but vanished, I believe that a once-powerful king led a migration through these highlands, leaving behind a number of gold-leaf figurines to divert the Spaniards who pursued his people. The king knew the conquistadors were obsessed by greed for gold." His dark eyes shone brightly as he warmed to his subject. "The Maya were highly intelligent. They realized, of course, the Spaniards would soon learn the figurines were of little value, and they hoped this would cause the enemy to give up the chase."

"Did it?" Melinda asked.

The professor shook his head slowly. "Hardly. A civilization that had made remarkable achievements in astronomy and mathematics, whose architecture and art rivaled anything the world had seen, was trampled underfoot in the march of progress. The Maya were enslaved by their conquerors and their ranks decimated by disease and poverty." He paused. "The king might have been far better off had he surrendered the real treasure."

"The *real* treasure?" Stefanie inquired.

"The real treasure," the professor nodded. "My research leads me to believe the king hid a fortune in gold, jewels and other priceless objects during his flight from the Spaniards, intending as a last resort to buy freedom for himself and his people—a king's ransom, if you will. *That* treasure never has been found. As I said, if only that figurine there could talk! There is evidence that particular Quetzalcóatl was fashioned by the same artisans who produced the glyphs you see over there. The glyphs, in turn, form a pictograph that I suspect provides clues to the whereabouts of the treasure. Unfortunately, without the missing tenth glyph..."

Melinda glanced again at the display case, then at the case featuring the collection of nine glyphs. Stefanie's gold-plated Quetzalcóatl might not be able to communicate, she thought. But the jade jaguar might have something to say for himself.

"Don't believe a word of it, my dear," she heard a woman say in a husky voice tinged with a vague French accent. "It's all wishful thinking—every last bit of it." Melinda looked around to see that a tall, willowy brunette, high-fashion svelte in a flamingo pink silk jumpsuit cinched to her slender waist with a silver-and-black-jade chain belt, had joined the group.

"Lindy," said Stefanie, "I don't believe you've met our hostess." She took each of the women's right hands in hers.

"Lindy, Nicole Patterson. Nicole—this is my old college roommate, Melinda Harding."

Nicole's thin, pink-glossed lips widened in a teasing smile and her gray eyes sparkled. "You Americans are so thoughtless, Stefanie! 'Old' is not a word that should ever be used to describe a woman! These musty antiquities you see all around you—they're old. But your Miss Harding here hardly fits into the same category! Like you, she's young, vibrant, and very attractive." She pulled her hands free of Stefanie's grasp and gave Melinda a hug, and Melinda felt nearly overcome by the heady scent of an expensive Chanel perfume. "Welcome to Hacienda Patterson. I've heard so much about you I feel I know you."

"Thank you," Melinda said, easing herself free of her hostess's embrace. "You have a beautiful place here, Mrs. Patterson."

"Please—I know you live and die by diplomatic protocol, but we're all friends here. Call me Nicole."

"Very well—Nicole it is. Now tell me, why shouldn't I believe the professor? I find his theory fascinating."

Nicole turned to Professor Lara and frowned. The frown accentuated the crow's feet around her high cheekbones and the hollows of gray around her eyes. *This woman has lived life to the edge and now is beginning to pay for it,* Melinda thought immediately. *She looks…what? Somehow used up.*

"I was joking," Nicole said.

"Actually, she is quite serious," Dr. Lara said with great solemnity. "Mrs. Patterson is convinced that if the word gets out, it will be in all those supermarket tabloids you have in the United States and the next thing you know the highlands will be swarming with fortune hunters poking metal detectors in every nook and cranny. Nothing attracts a crowd like the prospect of finding buried treasure."

Nicole nodded. "At the moment, this happens to be one of the more peaceful corners of the world. I, for one, would like to keep it that way. We certainly don't need a nine-teenth-century style gold rush to liven things up.''

"Why not?" Chad said. "You were saying the other day that these highlands are one of the best-kept secrets in the Americas. I agree. A treasure hunt would bring tourists by the thousands, and tourists spend money."

"It is not a question of money," Dr. Lara cut in. "It is a question of national heritage. Antiquities such as those you see here are the property of the Guatemalan people. They are our link with the past that has shaped us. To use them as mere inducements to promote tourism is unthinkable!"

"It's a moot point, anyway," Nicole said. "If there is a treasure, it could be concealed in any one of a thousand hiding places in these hills. I suspect it never will be lo-cated—certainly not until that missing glyph turns up, and lord only knows what happened to it."

"Where were the other glyphs found?" Melinda asked, trying to sound only casually interested.

"All over the countryside—from here to Petén, and as far south as Escuintla," Nicole replied. "A few of them were found hidden in caves. Some turned up in the Indian mar-kets. And one or two had come into the possession of pri-vate collectors. Over the years, the government was able to recover nine of them, but the whereabouts of the tenth glyph remains a mystery."

Melinda stole a glance at the glassed-in display of jade glyphs, and at the white felt hollow that awaited the last of the set.

"But enough of this," Nicole was saying. "Joel and I would like to have you and Chad come to supper the day after tomorrow—Saturday. Say eight o'clock?"

"I'd love to," Melinda said, "but I'm driving into Gua-temala City that day. I may not get back to Panajachel un-til quite late."

"Oh, dear," Nicole sighed. "Saturday's the only day we have open. Couldn't your trip wait until Sunday?"

"I'm afraid not. I have to swing by the embassy to pick up something." She looked again at the display of glyphs.

The time had come for the jade jaguar to return home.

THE PARTY WAS IN FULL SWING when Chad was summoned to another part of the hacienda a little after ten to take a phone call. When he returned to the salon, his jaw was set and the little-boy look was gone. He said he had to meet someone back in town, and that Melinda was welcome to stay at the party and ride back later with Stefanie and her group.

"I'll go with you," she said. "It's been a long day and Stuffy and I can get together tomorrow." She decided not to ask about the phone call. She didn't want to hear any more lies.

They said their good-nights and walked out into the courtyard. The fleecy clouds that had hung over the mountains earlier in the evening had thinned out to reveal a full moon whose bright glow danced off the black waters of the lake at the foot of the steep slope.

"What did you think of her?" Melinda asked as she climbed into Chad's rented Volkswagen and buckled her seat belt.

"Stefanie?" Chad mused. "She comes on a bit strong."

Melinda smiled. "She always has. But you get used to her." She became serious. "She's gone through a lot in her short lifetime. Her father killed himself after some big scandal on Wall Street, and then a few years later her husband drowned and she had to go to court to have him declared dead so she could collect his insurance. It had to have been a terrible ordeal."

Chad backed the car around and pointed it through the archway separating the hacienda from the road. "From what she said, while you were so busy talking to Lara, I got the impression you and her late husband were close at one time."

Melinda wondered if she detected a note of jealousy. "That really doesn't concern you."

"No, it doesn't."

For a while, they drove on in silence, and Melinda stole a glance at Chad. She shouldn't have snapped at him, she knew. He was just making conversation. "We were college sweethearts," she explained. "We even talked about getting married. Fortunately, we both came to our senses in time. It never would have worked out."

"Why not—or isn't that any of my business, either?"

Melinda ignored the subtle rebuke. It was a fair question, she thought. She'd asked herself the same thing for years and the answer never varied. "Tony Germaine was the playboy of the Western world: a good-looking, football-hero type whose family was quite wealthy. He always had more money than he knew what to do with and he never seemed to be truly serious about anything. Whenever he found himself in trouble, somebody was always there to bail him out."

"Funny," Chad observed, "from what you said a moment ago, I figured he was practically broke when he died."

"Oh? How's that?"

"Why else would your friend have been in such a hurry to settle the insurance claim? I'm not sure what the law is on this in New York State, but she would have gotten the money in time."

"I don't have any idea. That's just the way she is. Stuffy has always been aggressive when it comes to money. I suppose it's because of her background." She leaned forward in her seat, her fingers clutching the top ledge of the padded dashboard to steady herself, and peered out into the night. "Slow down. I think I saw something up ahead."

Chad downshifted into third gear, then into second. The Volkswagen, which had been moving along at less than fifteen miles per hour, lugged grumpily and slowed to a crawl.

He stared straight ahead, studying the narrow roadway il-
luminated by the headlamps. "I don't see anything."

"I'm sure I saw a reflection of some sort at that last
switchback," Melinda said. "Just for a second—when you
came around the curve and started downhill again."

"You probably saw the lights on the water below."

"Probably." Melinda settled back in her seat. "If there's
a next time I'll chip in and we'll hire a boat."

Chad laughed. "I thought you'd had your fill of boats?"

"Anything would be better than this road, especially in
the middle of the night."

"Cheer up. We're almost . . ."

Suddenly, he jammed on the brakes and the car ground
to a halt, its engine dying.

Ahead, parked at an angle so that it blocked not just the
roadway but also most of the turnout on the downhill side,
was a battered pickup truck. Its headlamps were turned off
and its hood was open. Two men were leaning over the engine. As the lights of the Volkswagen splashed upon them,
they straightened up and held their hands before their eyes
to block the sudden glare.

Setting his handbrake, Chad depressed the clutch of the
VW and turned the ignition key. The tiny, four-cylinder engine sputtered and came to life.

"Maybe we'd better get out and see if we can help them,"
Melinda suggested, starting to open her door.

"Stay put!" Chad ordered her. His bantering good humor of a moment before had disappeared, and in its place
was gruff wariness.

One of the men—a heavyset, middle-aged fellow wearing
jeans, a faded denim jacket and a straw sombrero—started
forward, his hands behind him, and Chad rolled down his
window.

"Buenas noches," the man said, stepping up to the open
window and bending down to speak to Chad. "You help us
out, eh, señor?"

"Sure," Chad replied coolly, as the stranger started to bring his right hand forward.

Before Melinda realized what was happening, Chad reached out through the open window and slammed the heel of his left hand against the stranger's jaw, sending him reeling back against the embankment on the inside of the roadway. At the same time, Chad's right hand wrestled the gearshift lever into reverse.

The car lurched backward and Chad grabbed at the steering wheel, one eye trained on the rearview mirror, and guided the car back up toward the curve they'd rounded a moment before.

"What are you doing?" Melinda cried, swiveling about in her seat to stare at the menacing blackness that was broken only by the dull red glow of their taillights.

"I'm getting the hell out of here, that's what I'm doing!" Chad growled. "That turkey was pulling a gun on us! Now turn around and keep an eye on them!"

"I don't underst—" Before Melinda could finish, she heard a sharp, popping noise, followed an instant later by a thump that sent a shiver up her spine. She turned to look forward, and saw a cobwebbed crack radiating from a round hole in the windshield.

"On second thought," Chad said, "duck down below the dash! This clown means business!"

Melinda tried to lower herself in her seat, but the seat belt held her snuggly in position. She groped for the buckle release, pressed it and crouched down until the top of her head was below the level of the dashboard.

The VW's engine howled in protest as Chad pressed the gas pedal to the floor, sending the car rocketing in reverse. Melinda could feel the vehicle sway as it swung around the uphill curve, and she had a vision of hurtling off the cliff and into the lake.

She eased herself back up into her seat, hanging on for dear life to the unfastened seat belt. "Who are those men?" she gasped. "Bandits?"

"Your guess is as good as mine," Chad replied. He had turned halfway around in his seat and was watching the road through the rear window, keeping a tight grip on the steering wheel as the car bounced over the rocks and ruts.

"But why *us*?"

"Why *not* us?" he countered. "We were coming from a party and maybe they figured we'd be easy pickings. Who knows?" He eased up on the gas pedal and the Volkswagen slowed.

"So what do we do?" Melinda asked.

"First, we turn around and then we head back to the Patterson place. It's a couple of miles and I don't really want to trust my skill at driving backward all that distance."

"There was another turnout a few hundred yards up the road," Melinda suggested. "It was on the inside, as I recall."

"We'll give it a try. Hang on."

Melinda struggled into her seat belt and cinched it tight. It wasn't much of a defense against bullets, but at least it made her feel somewhat more secure.

It took five harrowing minutes for the VW to reach the turnout. Twice, the little car nearly plunged off the roadway, and, in twisting the steering wheel to compensate, Chad scraped his side of the vehicle against overhanging rocks.

"I don't think the rent-a-car people are going to be too happy to see you when you bring this back," Melinda said, trying to ease the tension.

"Maybe not," Chad laughed dryly, backing into the turnout and switching off the headlamps, "but I'll sure be glad to see them again. I'll be glad to see *anybody* again— anybody but those thugs who were waiting to ambush us."

Melinda glanced around nervously, wondering why he wasn't pulling back out into the road and heading for the Patterson hacienda. "Don't you think we'd better put some more distance between us and *them*?"

Chad shook his head. "Let's hold off just a minute. There's another car coming down the hill. I got a glimpse of its lights."

"Do you suppose someone heard the shots?"

"Could be. Still . . ." Unbuckling his seat belt, he opened his door and slipped out of the car. As the door opened, the dome light came on and he reached back inside and flicked the switch, turning it off. "Stay put." he ordered. "I want to take a look."

And then he was gone.

From the car, Melinda could see no lights, no hint of movement on the road. Maybe the bandits had given up. Maybe they thought she and Chad were already back at the Patterson hacienda and had phoned the police. Maybe they . . .

"There's a path hidden in the brush just behind us," she heard Chad say. "It's going to be close, but I think we can just about squeeze in there if we're lucky." He opened his door and climbed in behind the wheel.

"You mean you're going to try to hide the car back there?"

"The way I figure it, we have two choices—run or hide. The way downhill is blocked, and we don't know who's in that vehicle on the uphill side. Hang on." He shoved the gearshift lever into reverse and inched back, maneuvering through fallen rocks and squarely into a clump of bushes that clung to the slope. Bits of gravel peppered the rear wheel wells as the tires clawed for traction.

Slowly, the bushes parted, their thorny branches gouging against the sides of the car as it moved backward, up onto the hidden path. A rock banged the underside of the rear axle as the vehicle rattled up the ever-steepening slope. And then the rear bumper struck something solid, and they came to a standstill.

"End of the line," Chad muttered, setting the hand-brake and turning off the ignition. Forcing his door open against the restraint of the thick brush, he bulled his way forward along the side of the car, one hand in front of his face to protect himself from the thorns, and pushed the bent-back branches forward until they concealed the Volkswagen from the roadway.

Satisfied with the camouflage, he got back into the car.

"And now we wait," he announced.

Melinda reached across to touch him, to reassure herself of his presence. His left hand was on the steering wheel, his right on the parking brake. Her fingers came to rest on the one closest to her, and it was wet and sticky. He sucked in his breath sharply.

"The thorns?" she asked.

Chad nodded.

"You want me to drive?"

"I'll live," he said curtly. He glanced at her, and letting go of the steering wheel, patted her on the hand that had reached out for him. His left hand was bloody, too, but there was a powerful, throbbing strength in it. "Sorry, Lindy. I didn't mean to bark at you."

"That's all right. I understand."

"Do you? Maybe you just think you do." Pulling away from her, he let go of the hand brake and reached out for the ignition. "They're getting close," he said.

Melinda could see headlights on the mountainside in the direction of the hacienda. Her view was obstructed by the tangle of brush in which the Volkswagen was hidden, but she also thought she could detect movement on the down-slope side of the road. "Those people who are headed down the hill—shouldn't we try to warn them? The bandits are apt to attack them, too."

"I don't think so."

"Why not?"

"Instinct, Lindy. I think they're working together to box us in. They're doing a pretty good job of it, too."

As he spoke, a small, dark sedan rounded the curve from the upslope side and swung into the turnout. It came to a halt no more than twenty feet from where Chad had concealed the VW in the brush. The driver left his headlamps on.

"I can make out two of them in the car," Chad whispered. "They seem to be waiting for the truck."

A minute later, the pickup came lumbering up the road, its lights out. The driver braked to a halt in the roadway and trotted over to the parked sedan. Melinda's window was rolled down, but she was unable to hear the conversation.

The man returned to the pickup. The driver of the sedan made a three-point turn and backed his car carefully into the turnout, grazing the rear bumper against the brush behind which Melinda and Chad were hidden. Cutting his wheels sharply, he pointed the vehicle back up the road. The pickup pulled forward a few feet and was then also backed into the turnout, ready to move quickly in either direction.

"What's happening?" Melinda asked, keeping her voice low.

"My guess is that the people in the sedan are going back up the hill to see if they can flush us out. Then they'll probably double back, beating the bushes for us. They'll know we haven't gotten past the truck."

"If they beat this particular bush, we've had it!"

"Tell me about it!" Chad peered out the cracked windshield, and Melinda supposed he was gauging the space between the pickup and the start of the trail upon which they were parked.

"So what do we do now?" she asked.

Chad turned to look at her, and even in the darkness she could tell he was worried. "Open your door quietly and get out," he whispered. "I'm going to tear out of here, and

they'll be right on my tail. You run back up the road to the
Patterson place and have them call the cops. Now move it,
Lindy. And if you see the other car coming, duck into some
bushes and hide.''

''I'll do nothing of the sort! I'm staying with you!''

''The hell you are. This is going to be dangerous.''

''Big deal. Have you ever been caught in a revolution?''

''What's that got to do with anything?''

''Plenty. I was right in the middle of a revolution a few
years ago in a dinky old South American country you
probably never heard of. There were bombs going off all
over the place, and I came through it just fine. Some country bandits don't scare me.'' Only part of it was true: she had
been caught in one of those nasty little revolutions while on
an assignment for the State Department. But she'd been
scared to death then, and she was scared to death now. All
she could do was hope he wouldn't see through her little
show of bravado.

''All right, Lindy—don't say I didn't warn you.''

Pressing in the clutch, he took a deep breath and turned
the key in the ignition.

The engine gave a feeble cough, sputtered, then died.

''Come on!'' Chad growled under his breath.

He tried again. This time, the engine caught, and he
quickly reached down and released the hand brake. The little car lurched forward through the brush, scraping the
bottom of the front bumper as it rolled onto the level ground
of the turnout.

The pickup was parked closer to the end of the trail than
either of them had realized, and Chad swung the wheel hard
to the left as the car came off the trail. Melinda's side of the
car grazed the left rear fender of the truck just as the front
left door of the pickup was thrown open.

Chad switched on the lights, and the twin beams caught
the driver of the pickup as he jumped to the ground. He
took one look at the snarling little Volkswagen barreling

down upon him and leaped back up into the cab, dropping his pistol in his haste. He was so close as the VW crunched by that Melinda could have reached out and touched him.

Chad veered onto the roadway and pointed the car downhill.

Up the slope, to their right, Melinda could see headlights. "We've got more company!" she yelled.

"So I see," Chad growled, checking the rearview mirror. "How far back do you figure they are?"

"A hundred yards or so. It's hard to say. There are so many twists and turns in this road."

Chad geared down as they came upon another switchback. "Uh huh," he muttered.

"What's the matter?"

"The oil pressure's gone. We must have put a hole in the pan when we backed onto that trail."

"How far can we get without oil?"

"Let's not even think about it."

They were coming upon the turn too fast and he started pumping the brakes. Just as they went into the turn, something thunked against the rear trunk lid and Melinda turned and saw that the pickup had joined in the pursuit and was less than twenty yards behind them. What's more, the man on the passenger side was leaning out the window, shooting at them.

Chad gunned the engine and sent the Volkswagen creaking through the turn in a controlled skid. A few seconds later, he was fighting the wheel to straighten out. The wheels on Melinda's side begin to sink in the soft earth of the shoulder and she gave an involuntary shriek. The lake was almost directly below them.

Chad eased up on the gas and again checked the rearview mirror. "He's still there—and closing," he announced between clenched teeth. "If we can just get down to the main road, we may have half a chance."

"It's only another quarter mile or so, as I recall."

"I'm not sure we have another quarter mile left in this baby. Look at the temperature gauge."

Melinda leaned over and looked. The needle on the gauge had moved well into the red zone.

A second later, the rear window cracked and a bullet smashed against the rearview mirror, between their heads.

"His aim is improving," Chad observed, stepping on the gas in an attempt to distance themselves from their pursuers.

"Not so fast!" Melinda yelled. "This curve coming up is a bad one!"

Going into the turn, Chad dropped down into a lower gear. This time, the engine gave a loud clunk and the wheels locked, sending the car into another skid.

Melinda remembered hurtling sideways off the side of the road and the whistling silence that followed.

And then blackness...

Chapter Four

The sharp tug of the seat belt against her lap and across her chest seemed to be squeezing the last bit of breath from her body as the Volkswagen flipped end over end in a seemingly slow-motion arc that carried it far out over the water, as if hurtling her into another world, a world turned upside down, a world in which she looked up at a dark, shimmering stillness and down at the stars. It was a dizzying world, a world filled with ominous and mind-numbing silence. It was another world, but it was more. It was a strange new dimension: a moment of terror suspended in time, a microcosmic eternity in which the only reality was Chad's strong right arm pulling her close, cushioning her head against his shoulder, trying to protect her from the impact that had to come.

And then she got the merest glimpse of jagged shards of broken windshield bowing inward from the pressure as the car slammed into the water nose first, flopped over on its top and then dropped like a rock, the cold water spilling into the interior through open windows.

"Lindy..."

That was all she heard him say. His voice was cut off by a rush of water, giving way to a series of amplified creaks and groans as the car settled to the bottom. His hands went limp, fell from her face.

She tried to speak, but could say nothing. When she opened her mouth, she choked. *I've got to get out of here,* she thought. *Correction: we've got to get out of here. We—Chad and I. Now!*

She groped between the bucket seats for the buttons that would release their seat belts. She found Chad's, pressed it and felt his body float free and nudge against the floorboards. Then, releasing her own seat belt, she pushed down on the door handle and shoved.

The door wouldn't budge.

She tried to remember the things she'd read about escaping from a vehicle that had gone into the water.

First thing: don't panic. Hah! she thought crazily.

Second thing: equalize the water pressure against the door by rolling down the window, thus making it easier to open the door. But the window was already down. So was Chad's.

Next step? Think!

Go out through the door and swim clear. Just like that...

She grabbed at the collar of Chad's suit jacket and pulled him off the floorboards. Reaching across, she tried to force open his door. It, too, was jammed.

Then it would have to be the window. Squirming about, still holding onto the collar of Chad's jacket with one hand, Melinda felt blindly for the open window. It took long seconds to locate it, seconds that seemed an eternity as her lungs began to ache for air.

She started to swim out through the window, head-first, then decided against it. She couldn't let go of Chad because she might never be able to find him again in this impenetrable blackness, and if she tried to squeeze the two of them through the window at the same time they'd probably both get stuck.

The pressure began to build behind her eyeballs and she knew time was running out. She had to have air. So did Chad.

Steeling herself to move slowly, deliberately, she felt around with her feet until she found the opening, and then she moved through it, feet first, propelling herself by pushing against the dashboard with her right hand while her left hand clung to the collar of Chad's jacket.

Then she was free of the car. She kicked out with both legs and started for the surface.

And promptly lost her grip on Chad.

He was caught in the window, she realized. Turning a somersault in the water, she swam back to the open window and forced her hand into a tiny opening between one corner of the window and Chad's back.

One of his pockets had caught on the window handle. Ripping it free, she grabbed his collar again and struck out for the surface, kicking hard and fast.

Her head splashed above the surface and she could see the moon and the stars shining down upon her. Her heart pounding, she raised her face to the heavens and gulped down the cool, night air, feeling the pressure drain from her body.

You're going to be all right, Melinda told herself. *You're not far from shore. All you have to do is swim in and...*

And what?

Here in the water, all she had to worry about was drowning. On shore, there were men who were trying to kill the two of them, she and Chad.

Chad.

She wiped at her eyes with the back of one hand and looked around. Somehow she had lost her grip on Chad's collar and he was floating facedown in the water, showing no sign of life. Gunmen or not, she had to get him to the shore, had to revive him. Every second counted.

Turning him over so that his face was above water, Melinda started swimming toward the rock-crusted beach, holding tight to the collar of his jacket with one hand. Glancing up, she thought she saw lights moving down the

cliff above the beach. Was there a footpath from the roadway to the shore? She had no idea. All she knew was that she
had to get Chad back on dry land.

And then the fingers of her free hand came down upon an
outcropping of rock, and she stopped swimming and
straightened up in the water. It was only chest deep as she
stood upright. She looked up again at the cliff, and seeing
no more lights, dragged Chad to a muddy patch of shore
between two boulders. It took every ounce of strength she
could muster, but she finally managed to wrestle him to an
upright position, bending him, stomach down, against the
more rounded of the two boulders.

Quickly, she pressed the heels of her hands against his
back, just under his shoulder blades, and the water came
gushing up from his lungs. How long had they been under-
water, she wondered. A minute, two minutes? It was impossible to say. Every second had seemed endless.

Grasping him by the shoulders, she pulled him down on
the beach until he was flat on his stomach, his arms above
his head, his head turned, cheek against the mud. She leaned
forward and held her right ear to his lips. Was he breathing? She couldn't tell.

Don't die, she pleaded silently. *Please don't die!*

Hiking up her tight skirt, she straddled his waist and began shoving the heels of her hands against his back, just
under his rib cage. She wished she'd paid more attention
during the first-aid course she'd taken years before.

Good air in, bad air out, good air in, bad air out, she kept
telling herself. Wasn't that how it went?

It didn't seem to be working.

Turning him over on his back, she knelt beside him,
forced open his mouth and placed hers over it, forcing her
breath into his lungs. All at once, she was aware that his
hands were pressing against the small of her back, pulling
her tightly against him. The lips that, a few seconds before,

had been so cold and so lifeless were now warm and search-ing.

She pulled herself free. "Damn you!" she whispered fiercely, experiencing both a strong sense of relief and more than a little irritation with him. "How long have you been conscious?"

"So who's conscious?" he said weakly. In the pale glow of the moonlight she could see he was grinning. "I think I've died and gone to heaven. Your artificial respiration is something else, Lindy."

He reached out for her, but she rolled free and stood up, edging in close to the cliff where there'd be less chance of being seen from above. "If you're through playing games, we'd better see about getting out of here. I think those men who tried to kill us are coming down the cliff."

Chad sat up and shook his head groggily. "Give me just a second, huh?" He took several deep breaths and then wriggled backward, forcing himself to his feet at the base of the cliff alongside Melinda. "I must have hit my head on something when we went into the water. I blacked out and didn't come to until you dumped me across that rock and pumped some of the water out of me." He put his left arm around her and hugged her. "Thanks."

"You came to my rescue when I needed help. I was just paying you back." Melinda took a tentative step toward the water's edge and peered up at the cliff. "You feel like an-other swim?"

"Not really." He leaned forward and cocked back his head to look up toward the road. The gunmen *had* found a path down the side of the cliff. Flashlights were bobbing about, less than forty feet above their heads, and the move-ment was sending chips of rock and bits of dirt bouncing down the almost perpendicular incline. "But then I'm not at all sure we have much choice, do we?" He glanced around. "The way those boulders are stacked up at the foot of the cliff, we can't walk six feet in either direction."

Melinda looked out thoughtfully at the darkness of the lake, then made up her mind. "I have an idea. You stay here and I'll swim out a ways and start shouting to divert them. I'll make so much noise they'll think the two of us are together and they won't bother to search down here. While they're scrambling back up the cliff, I'll strike out for Panajachel and get help. What do you think?"

Chad dropped to his hands and knees, pulling her down with him. "No way. You go, I go. Those turkeys are probably so busy clinging to the side of that cliff that they're not going to risk looking down. Come on." Stripping off his jacket, he wadded it up and shoved it into the gap between two nearby boulders and then crawled into the water, with Melinda following him.

After the chill of the night air, the water was surprisingly warm, she noticed. Even so, they couldn't remain in the lake too long. Once their pursuers spotted them, they'd be easy targets in the moonlight.

Splashing as little as possible, and staying close to the shore where the ripples caused by falling rocks and dirt would conceal their movement, they swam toward the cleared beach of Panajachel, still a mile in the dark distance. Twice, they looked back to see flashlight beams playing across the water, searching.

Melinda paddled in close to Chad. "They probably think we're still in the car," she whispered.

"Maybe," he said softly. "And maybe not. In any case, I don't think we'd better risk going back to the hotel until it's light."

"That'll be hours!" Melinda protested. "We can't stay out here all night!"

"I have no intention of playing porpoise till the break of dawn. I seem to recall a boat shed on the beach at the edge of town. We'll hole up there for a while."

Fifteen minutes later, they came up out of the water under a dock that extended out from a rickety frame building sitting on pilings on the shoreline. A quarter mile away, Melinda could see the curving white facade of Del Lago looming against the nighttime sky. The hotel looked so inviting with its implicit promise of a hot shower, dry towels and a warm bed. So inviting—and so forbidden.

Staying in the shadows of the heavy pilings supporting the dock, they crept up onto the beach and looked around. There were several summer homes nearby. All of them were dark. In the distance, toward town, the sound of rock 'n' roll music could be heard, wavering on the midnight breeze that blew in off the lake.

When they had come to a point where the dock was only waist high, Chad swooped Melinda into his arms and lifted her easily onto the wooden platform. "Keep low," he cautioned, vaulting up onto the dock beside her. "I don't think anybody's watching, but let's not take chances."

They crept along the planking to the door of a large, plywood-walled shed with a single, unwindowed door. The door was firmly held shut with a thick hasp and heavy padlock.

"I guess we'll *have* to head for the hotel," Melinda observed, her teeth chattering. "We'll both end up with pneumonia if we stay out here much longer."

"We can't have that," Chad said. Fishing into his pants pocket, he came up with what looked like a pipecleaning tool. He unfolded a thin metal rod from the tool and inserted it into the padlock. Almost as quickly as if the rod had been a key, the padlock popped open.

"After you, m'lady," he said, sweeping out his arm in a flourish of welcome.

Melinda stepped past him into the pitch blackness of the shed. "You have some unusual talents for a travel agent."

"I'm one of those people who're always losing their keys," he explained with a chuckle, removing the padlock and quietly closing the door behind them.

"I don't believe that."

"Would you rather believe I'm a reform school graduate who majored in breaking and entering?"

I don't know what to believe, she thought. "Do you suppose we can turn on a light? There are no windows in here, so there's no way anybody can see in."

"Afraid not," he apologized. "If somebody comes busting in here, I want the advantage of having my night vision at its peak."

She could feel him move away, patting at the walls and fixtures of the shed. "Chad?" she called out softly.

"Quiet," he cautioned. "Just stay put so I'll know where to find—*ouch!*"

"What did you do?"

"I barked my shins against a big chunk of metal of some sort—an outboard motor, I think. Now quiet down."

Several minutes passed without either speaking again.

As suddenly as he'd left her side, she sensed his nearness.

"There's a bunch of kayaks stacked against one wall, and some beach umbrellas and folding chairs toward the back. I also found a blanket and an old tarp."

"Great," Melinda sighed. "All the comforts of home."

"They'll have to do. Now take off your clothes."

"What?"

"I said, take off your clothes."

"I'll do nothing of the sort!"

"Keep your voice down and listen to me, damn it. I have no intention of jumping your bones—"

"I should hope not!"

"But we've both got to get out of these wet clothes and dry off or we're going to be stiff as boards if and when we have to take off in a hurry. All right?"

Melinda ran her hands down her sides. She'd lost her sweater and her shoes, and her strapless white sheath was wringing wet and fast becoming cold and clammy against her skin. "I left my purse in the car," she murmured in a barely audible voice.

"I'll buy you another. Now take off your clothes."

"It…it was my favorite purse. I…I bought it four years ago in Buenos Aires. It was soft white leather and it had a…a little silver chain so you could sling it over your shoulder, and it…it just matched my shoes."

"It's probably still with the shoes. They can console one another."

"That's not very funny!"

"What did you have in it?"

"In what?"

"The purse, damn it!"

"A comb, lipstick, hanky, my room key—a few quet-zales."

"What about your passport and credit cards?"

"I left them in the hotel."

"You're stalling. Take off your clothes."

Melinda took a deep breath. "Just the dress."

"Everything," he corrected her. "Slip, pantyhose and whatever else you're wearing underneath."

"What I'm wearing underneath is none of your busi-ness!"

"I'm not going to touch you. Promise." She could feel him bend down and place something on the floor by her feet. Then he straightened up. "Here, I'm holding out a blanket. Take off your clothes and wrap yourself in it."

Melinda started to protest further, then changed her mind. He was probably right, she knew. She tugged off her soaked dress, dropped it on the floor at her feet and then pushed down her half-slip, kicking it out from around her ankles.

"Finished?"

She hesitated. "No."

"Well, hurry up. I'm next."

"You're going to get undressed, too?"

"You better believe it."

Melinda bent down and felt around for her dress and slip.
"I think I'll take my chances with the bandits."

"Think again. This is no time for false modesty."

"There's nothing false about it. I've no intention of—"

She felt his hands on the sides of her upper arms, lifting
her upright. Without speaking, he put his arms around her
and unsnapped her bra, let it fall, and then peeled down her
bikini panties until they were rolled around her knees.

"You can do the rest," he said, stepping back.

"I . . ." She finished stripping off the panties, and as she
straightened up he enfolded her within the rough, scratchy
warmth of the blanket. In the darkness, she could hear his
slow, even breathing, and she realized he was taking pains
to avoid letting his hands come into contact with her naked
body.

He guided her to the tarp he'd spread out on the floor.
"Now sit down right here. I'm going to find a way to bar the
door. I don't want any surprise visitors."

She heard him slide something heavy across the floor. A
minute later he was back, sinking onto the tarp beside her
with a sigh of exhaustion.

"Feel any better?"

"Lots," she admitted. "The goose pimples are gone."

She stiffened as he put one arm around her. And then she
relaxed, leaning her cheek against his chest.

She reached one hand out from under the blanket and
touched him. He was still wearing his wet clothes. "I
thought you were going to get undressed, too."

"I decided I'd better not."

"Why?"

He shrugged. "We only have the one blanket. If I got
undressed and climbed in with you, I'm afraid I'd never be
able to keep my promise."

"Your promise?"

"I said I wasn't going to touch you—remember?"

"I . . . I remember."

"Lindy, I may come on like a Boy Scout at times, but that doesn't mean I don't get some strong urges when I'm around you."

"Oh." She settled back against his chest, drawing warmth as much from his closeness as from the blanket. "Chad?"

"Yes?"

"What do we do now?"

"We wait until just before sunup, and then you get dressed and we slip back to the hotel. They'll probably have given up on us by then. But on the off chance they're still watching the hotel, we'll try to get over the wall in back, on the lake side."

"Why us, Chad? Why did they single us out?"

"Who knows? We were the first to leave the party. I suppose that was why."

Melinda closed her eyes and tried to remember the State Department advisories she'd read. There'd been sporadic rebel activity in these hills in years past, but no reports she could recall of bandits preying on tourists. Guatemalans, in fact, were far more hospitable toward foreign visitors than were the residents of many other Central American republics. And besides, surely ordinary bandits would never be so persistent—which meant that they probably weren't ordinary bandits at all.

"Chad?"

"Yes."

"Who are you? I mean—really?"

"I've already given you my name, rank and serial number. That's all that's required under the Geneva Convention."

"Seriously!"

"I'm a poor, overworked travel agent from New York who, at the moment, finds himself holed up with a very desirable young lady who isn't wearing a stitch of clothing.

Any minute now, I may yield to temptation and put a move on you." He paused. "That satisfy you, Lindy?"

"You're no more a travel agent than I am, Chad."

Even through the heavy barrier of the blanket she could feel his muscles tense. "All right, have it your way. I'm not a travel agent."

"Why'd you lie about it?"

His other arm came around and encircled her and he buried his face against the softness at the side of her neck. "Lindy," he said, "I'm in a business that forces me to do a lot of things I don't especially like. Lying is one of those job requisites—probably the *least* objectionable of them, if that tells you anything. I make no apologies for what I am nor for what I have to do. Someday, if everything works out, I hope you'll let me try to put things in perspective for you, but I can't do it just yet."

Melinda's free hand gently lifted his head until they were nose to nose, a breath apart. She was unable to see Chad's face in the darkness, but she sensed a wistful sort of sadness in his eyes, a yearning that had all but despaired of fulfillment.

Without any conscious design, their parted lips brushed, lingered for a moment, then joined in a long, soft, bittersweet kiss that sent an ache through Melinda's soul. She had known passion before, but this was a kiss that went beyond mere passion, soaring into new heights of hunger and tender longing. She closed her eyes, and in so doing opened them to the brightness of new hope. *If only this moment could last,* she thought. *If only we could shut out the badness and just be two people who are discovering each other, two people without fears and regrets and the hesitation born of uncertainty.*

The skin at the back of his neck was cold under her touch, and she squirmed about to draw one corner of the blanket around his shoulders. Her lips left his and nuzzled the roughness of his cheek. "Chad?"

"Uh-huh?"

"Chad, take off your clothes and get in here with me. You're going to catch your death."

He gave her a little hug. "You make it tough for a guy to keep his promise, Lindy."

"Chad?"

"Uh-huh?"

"Have you known a lot of women—in your business, I mean?"

"A few."

"Did you have to lie to them, too?"

"What kind of a question is that?"

"I'm just curious. Did you?"

"I did whatever I had to do. Satisfied?"

"No." She again rested her cheek on his damp chest. "When you kissed me a moment ago—were you lying then?"

"Would you believe me if I said I wasn't?"

"I don't know what to believe."

"Try to get some sleep, Lindy. I'm going to move over by the door and keep watch."

Melinda yawned. "You're evading the issue. I'm not really worried about you."

"You should be. Now try to get some sleep."

THE POLICE OFFICER was gone, his swarthy face wrinkled in a troubled frown, undoubtedly wondering why it had been his lot to be forced into a second confrontation with this beautiful but crazy gringa who now claimed she had been waylaid by bandits on the cliff road.

"Ask Mr. Young," Melinda had informed the doubting officer, in her usual flawless Spanish. "He'll tell you what happened. They had guns, and they tried to kill us."

"There have been no bandits in this district for years." The officer bristled, drawing himself erect as if to imply Melinda had insulted his integrity by suggesting that miscreants would dare operate on his turf. "There are only honest, hard-working people. I wonder if you and your companion could not have mistaken their motives. Perhaps they only sought your assistance in repairing their stalled truck."

"They had a strange way of asking," Melinda grumbled. "If you send a crew to fish out that car we were riding in, you'll see the bullet holes in it. Now, if you'll excuse me, I'm quite tired...."

She and Chad had climbed the high, stone wall separating the hotel from the beach and had slipped into the back of Del Lago before the sun had climbed above the mountains to the east. There had been two locked doors to get through, but Chad had made short work of them with his pocket tool. He had escorted Melinda to her room, using the stairs to avoid being seen by the night clerk and porter, unlocked her door—again with a few flicks of his pocket tool—and, after a kiss on the cheek, told her to expect a call later in the morning from the *Policía Nacional*.

As soon as he'd left, Melinda had locked the door behind her and inspected herself in the full-length mirror mounted on the bathroom door. Her hair was a fright, her new silk sheath a ripped, sodden, misshapen mess. Her sweater, high-heeled sandals and purse were at the bottom of the lake. She'd made no effort to salvage her bra and panties, choosing instead to stuff them in the cockpit of one of the kayaks stored in the shed where she and Chad had spent the night.

Stripping off her dress, she'd stood under a warm shower a full twenty minutes, until the last of the chill had washed away. She had then wrapped her hair in a white towel, donned her terry-cloth robe, phoned room service for a pot of coffee, and sat down to wait for the police.

Now that she'd taken care of that detail, all she had to do was attempt to figure out *why* all this had happened to her.

If what the police officer had said was true—that there were no bandits operating in the Panajachel area—then only two clear possibilities were left: the attackers were after her, or they were after Chad.

But why? She'd done nothing to present a threat to them—to anyone, for that matter. All she wanted to do was keep a years-old promise and then be on her way to Washington. The only person in Panajachel, or in all of Guatemala, who knew the real reason she'd come here was Stefanie. And Stefanie certainly had no reason to harm her.

No, it was far more likely that Chad was the target.

What did she know about Chad Young? Not much, not much at all. He was bright, good-looking and a highly accomplished liar. Oh, yes, he also possessed some rather remarkable skills at opening locked doors without using a key.

Who are you, Chad Young, she wondered for the umpteenth time.

She was sitting on the edge of her bed, and, without realizing it, reached out and touched the telephone on the night table. Washington must know something about him.

She picked up her wristwatch and stared at it as the sweep second hand made one full circuit of the Roman numerals arrayed along the rounded edge of the thin, gold-and-black face. Obviously, the timepiece had survived its dunking of the night before. She saw that it was ten o'clock straight up—eleven o'clock Washington time. If she placed the call now, she just might catch her friend Peg at the Passport Agency before the woman went to lunch.

She lifted the receiver. Within ten minutes, she was talking again to her friend.

"Any luck with the mysterious Mr. Young?" Melinda asked straight out.

"None at all." Peg sighed. "I've drawn blanks everywhere I've looked. I even checked with one of my contacts at the FBI. There's simply no record of the man. Are you sure you've got the right name?"

"I've got the name he gave me."

Her friend giggled. "Come on, Lindy! You know as well as I do you can't believe everything a man tells you! Maybe he has a wife and ten kids squirreled away somewhere and he's living a double life."

Melinda wasn't amused. "At this point," she said, "nothing would surprise me."

After she hung up, she leaned back on the bed, intending only to close her eyes for a few minutes. But the strain of the previous night caught up with her and she soon fell asleep.

Shortly after noon, she was awakened by the soft *tweet-tweet* of the phone. Making no attempt to sit up, she groped out for the receiver, her sleep-fogged mind telling itself it was on the edge of the discovery of a great truth. Only in the United States did telephones ring with insistent brassiness; elsewhere in the world, in all the countries she'd visited, the rings were gently muted, almost apologetic. Why was this? Was it a sly jab at the great American caricature of loud-mouth pushiness? Good question. She'd have to ponder it at length. Sometime. Not now.

Tweet-tweet.

"'Lo," she mumbled, sliding the receiver across the bed and wedging it between right ear and pillow.

"Lindy! Are you all right?"

It took a few seconds for Melinda to recognize the voice. "Stuffy?"

"Of course it's me! I'm up here at the Pattersons with some other art dealers. The police just came by and told us what happened last night. I was shocked."

"That makes two of us, Stuffy."

"Were you hurt?"

"I'm fine—now."

"What about that good-looking fellow you were with?"

"He got a bump on the head and he swallowed a lot of water, but otherwise he's all right."

"Did you get a good look at the people who attacked you?"

"Not really. One of them was in the headlights for a minute, but he had his hand up over his face as if shielding his eyes from the brightness."

"The police said there were two of them."

"At first. Later, some accomplices showed up in a car. They must have been hiding back there on the road above the hacienda."

Stefanie clucked sympathetically. "Crime seems to be rearing its ugly head everywhere you look these days. It hasn't been safe to walk the streets of New York for years."

"That's the funny thing about it, Stuffy. I've never heard of any bandits in this part of Guatemala."

"Don't be so sure about that. Nicole Patterson tells me that robbery and murder are fairly common. You just don't hear much about it. After all the bloodshed a few years back when the army was chasing the rebels in these parts, a garden-variety holdup is pretty small potatoes." She paused. "I don't mean to frighten you, Lindy, but it might be a good idea for you to cut short your visit. Those bandits are probably afraid you could pick them out of a police lineup. Who knows what they might do?"

"I came here to do something, Stuffy. I intend to do it."

"It's not worth risking your life, Lindy. I can handle things." She lowered her voice. "Where's the jade jaguar now?"

"My folks mailed it to me in care of the State Department, with a request to forward it to the embassy in Guatemala City. It should be there by now."

"Well, then, just have them hold the package for me. I'll be down in the capital in a few days. I'll pick it up and see that it gets back where it belongs."

Melinda hesitated. The offer was tempting, but she knew she couldn't accept. And her main reason had nothing to do with the original purpose of her visit to Guatemala. It had to do with a man named Chad Young. "Sorry, Stuffy, but it's something I have to do myself. I plan to drive down to the capital tomorrow and pick it up."

Stefanie sighed. "All right, be stubborn. As long as you're going to stick around, let's plan on getting together again. We have so much to talk about. Do you have plans for tonight?"

"Not really."

"Good. I'll meet you in the lobby at seven. I've halfway promised Joel and Nicole I'd join them at their gallery in town for a new showing of Indian primitives. I'm not much interested in primitives, but I don't want to hurt their feelings. We'll stop by the showing, then go off and have dinner somewhere and catch up on our girl talk. All right?"

Melinda thought about it. "You're not worried about getting robbed?"

Stefanie laughed. "I'll borrow some of Joel's armed guards. He's got a whole bunch of them on the payroll, keeping an eye on things. He'll never miss two of them for an evening. See you at seven."

Melinda was getting dressed to go downstairs to the hotel dining room for lunch when the phone rang again.

"Señorita Harding?"

"This is she."

"Señorita, this is Juan Lara Saavedra. We met last night at the Patterson hacienda. Do you remember?"

Melinda had a mental picture of a rumpled little man with glasses propped precariously above his bald pate.

"Of course, Dr. Lara," she said, trying to put him at ease. "What can I do for you?"

"I have a favor to ask of you, señorita. I must return to the capital tomorrow. Unfortunately, my assistant has taken the car to look in on a university project at Huehuetenango and he won't be back until tomorrow night. I believe you mentioned you are driving to the city?"

"That's right. I plan to leave first thing in the morning."

"I know it is an imposition, but would it be possible to ride back with you? I am to speak at a luncheon at the National Palace and it completely slipped my mind. I would take the bus, but the service is rather undependable."

"Of course, professor. I'd be delighted to have the company. It will give me the opportunity to hear more about your work. Shall we meet in the dining room at six?"

"I am in your debt, señorita."

Melinda was on her way out the door when the phone rang again. This time, it was Peg Hodgson in Washington.

"I'm glad I caught you before you left the hotel," the woman began. "I've got some news for you about your friend Chad Young."

Melinda pricked up her ears. "What did you find out?"

Peg lowered her voice. "We're off the record? I mean, you'll forget where you heard this?"

"Oh, for heaven's sakes, Peg, we've been friends for years! You know I'm not going to put you on the spot!"

"All right, Lindy, that's good enough for me. What I have comes from the department's security office. I have a friend over there—a very good friend, I might add. I didn't mention your name, of course, just that I was asking on behalf of a third party. He told me in no uncertain terms that you'd better lay off this fellow Young."

"Did he say why, Peg?"

"No. He just made it clear that Mr. Young is—and I'm quoting him word for word—strictly bad news."

Chapter Five

It was *him*. There could be no doubt about it. The man walking into the gallery with Chad was the same man who'd been with him the day before, skulking through the mountains below Sololá, submachine guns slung around their necks. He was big and solidly built, middle-aged and, even with the aviator-style sunglasses he was wearing, Melinda had the distinct impression his eyes were darting about the gallery, taking in everything and everyone.

The day before, he—Chad, too, for that matter—had been wearing coveralls splotched with ocher and brown camouflage dye. Now, though, the two of them looked as if they might have just come from a corporate board meeting. Or, perhaps, from a funeral. The mystery man was darkly handsome in a navy-blue suit, starched white shirt and black tie, and Chad was almost as formal in a three-piece gray pinstripe suit, a blue, oxford cloth button-down shirt and maroon-and-blue-striped silk tie.

Nicole Patterson, looking almost preppy in a loose-fitting double-breasted navy blazer and white slacks, also had spotted the two men. "Don't get any ideas, my dear," Melinda heard her whisper in a voice tinged with the faintest of French accents. "I know you're a friend of the American, but that man with him is—how do you say it—a nasty piece of work."

Melinda felt the color drain from her cheeks. She was startled not so much by Nicole's words as by the sudden awareness that Joel Patterson's wife knew of her interest in the man who'd arrived at the gallery with Chad.

She turned slowly to face Nicole. "How so?" she asked, raising her champagne glass to her lips.

Nicole's thin lips widened into a knowing smile. "Corruption always has been such a problem in these developing nations. To be perfectly candid, my dear, Major Ramirez has raised avarice to an art form. If Joel and I could put together a visual chronicle of his, ah, achievements, we would have students of aberrant behavior beating down our door."

"*Major* Ramirez?"

Nicole nodded. "He's an officer in the Guatemalan army. The word I get is that the major has been in trouble for years—gambling, soliciting bribes, dabbling in the black market and that sort of thing. I hear the government is finally pulling together the evidence it needs and is about to arrest him and send him to prison." She glanced questioningly at Melinda. "Rather an unusual choice of companions for your friend from New York. I wonder what those two could possibly have in common."

"So do I," Melinda said.

Chad and Major Ramirez had shaken hands with the towering Joel Patterson, who'd stationed himself at the door to greet his guests. Now they were on their way over to where Melinda and Nicole were standing, alongside a display of vibrantly colorful oils by a Quiché Indian artist.

Nicole quickly excused herself and walked off to seek the company of other guests. Melinda, feigning a sudden interest in the oils, turned as if to examine them more closely. She wasn't at all sure she could stand up to another verbal sparring match with Chad. She was beginning to like him too much, and it hurt to know that he was telling her one lie af-

ter another. Maybe, she told herself, it would have been
better if their paths never had crossed.

"I sort of thought you'd be here," Chad said, stepping up
behind her and putting his arm around her waist. "I have
someone here I'd like you to meet."

"Major Gilberto Ramirez Soledad, *a su servicio*," the
major intoned, taking Melinda's left hand in his right as she
turned to face the two men. He bowed stiffly from the waist
and brushed his lips across her fingertips. "I have seen you
from a distance, señorita, and I was utterly enchanted. But
close up—"

Melinda nodded curtly. "I, too, have seen *you* from a
distance, Major Ramirez."

The two men exchanged glances.

"It was yesterday—up in the hills," Melinda went on,
switching to rapid-fire Spanish to see how Chad would
react. "You and your gringo friend here were tramping
around playing war games, just the two of you."

Chad grinned. "We were hunting. We..." He realized she
was deliberately testing him, and his grin widened in sheepish admission of guilt. "Made a liar out of myself again,
didn't I?"

"I'm getting used to it," Melinda said dryly. She re-
verted to English. "Give me a straight answer for a change.
What were the two of you doing?"

"Hunting—honest!"

"With machine guns? Oh, come on, *Mr.* Young! You can
do better than that!"

"Ah," said Ramirez, "it is true, señorita. Not very
sporting, I grant you, but a middle-aged man such as myself needs all the help he can get. My eyesight is not what it
used to be, nor are my reflexes as sharp. Consequently, I
require a weapon capable of firing a great many rounds in
a short time." There was a sparkle in his dark brown eyes as
he turned on the charm. "Is it not shameful?"

Melinda glanced sharply at him. Nicole had wondered what the two men could possibly have in common. Now Melinda could provide an answer: both Chad Young and the soon-to-be-disgraced Major Gilberto Ramirez were capable of lying through their teeth without batting an eyelash.

"Are you stationed in this district, Major?"

"*Sí, señorita*, but only temporarily. The generals in the capital have plans for me, so I have been stationed at the barracks at Sololá to await their pleasure."

That's not the way I heard it, Melinda thought. "What sort of plans—or is it a military secret?"

"Are you enjoying the show?" Chad cut in, obviously wanting to change the course of the conversation.

"It's fine. Tell me, Major Ramirez, do you . . ."

"Ah!" The major was smiling and looking past Melinda, toward the door. Melinda looked over her shoulder, to see Joel Patterson bend down to give a hearty greeting to Dr. Lara, who looked even more rumpled than when she'd last seen him. "You must excuse me, señorita," Ramirez apologized. "I must pay my respects to Dr. Lara. I am a great admirer of his work."

Melinda watched him cross the room. The man didn't walk, he swaggered, she noticed.

"I take it you're not overly impressed with the major," Chad said in a low voice.

"Not really," Melinda said. "But, then, I've always been prejudiced against thieves and grafters. Nicole Patterson told me all about him."

"Oh? And what did Nicole say?"

"She said he's about to be cashiered from the army. I think she was surprised to see that you'd taken up with him."

"The major and I aren't exactly bosom buddies, Lindy. However, we do have some mutual interests."

Melinda studied Chad over the rim of her champagne glass. "What sort of mutual interests?"

"Let's see. We like outdoor sports—hunting, hiking, that sort of thing." He grinned. "We also share a healthy admiration of female beauty. Which reminds me, that's a nice outfit you're wearing tonight."

Melinda glanced down at the royal-blue wool cardigan jacket and green-and-white plaid, full-cut pleated wool skirt she'd dug out of her bag. The jacket and skirt had been too heavy for warm and humid São Paulo and had been packed away for years. She'd tried to steam out the wrinkles by hanging the outfit in the bathroom and running a hot shower, but it hadn't helped much. Still, it was nice of Chad to let her think otherwise. Nice—and also quite convenient for him, what with his knack for changing the subject.

"It's all right, I suppose," she said grudgingly. "But what about..."

Stefanie suddenly appeared out of nowhere and slipped in between them, linking her arms with theirs. "I hope you can talk some sense into this girl," she said, addressing herself to Chad. "After that terrible business on the road last night, I've told her that if she has any sense she'll get out of here."

"I'll try," Chad said. "But I doubt if she'll listen."

"I'm serious," Stefanie said, frowning at her former roommate. "The more I think about it, the more I worry. You're not safe in Panajachel, not with those bandits after you."

Melinda shook her head. "We don't know that for sure."

"I told you, Lindy, they probably think you can identify them." Stefanie glanced at Chad for support. "Don't you agree?"

"Reluctantly, yes." He smiled. "My irresistible charm aside, what is there to keep you here?"

Questions, Melinda thought. *Questions and a frustrating shortage of answers.* "As a matter of fact, I'm leaving first thing in the morning."

Stuffy's somber expression brightened. "You are— *really*?"

"I'm driving into Guatemala City to pick up something at the embassy. Then I'm coming back here."

"But *why*, Lindy?"

"You know why."

Stefanie looked quickly at Chad, then gave an almost imperceptible nod. "I told you I can handle things for you."

Chad was mystified. "Mind letting me in on what you ladies are talking about?"

Melinda shot a triumphant glance in his direction. "Yes," she said. "I *do* mind. All right?"

Stefanie laughed. "That's telling the man, Lindy!"

Melinda nodded. "If Mr. Young can have secrets, so can we."

Chad eyed her strangely. "Hey, my life is an open book."

"I'm sure it is," Melinda retorted. "But it seems to be written in Sanskrit, and I don't read Sanskrit."

"I WON'T EVEN ASK YOU how your love life's been," Stefanie said as they sat down across a candlelit table from one another in the dining room at Del Lago. "It's written all over your face."

Melinda, taken aback, put down the wineglass she'd raised to her lips. She'd been eagerly looking forward to this dinner get-together with her old friend. It should have been a time for smiles and nostalgia, for remembrances and renewals. But this opening remark was something else, something unexpected. She stared at Stefanie. "You mean Chad Young?"

"I mean Chad Young," replied Stefanie with a nod.

"That's ridiculous!" Melinda scoffed, looking away to avoid eye contact. "I hardly know the man. We've had exactly one date and that, as you well know, turned out to be a lesson in survival techniques." She opened the menu in front of her and pretended to read it. "Let's order. I'm starved."

Stefanie giggled and signaled to the waiter. "Let's have another drink first and talk. I want to hear about Chad."

"There's nothing to tell," Melinda insisted. "He fished me out of the lake two days ago when my sailboat capsized. Then he invited me to go with him to that reception at the Pattersons last night. He said they had a surprise planned for me. That's the extent of it—believe me, Stuffy."

"You say he's a travel agent?"

"*He* says he's a travel agent."

Stefanie cocked her head in bemused skepticism, sending her bob of golden hair dancing to one side of her forehead. "In other words, you don't think he's telling you the truth?"

Melinda took a deep breath. "Stuffy, all I know is that I don't want to talk about him."

"Oh? It sounds serious, girl. Would it surprise you to know that he wants to talk about *you*?"

"What do you mean?"

Stefanie finished her first rum collins and reached for the fresh drink the waiter had brought. "He's been asking questions about you."

"Asking *who*?"

Her friend shrugged. "People around town. The domestic staff at the Pattersons'. Some of the employees here at the hotel. Our friend over there." With a nod of her head she indicated a small, dark man sitting at the bar, nursing a bottle of Gallo beer. "The fellow Joel sent along to keep an eye on us this evening. He told me Chad had even tried to pump him."

"What sort of questions has he been asking?"

"What you were doing in Guatemala, whom you were seeing—that sort of thing." Again, Stefanie giggled. "You suppose he's jealous?"

"Oh, come off it! I told you, I hardly know the man!"

Stefanie took a sip of her second drink. "Joel suspects he's a con artist of some sort. That or maybe an art thief who's trying to get his hands on some valuable Mayan pieces. When Chad first showed up here in Panajachel a month ago, Joel checked him out with a travel agent friend in New York. I guess Joel has been taken to the cleaners a couple of times in his life, and he has no intention of letting it happen again. Anyway, his friend had never heard of Chad—and neither had anybody else he checked with. Chad has no office listing in New York, no membership in any trade groups, none of the professional affiliations you might expect of somebody in that business."

Melinda shook her head slowly, less in disbelief than in resignation that her worst fears about Chad were being realized. Still, something bothered her and she couldn't quite put her finger on it. There were too many holes in Chad's background story—almost as if he were purposely encouraging others to distrust him. It made no sense whatsoever. "If Joel Patterson is so convinced that Chad is a phony, why on earth did he invite him into his home? Good lord, Stuffy, he greeted him like a long-lost brother!"

"You'd have to ask Joel," Stefanie replied. "I got the impression he wants Chad close at hand so he can keep an eye on him." She put down her drink and leaned forward on her elbows. "Enough talk of conspiracy theories. Bring me up to date. What has my old roommate been doing these past few years?"

Melinda filled her in on her three-year tour of duty as a consular officer in São Paulo, the highlight of which had been her role in arranging a hemispheric conference on economic cooperation.

"I hate to say this, Lindy, but it all sounds frightfully dull." Stefanie smiled. "Whatever happened to the free-spirited young lady who faced down the jade jaguar years ago in that cave?"

"We all have to grow up sometime, Stuffy," Melinda said. Then she laughed. "Coming here was something of a rite of passage, I suppose—I mean, seeing that the jade jaguar gets home safely after all this time."

Stefanie turned serious. "I still think you ought to let me handle it from here on out. It's not safe for you to come back here."

"That's silly! One isolated little incident doesn't change things, Stuffy. What happened last night could have happened to anyone."

"That's just the point," Stefanie said, lowering her voice. "It might not have been 'one isolated little incident.' Those men on the road just might have been gunning for you. It's something to think about...."

MAJOR RAMIREZ HELD all the bargaining chips, and he knew it. "I shall put two men on it at once, my friend. Your Melinda Harding has nothing to fear, believe me. In exchange, however..." His words trailed off.

Now the rub, Chad thought. *You scratch my back, I'll scratch yours.*

"...a small favor," Ramirez continued. "For a man of your talents, it will be but the work of a few hours." He slipped out of his jacket, slung it over the back of a chair and loosened his black tie. "Would you care for a brandy?"

"I'll pass. What's the favor, amigo?"

Ramirez removed a bottle from a cabinet back of his desk and poured himself a stiff jolt. "I have just received word that a shipment is coming down from the north tonight, from those Zaculeu digs near Huehuetenango, you know. There will be three trucks and a police escort. I think it would be well worthwhile to intercept the shipment."

Chad took off his suit coat and draped it over the back of a chair. He settled down on a nearby cot and stretched out, lacing his fingers behind his neck and staring up at the ceiling. "In other words, you want it hijacked."

"Your choice of words pains me, my friend." Ramirez smiled and sipped at his brandy. "I merely want the trucks stopped and a slight adjustment made to their cargo."

"What sort of an 'adjustment'?"

"I want you to pry open several cartons in each of the three trucks, and then . . ."

When the major had finished explaining, he poured himself another glass of brandy, kicked off his shoes and planted his feet atop his desk. "As I say, for a man of your talents it will be the work of a few hours."

"Am I supposed to do all this on my own?" Chad demanded.

"Of course not, my friend. I shall assign several of my best men—excellent shots, all of them, and experts in hand-to-hand combat. The convoy guards are from the *Policía Nacional*. They will never know what hit them."

Chad sat up and eyed Ramirez questioningly. "If you don't mind me asking, why can't you do it yourself, amigo?"

Ramirez shrugged. "My face is too well known and I should almost certainly be recognized. The only way to prevent that from happening would be to kill every man in the convoy. And that, my friend, seems a bit extreme, eh?"

Chad snorted his disapproval of the idea. "The home office didn't send me down here to play Jesse James, amigo. Why don't you put the arm on one of your own people to ramrod the operation?"

"I trust you, my friend. You have too much to lose if something goes wrong—and that now includes the protection I am able to extend to your lady friend, of course. Besides, I am not all that sure of my own people. This is a delicate business we are in. I suspect some of my men are playing both ends against the middle. May I count on you?"

"I don't know that I have a choice," Chad grumbled, thinking of Melinda and what Stefanie had said about the "bandits" trying to silence her.

"True." Ramirez nodded. "Now help yourself to that Uzi in the closet, and I will summon my men."

IN THE DREAM, Melinda was sailing in the middle of a blue lake, so far out from shore nothing could be seen on any horizon but a blurred shimmer where water met the brightness of the sky. The wind was singing through the rigging, puffing out both mainsail and jib and causing the little boat to heel hard as its bow sliced through the water, misting her face with cool spray.

Someone was chasing her, calling her, trying to get her to come about and stop. Afraid of what she would see, she didn't dare look back . . . at *him*.

"Lindy!"

It had to be Chad. She could hear him calling to her, softly. She didn't want to face him again, didn't want to listen to more of his lies. Lies hurt. Most of all, *his* lies hurt.

"Lindy!"

Trying to shut out the sound of his voice, she stared hard at the horizon, concentrating on it, wondering what had become of the volcanoes and the mountains that surrounded the lake.

Nothing had gone right since she'd met him.

No, not true. Meeting him, being with him, was right.

Listening to him was something else quite different. When she listened to him, she knew he was lying to her.

So be it. She didn't need any new attachments, not now, not when she was stepping up the ladder to a new level in her Foreign Service career. She certainly didn't need any attachment to someone like him.

So who's lying now?

"Lindy!"

She found herself sitting upright in bed, naked atop the sheets, trying to blink away the mind-numbing daze that separates wakefulness from sleep. Outside the sliding screen door of the balcony, the nighttime sky crackled with lightning and a cold wind was blowing a spray of the rain into the room.

"Lindy? Open the door—please!"

She groped across the nightstand for her watch, found it and squinted at the luminous dial. It was almost four o'clock. What on earth could he want at this hour of the morning?

Planting her feet firmly on the carpeted floor, she stood up groggily and made her way to the hallway door, pausing long enough to pull on her terry-cloth robe.

The door was standing ajar, secured only by the chain she'd attached before she'd gone to bed. She remembered that he was very good with locks.

Peering out into the lighted hallway, she could see his silhouette standing there in front of the door, hand poised to rap again. "Chad?"

"Let me in, huh?"

"Do you know what time it is?"

"I know very well what time it is, Lindy. Are you going to open this door or do I have to use these bolt cutters?" As he spoke, a pair of heavy pincers nosed through the opening and came to rest on the chain.

"You wouldn't!"

"The hell I wouldn't. I want to talk to you."

Melinda hesitated. "Are you alone?"

"Of course I'm alone. Now open up!"

Turning on the room lights, Melinda pushed the door shut, fumbled for the chain and then opened the door. She stepped back. "I'm warning you, I can scream awfully loud if you try anything."

Chad stepped into the room, shut the door behind him and chained it. He still was wearing the three-piece, gray pinstripe suit he'd worn much earlier that night, when he'd shown up at the art gallery with Major Ramirez. Now, though, the suit was wet and shapeless, and there was a dark stain on his upper left arm, spreading from a tiny, round hole.

"You could have screamed last night when there was only a thin blanket separating us," he said. "But you didn't."

"Last night was…" Melinda's eyes widened as she stared at the stain. "Oh, my God, you've been shot!"

He nodded, and for the first time she noticed how white and cold he looked standing there, soaked and disheveled. "That's right—I've been shot," he said weakly. He took another step toward her, then stopped and leaned against the wall, breathing hard.

"How did it happen, Chad?" she demanded. "For God's sake, *how*?" She saw him looking at the balcony door, saw that the wind was picking up and the rain now was coming in hard. Without taking her eyes from him, she moved to the balcony door, slid it shut and drew the drapes. "Take off that jacket. I want to have a look at your arm."

Chad gingerly slipped off his suit coat and hung it across the back of a chair. The left sleeve of his shirt had been punctured and was soaked with blood.

"I've got to get a doctor!" Melinda gasped.

"No, no doctor," Chad said defiantly. He settled wearily into the chair on which he'd placed his jacket. Kicking off his shoes, he planted his stockinged feet on the edge of the bed. "Let's talk, Melinda Harding," he said, loosening his tie.

"I'm going to phone the desk and have them find a doctor," she said. She started for the phone on the nightstand between the beds, but he caught her arm and stopped her.

"No doctor," he growled.

She turned to face him, started to argue with him, then thought better of it. He obviously was in no mood to listen to reason. "All right, then, take off your shirt and let me see your arm. Then we'll talk."

"It's nothing serious."

"Any bullet wound is serious, you idiot. Now off with the shirt."

Chad slowly unbuttoned the blue, oxford-cloth shirt, then leaned forward in his chair and eased his arms out of the sleeves. There was another splotch of wet blood on the sleeve of his T-shirt.

He dropped his shirt to the floor and looked at Melinda. "Satisfied?"

Kneeling beside the chair, she gently rolled up the sleeve of the T-shirt around the hard, taut muscles of his upper left arm. The wound was a shallow one, she saw. A bullet had creased the flesh about three inches down from his shoulder, leaving an ugly gouge that was still pulsing blood.

She wadded up the shirt he'd dropped and pressed it against the wound, placing his hand over the compress. "You're lucky," she said, rising to her feet. "That bullet could have hit an artery."

"Any number of things *could* have happened," he said softly. "And you're right, I am lucky. I met you."

Melinda felt a faint flush of pleasure. Suddenly shy, she turned away from him, and picking up her carry-on bag, tossed it onto the bed. She rummaged through it and brought out a bottle of expensive Scotch whisky still in a gift box. "I picked this up in the duty-free shop at Rio. It was supposed to have been a present for my dad, but medical emergencies come first."

She fetched a clean, white washcloth from the bathroom, then opened the bottle and soaked the cloth. "This is going to sting a bit, but at least it will help clean out the wound," she said, replacing the wadded-up shirt with the more antiseptic compress.

Chad sucked in a sharp breath as she pressed the washcloth against the wound. "This stuff is better taken internally," he joked.

"Hold that cloth where it is and I'll see what I can do." She put the bottle on the dresser next to the chair, went to the bathroom and brought out a clean glass and a towel. Setting the glass next to the bottle, she carefully wrapped the towel around the washcloth and tucked in the edges to secure it. "Help yourself," she said, looking at the glass and bottle.

Chad poured himself a small measure of liquor and sniffed at it appreciatively. *"Salud,"* he said, raising his glass to her.

Melinda sat down on the end of the bed and folded her arms across her chest. "Now suppose you tell me what happened."

"I had an accident."

"What sort of an accident?"

He took a sip of the Scotch and closed his eyes, savoring the liquor. "You mind if I spend the night here?"

"I certainly *do* mind!" Melinda said sharply, pulling her robe more tightly around her. "You have your own room. You've come this far, I should think you could make it the rest of the way under your own steam. What floor are you on?"

"Four—one up."

"I'll walk you to the elevator, if you like." She started to stand up, but something in his eyes told her to remain seated.

"I don't want to go up there," he said.

"Why not?"

"I'm expecting visitors anytime now. I don't want to be there when they show up."

"You mean the police?"

He opened his eyes and took another sip of Scotch. He didn't answer her question.

"Chad, why did you come here?"

"I wanted to talk to you."

"Talk about what?"

"You."

"What about me?"

He finished his drink and put aside his glass. "I want you to do something for me."

"Do what?"

"I want you to get the hell out of here. As soon as it's light, I want you to pack up and get in that rental car of yours and head straight back to the capital. As soon as you get there, I want you to head for La Aurora Airport and book a seat on the next flight out of Guatemala. I don't care where it's headed—Mexico, the States, El Salvador, wherever."

Melinda studied him. He didn't show a flicker of emotion.

"Has Stefanie been talking to you?"

"No."

"Then why?"

"Because I don't want to see you get hurt. Isn't that a good enough reason?"

"What do you mean 'get hurt'?"

"Just that. I almost got you killed last night. I don't intend to let them have another crack at you."

Melinda took a deep breath to clear away the confused medley of thoughts that suddenly assaulted her mind. Reason told her to take his advice, to pack up and stay away from Panajachel. Her heart told her something else, something quite different.

"Who's after you?" she asked, her tone softening.

"It doesn't matter. Will you do as I ask?"

She leaned forward on her elbows and looked at him. "I might be able to help you."

"I doubt it."

"Really, Chad. I know people at the embassy in Guatemala City. If you're in trouble, they might be able to help you get squared away. You'd have to level with them, of course, but it'll all work out."

"That won't be necessary."

Melinda squirmed around on the bed and tucked her legs under her, covering them with the skirt of her robe. "Is it Major Ramirez?" she asked. "Is he the one who's giving you a bad time?"

Chad looked at her strangely, as if he were wondering how much she actually knew. "Hardly."

"I told you he has a bad reputation. I don't know how the two of you met, but you really shouldn't be associating with him. They say he's apt to be arrested almost any day now."

"Who's 'they'?"

"Nicole Patterson. If you'll remember, I talked to her at the reception last evening and she told me all about the major."

"You don't believe everything everybody tells you, do you?"

"No, I—" Melinda started to say that she especially didn't believe what *he* told her. But something held her back. She looked down, avoiding those searching blue eyes of his. As she did so, she noticed that his stockings were soaking wet. "Take those socks off—right now," she instructed him, clambering over his legs and heading for the bathroom. She returned with a dry towel and tossed it to him as she climbed back onto the bed. "You're going to catch pneumonia unless you start taking care of yourself."

"I try," he said, straightening up in his chair and one-handedly tugging off his wet socks. "I try, but it's not always easy."

Melinda watched him rub down his feet and ankles with the towel. "Chad?"

He looked at her.

"Chad, what brought you to Guatemala?"

"I told you, I'm a travel agent."

"If you're a travel agent, then I'm the secretary of state." She hesitated. An idea had been taking shape in the back of her mind since her first phone call to Peg Hodgson in Washington. It was just a shot in the dark, but perhaps now

was the time to put it to the test. "Was he a friend of yours?
A relative?"

"Who?"

"Mark Cronin."

Chad's face wrinkled into a frown, and Melinda couldn't
tell if he was perplexed or agitated. "So who's Mark
Cronin?" he demanded, reaching for the bottle of Scotch.

"That's what I want you to tell me."

He poured himself another drink, avoiding her eyes. "I'd
be happy to, Lindy, but I don't have the foggiest idea what
you're talking about. I don't know any Mark Cronin."

"I think you do, Chad." She hesitated. Maybe she was
making a mistake, but she couldn't quit now. She *had* to
find out the truth. "Mark Cronin was a pilot who disappeared on a flight over this area several months ago, and he
hasn't been seen since."

He smiled at her. It was a warm, open smile, devoid of
any overt tint of deceit. "And you put two and two together and figured I came charging down here to find him?"

"Be honest with me for once, Chad. Isn't that why you're
here?" She wanted him to say that it was. It would explain
so many things, even help justify some of the lies he'd told.
Maybe Mark Cronin had been on some sort of secret mission—for the CIA? And maybe the governments of both the
United States and Guatemala were playing their cards close
to the vest. Maybe Mark Cronin was being held captive, if
not by bandits then by some rebel group. Maybe Chad had
hired the disreputable Major Ramirez to help make contact
with the men who were holding Mark Cronin. Why not? It
would explain a great many things, even the gunshot wound
Chad refused to talk about.

"I put two and two together," Melinda admitted.

"Sometimes two and two don't add up to four. Sometimes..." Chad's free hand went to his face to block a
sneeze.

"You *are* coming down with a cold," Melinda scolded him.

"I'll live," he said. "Why don't you cut those lights and get back into bed?"

"It's almost time to get up anyway," she replied with a shrug. "I might as well stay up. I promised to meet Dr. Lara in the dining room at six."

"Oh? How come?"

"He asked me to give him a lift back to Guatemala City. He came up here with a research assistant, but the assistant is in Huehuetenango with the car and the professor has to be at the National Palace for a luncheon."

The mention of Huehuetenango brought a flicker of interest to Chad's dark-blue eyes. "You'll have another passenger, too, Lindy."

"You?" She hoped he'd say yes.

"One of Ramirez's people is going to ride along to keep you out of trouble."

Melinda shuddered. "I'd rather take my chances with the bandits."

"Don't be too sure about that." He eased his wounded left arm around in front of him and checked his watch. "I'd better get out of here."

She looked at him searchingly. "I thought you wanted to stay?"

"I did," he said, draining his glass and setting it aside. He stood and gathered up his shirt and jacket. "But, on second thought, it probably isn't a very good idea. There are some things I've got to take care of, then it would probably be wise for me to disappear for a while."

Melinda got up off the bed, and as she rose to her feet her body brushed his in the narrow space between the foot of the bed and the chair where he'd been sitting. Before she realized what was happening, she was in his good arm, her eyes closed, her head bent back, her auburn hair spilling down her back. His lips brushed the softness of her cheek and came to rest on hers. His mouth opened, and he murmured something that was lost in the warmth of a kiss.

Her fingers pressed the back of his neck, pulling him more tightly against her, and her tongue touched his. *Stay,* a little voice within her cried. *Stay with me for what's left of tonight. Stay and tell me no more lies.*

She could feel his hand stroking her back, coming lower with each movement, pressing her body against his. "I've wanted you from the moment I first saw you," he murmured. "You have no idea how much I've wanted you, Lindy."

She pulled back her head and pressed the tips of two fingers against his lips. "Don't say anything," she whispered "Not now."

His lips again brushed hers, then he pressed her head to his chest as he stroked her hair. "Hear me out, Lindy," he said in a voice so soft she could barely make out the words. "I've lied to you about a lot of things, and I'll probably lie to you again. I don't like to do it, but I have to—for your own good, as well as mine."

"Chad . . ."

"Let me tell you a story—a true story—and then I've got to get the hell out of here. Once, there was a guy who had a job that wasn't very pleasant. He started feeling sorry for himself and he decided he had to have someone to talk to, someone to share his troubles with. He met a woman and he fell in love, and before he knew what he was doing he was telling her things—things he should never have told anyone. The woman told someone else, and someone else told someone else. And one night a killer came to their apartment and, mistaking the woman for this non-hero of ours, started blasting away. Our non-hero swore then and there it would never happen again, no matter how much he had to lie. End of story." He pushed himself away and moved toward the door, slinging his still-wet jacket over his uninjured right shoulder. "I've got to get out of here, Lindy, for your sake as well as mine."

"Chad?"

He glanced back over his shoulder at her, but said nothing.

"Will I see you again?"

"Count on it."

"When?"

"Probably when you least expect it." He turned off the room lights and reached for the doorknob.

"Chad?" She groped out for him in the darkness, wanting to assure herself he was still there. "Chad, is there still..." She wanted to ask if there was anyone else in his life now, but the words she'd framed in her mind refused to form on her lips. Was it because she didn't want him to lie to her again, especially not about *that*?

He pulled her close and kissed her lightly on the forehead. "Make sure you secure that chain after I leave. And keep the balcony door shut, huh?"

"You've all but said they're after you, not me," she reminded him.

"I still don't want to take any chances."

"Chad?"

"Uh-huh?"

"I may stay overnight in the capital. If I do, I'll be at the Camino Real. You can reach me there."

"I told you, Lindy, I want you on the first plane out of the country."

"Chad, I can't leave just yet. I have something I have to do."

"You mean that business you and your friend were talking about? It's not worth risking your life for, is it?"

"It's you they're after—not me."

"Don't be too sure about that, Lindy."

Chapter Six

Melinda kept her eyes straight ahead, wishing that Ybañez would stop his incessant babbling.

"I shall leave you in Chimaltenango, señorita," he was telling her for the ninth or tenth time as the road straightened out on the approaches of Patzicia, where it would join the main highway. Ybañez zipped shut the soft, black plastic case he'd carried across his lap all the way from Panajachel. Melinda couldn't be sure what was in the case, but she suspected it was a shotgun. Ybañez was careful not to let her get a glimpse of the contents.

"Just say when," Melinda sighed. She'd certainly be glad to see the last of the man. He'd talked almost constantly for the past hour and he'd said absolutely nothing.

She glanced at the rearview mirror. Dr. Juan Lara Saavedra was dozing peacefully in the back seat, head bowed, chin bobbing on his chest, thin fingers laced across his midsection.

I envy you, professor, she thought. *You don't have to listen to this character. You can close your eyes and tune him out.*

Ybañez had been waiting for her, slouched against one of the front fenders of her locked Nissan, when she and the professor had come out of Del Lago a little after six. The note Chad had left her at the desk told her to expect him.

Ybañez is one of Ramirez's men. He may not be Mr. Personality, but he knows how to follow orders. If you run into problems, do as Ybañez says and everything will be all right.

Thus far, the only problem Melinda had encountered had been Ybañez himself. Before the introductions were completed, Ybañez had spread out a road map on the hood of the Nissan and traced his finger along the red line indicating the road that went through Sololá and connected with the Inter American Highway at Los Encuentros. "We go this way," he announced.

"Why?" Melinda demanded, feeling argumentative.

"Because I say so," Ybañez said gruffly.

"Is it less dangerous than that way?" She pointed to a secondary road that meandered through Santa Catarina Palopó and Patzún.

"That way," he said scornfully, "is slower."

"I'm not in all that much of a hurry." Melinda smiled at the professor, who was standing at the passenger-side door, a scuffed briefcase in one hand. "As long as Dr. Lara doesn't have to be at the National Palace until noon, we might as well see some different scenery."

"We go this way," Ybañez insisted, tapping the map with a blunt forefinger.

"Yes, master," Melinda said with all the exaggerated humility she could muster. "Whatever you say, master. Your slightest wish is my command."

The sarcasm was lost on Ybañez. Clearly, he considered her subservience as his due.

They got into the car and headed up the road from the beach into town, where Melinda promptly turned off onto the route of her choosing. Ybañez swiveled around and fixed a steely glare on the road sign that was disappearing behind them. He sputtered and fumed and shouted for her to stop and turn around. When that failed, he muttered several expletives in Spanish—to which Melinda promptly responded in kind, topping them off with a random selection of the choicest Portuguese insults she recalled from her three years in São Paulo.

Ybañez fumed and sputtered, his face dark with rage. And then he slumped back in his seat and stared straight ahead in a sullen silence that lasted all of three minutes before he started complaining about Melinda's driving.

"I am afraid you have ruined the poor man's day," the professor said in English. He smiled. "But you will enjoy the scenery. It is magnificent."

It was, too. Not recommended for the timid or impatient traveler, the road traversed a cloud-misted landscape where terraces had been hacked out of the steep hillsides to make way for squat rows of corn and beans and evenly spaced stands of fruit trees. Even at this early hour, sturdy, solemn Indian women, wearing colorful blouses, or *huilpiles*, and heavy, wraparound skirts, trudged along the shoulders of the road, bundles on their heads, while bronze-skinned youngsters with burled staffs tended flocks of sheep and goats in rock-studded fields the size of postage stamps.

But Melinda was soon lost in her thoughts, oblivious to the scenery and to Ybañez's grousing. She had several things on her mind, but one subject above all kept returning again and again. Who was Chad Young and would she ever see him again? Or would he become just a memory, as fragmented and wispy as all the lies he'd told her?

Ybañez had begun lecturing Melinda on the need for caution, his voice a droning rumble against the whoosh of the wind spilling in the side windows. "After I leave you, do not stop until you are in the capital," he intoned, reciting instructions he'd committed to memory. "Go directly to your embassy, have the rental agency come pick up this car, and then arrange a seat on the next flight to the United States. Do you understand what I am telling you?"

"I understand quite well," Melinda said absently.

"Another thing: remain in your embassy until it is time to leave for the airport. Have someone drive you."

Now *that* was too much. She realized Ybañez was simply parroting orders he'd been given by Chad, but Chad had no right to tell her how to run her own life!

"The embassy staff has more important things to do than to play nursemaid to me," she protested, reverting to English.

Ybañez stared at her uncomprehendingly. *"¿Cómo?"*

Melinda repeated what she'd said, in Spanish this time.

"You will do as you are told, señorita," Ybañez grumbled, annoyed that the orders were again being questioned.

Melinda decided against further argument. It wouldn't do a bit of good, she knew. Once she dropped off her unwelcome passenger in Chimaltenango, she'd be free to do things her way.

Ten minutes later, she and the professor were alone in the car, having left Ybañez at a bus stop on the bustling main drag of Chimaltenango, a drab little city that served as both a departmental capital and as a trading center for the highlands. On the eastern outskirts of town, she spotted a restaurant with a thatched roof and tables set out in the open air. On impulse, she swung off the highway and parked in front of the building. The place looked clean enough, there were no other cars in evidence, and she wanted a cup of coffee.

No, you don't, she forced herself to admit as she and the professor got out and locked the car doors. *All you want to do is assert your independence.*

They sat down at an oilcloth-covered table where she could watch the highway, and Melinda smiled at the waiter who came hurrying forward from the kitchen.

"Black coffee, please," she said. She looked at the professor, and he seconded the order.

When the waiter had gone to get the coffee, the professor fished in his jacket pocket for a pipe. "I want to thank you again, Miss Harding, for allowing me to ride back to the capital with you."

"It's no trouble at all, Dr. Lara."

The professor fiddled with his pipe, then put it aside on the table. "I have a confession to make," he said. "What I really wanted was an opportunity to speak with you."

Melinda looked at him. He seemed nervous.

The waiter brought their black coffee. When he was gone, the professor continued. "How well do you know the Pattersons?"

"I'd never heard of them until two days ago."

"And the others who were at the reception—all those art dealers?"

"One of them, Mrs. Germaine, is a college friend whom I hadn't seen in years. The others were complete strangers. Why?"

The professor hesitated. "May we speak in confidence?"

"Of course, Dr. Lara."

He pushed aside his coffee cup, untouched, and leaned forward on his elbows. "I received a rather disturbing report in Panajachel. A certain item recovered from our Huehuetenango site has turned up in New York, where it has been purchased by a private collector unaware of its historic value."

"What was this item?"

"A ceramic bowl used in ceremonial bloodletting—a very handsome piece that could shed a great deal of light on our research. The history of the Maya is inscribed on such pieces as this. In their own time, of course, the Maya had more mundane media: cloth, parchment and fig-bark paper, for example, but over the centuries most of these crumbled into dust and were lost forever. Ceramic, on the other hand, is durable."

Melinda thought about it. "Are you suggesting that the Pattersons or one of their guests stole this bowl?"

The professor shook his head quickly. "I am suggesting nothing. I am merely assessing various possibilities." He paused. "Frankly, I would find it hard to believe that the Pattersons had anything to do with this incident. Joel and Nicole are quite well-to-do, you know, and the few thousand dollars they would earn on this transaction would hardly be worth the risk of deportation and possibly even prison."

"Then—"

"I cannot say about the others. All of them have visited Guatemala in the past—several times, in fact. It is possible they could have co-opted one of Joel's people, or perhaps even someone from my research staff. I do know that a very strange thing happened a few days ago, about the time these art dealers arrived in Panajachel. Do you remember that gold Quetzalcóatl I pointed out to you?"

Melinda remembered. She remembered quite well.

"That figurine miraculously appeared on a workbench at the hacienda. A shipment had come in from Huehuetenango the night before, but the Quetzalcóatl did not appear on the manifest. No one knew where it came from."

"Why are you telling me this, Dr. Lara?"

The professor smiled. "I have heard good things about you, señorita. You are not only an officer in the government of the United States, but you are someone I believe I can trust. When you return to Washington, I would appreciate it if you would see what you could find out about these art dealers who deal with the Pattersons."

"I'm not a detective, professor."

"No, but you are an intelligent young woman and you have certain connections. With the information you could develop, we could possibly put a stop to this trafficking in antiquities that robs us of our national heritage."

Melinda looked about for the waiter to ask him to bring her more coffee. As she turned, she saw that a lean, wiry man of about fifty had taken a seat two tables away and was eyeing her through dark glasses. He was wearing a brown leather jacket, unpressed khaki pants and a practiced scowl.

Where'd he come from, she wondered. She'd seen several cars and trucks pass by on the highway in front of the restaurant, but none had stopped.

Spotting the waiter, she signaled to him.

Turning back to the professor, she lowered her voice to keep from being overheard by the man two tables away. The chances were he didn't speak English, she knew, so she switched to that language.

"I'll do what I can," she said. "I can't promise anything, though. But if..." She hesitated, unhappy with the thought that had just occurred to her, then decided to proceed. "If by some remote chance my friend turns out to be involved, what will happen to her?"

The professor shrugged. "Nothing—nothing at all as long as she does not return to Guatemala. As you say in diplomatic circles, she would be persona non grata. And the government would, of course, take steps to see that none of the wholesalers in this country have any further dealings with her."

"I see." Melinda considered the problem for a moment. "I'm not all that familiar with Mrs. Germaine's operation, but I gather that she does a good deal of business in this part of Latin America." She lowered her voice still further. "You said we're speaking in confidence?"

"You have my word on that, Miss Harding."

"All right, then, suppose—just for the sake of argument, you understand—that Mrs. Germaine has been dealing in illegally acquired artifacts. What if she saw to it that those artifacts were returned to Guatemala? Could she continue to do business here? This is all hypothetical, you understand."

The professor nodded gravely. "I'm sure we could work things out."

"All right, Dr. Lara, I'll see what I can find out."

She glanced back over her shoulder and saw that the stranger was still sitting there, still watching her intently. He'd ordered nothing from the waiter, and the latter seemed to be going out of his way to avoid the nonpaying customer.

"Do you want something?" Melinda demanded, staring at the man.

He said nothing. Nor did he move.

"I think we'd better get back on the road, professor," Melinda said, standing up and dropping a quetzal note on the table.

Driving away from the restaurant, she watched in the rearview mirror to see if the man would follow her.

He didn't.

A few miles beyond El Tejar, before the road widens to begin its climb through the mountains ringing the capital, she realized that the same two motorcyclists had been in back of the Nissan for some time. She'd seen them first in Chimaltenango, just after she'd dropped off Ybañez, but had thought nothing of them; they were simply part of the passing scene. Now, though, they were staying no more than one hundred feet in back of her, riding close together, slowing when she slowed, speeding up when she accelerated.

Am I becoming paranoid, she wondered. *I can't go jumping at every shadow.*

"Is something wrong?" the professor asked.

"I think we're being followed."

"But why?"

"I don't know. I suppose they're friends of Ybañez."

The morning rush hour was well under way as she began the steep, winding descent into the city. After a detour to drop off the professor at the University of San Carlos campus, she headed straight for the embassy on the broad, tree-lined Avenida de la Reforma. Checking the rearview mirror, she could see no sign of the motorcyclists.

It was almost ten o'clock when she got to the embassy.
Leaving her rental car parked on a sidestreet, she walked
around the corner, showed her identification card to both
the Guatemalan guards and the United States Marine corporal on duty at the front gates, and was admitted to the
office of the chargé d'affaires.

"Thank heavens you're all right, Miss Harding!" the
chargé exclaimed, pumping her hand and steering her to a
chair on the visitor side of his desk. "The Guatemalan authorities told me you'd had a nasty experience in the highlands."

"It was a close one," Melinda admitted, sitting down and
primly crossing her legs and folding her hands in her lap. "I
had no idea there were bandits in that part of the country."

The chargé nodded. "I've been here almost three years
and this is the first such incident I've heard of in the Sololá
area. Elsewhere, yes—on the Pacific highway and in Petén—but not Sololá. You were lucky, young lady."

"Very lucky," Melinda agreed, thinking of Chad Young.

After a few minutes of polite conversation, the chargé
glanced at his watch. "I have an appointment downtown,
but perhaps you'd care to join us at a reception and late
supper here at the embassy tonight. Typical diplomatic do,
you know: some Argentinean business people are looking at
a joint venture here with an American firm, and we're act-
ing as middleman. Since you're familiar with Argentina,
we'd love to have you join us. I promise we won't keep you
late, Miss Harding. We've got you booked on a seven
o'clock flight tomorrow morning—TACA to Houston, with
direct connections to Washington."

Melinda eyed the chargé quizzically. "What made you
think I'd want to leave so soon? I just arrived in Guatemala
a few days ago and I still have a week's leave before it's time
to report to my new assignment."

The chargé frowned. "The National Police indicated to us that you were anxious to be on your way. In fact, they said you told them you wanted to be on the first flight out."

"I see. . . ."

She *didn't* see. She'd made no such statement to the officers who had questioned her in Panajachel. It was Chad's idea that she leave the country—Chad's and the major's *and* Stuffy's. It was unlikely any of them would have had much to say to the police.

Melinda started to get out of her chair, then hesitated. "Tell me, have you ever heard of an American named Chad Young?"

"I'm afraid not. What's he do?"

"He's a travel agent. I met him in Panajachel."

The chargé shook his head. "You can check with the consular office, but Mr. Young hasn't come to my attention."

"What about Joel and Nicole Patterson?"

"Of course. They're art dealers in Panajachel. A fine couple—very respectable, and quite highly regarded by the government here. I've been in their gallery myself. Even bought a few pieces from them." He wheeled around in his swivel chair and scooped up a small piece of jade from the credenza in back of his desk. "This is my latest acquisition." He placed a carved glyph on the desk in front of Melinda, and she blinked.

It was a jade jaguar, with fire opal eyes.

"It's a reproduction, of course," the chargé confessed, "but it still cost a pretty penny. I bought it for a gift, but then decided to keep it myself. What do you think of it?"

"It's lovely," Melinda said softly. "Do you know where the . . . ah . . . original might be?"

The chargé shook his head. "I have no idea. Joel Patterson told me that the design for this jaguar was based on Mayan cave paintings he'd found in various areas. As I understand it, several fairly similar glyphs have been found in the highlands, and scholars who've studied them say they tell a story—part of a story, at least. Some of the glyphs in the set are still missing, so there's no way to complete the translation.''

"Come to think of it," Melinda ventured, "I did hear something in Panajachel about those glyphs."

"That's right, Miss Harding. The story has something to do with the migration of the Mayas. Someone who's more conversant in anthropology and archaeology should be able to tell you." Again he checked his watch. "Now you must excuse me, Miss Harding," he said, standing up. "I really must head downtown. Don't forget the reception tonight. We'll look forward to seeing you at seven."

Melinda thanked him for the invitation and asked directions to the embassy administration office, where she signed a receipt for a small parcel addressed to her.

"It came in by diplomatic pouch," a secretary informed her. "I guess the people in Washington were afraid you might not get it in time if it were sent regular mail." She gave Melinda a mock frown. "No contraband, I trust?"

"No contraband," Melinda laughed. "Just something I borrowed and promised to return."

She dropped the parcel into her shoulder bag, and then thought of how her room in Panajachel had been searched. "I just remembered: I have a lot of running around to do today. I don't suppose I could ask you to hold onto this until tomorrow?"

"Of course."

Leaving the embassy, Melinda looked up and down Reforma. There was no indication she was being watched. Major Ramirez probably had called off his watchdogs, she decided.

Eight blocks south of the embassy was the elegant Hotel El Camino Real. She registered at the desk and immediately went up to her room, showered and changed into the one suit she'd packed in her carry-on bag. The suit was a lightweight, solid gray tropical worsted with a flared skirt and squared shoulders. Very businesslike, very all-together. Just the thing for getting to the bottom of a mystery in a big city.

And the capital *was* a big city: almost two million people, more than a third of the country's population. It occupied the center of the Valley of La Ermita, rimmed—like Lake Atitlán—by volcanoes. In some ways it was a very modern metropolis, complete with daily traffic jams, shiny new high-rises and twinkling neon. But in other ways it was a throwback to another era: a collection of musty-smelling, tightly knit neighborhoods crisscrossed by narrow streets and alleys, with pockets of affluence carefully concealed behind high, stuccoed walls.

Melinda took a cab to the Public Library, on the edge of a vast recreational and cultural complex that included a bullring, a hippodrome and several superbly laid out museums.

She had no trouble finding what she sought. Extensive research had been done on the Maya, by both Guatemalan and foreign anthropologists, and there was a whole shelf of books on the legend of the jaguar.

The jaguar, she learned, was the savage alter-ego of a Mayan king killed in battle with the conquistadors. The king's body had been carried to the highlands to be buried with his treasures. And, it was said, the jaguar would stand guard over his master's tomb until the day the king rose to again confront his enemies.

As she scanned the books, an idea began to take shape in her mind. It was a bizarre idea, an idea unsubstantiated by any hard evidence. And yet it just might make sense.

She checked the time. It was one o'clock. The professor had said he'd be going to a luncheon in the grand ballroom of the National Palace. Perhaps she could still catch him. She had to talk to him again.

MELINDA KNEW she was being followed. An aging black Mercedes sedan with dark film obscuring its windows had trailed her cab all the way from the library, never getting any closer than a half block nor dropping back any more than twice that distance. What was more, the driver of the Mercedes obviously wanted her to know he was there. Twice—without any urging from Melinda—the cab driver had zoomed through intersections as the traffic signals were changing from yellow to red. And twice the Mercedes had run the red light to stay on the tail of the cab.

The cab driver noticed it, too. "You are not in trouble of some sort, are you, señorita?" he asked worriedly, studying her reflection in his rearview mirror.

"Not that I'm aware of," Melinda assured him, trying to sound confident. "Why do you ask?"

"I think the police are following us." He reached up to adjust the rearview mirror, giving himself a better look at the car that was following them. "If it is the police, they might arrest me for speeding—and then where would I be? I have a wife and seven children. How would they eat if I were in jail?"

Melinda glanced back over her shoulder. "I'll give you an extra five quetzales if you lose him."

The driver sighed. "What is five quetzales if one is behind bars, unable to feed his family?"

"Ten quetzales."

"I don't know, señorita . . ."

"Twenty quetzales—and that's my final offer. Twenty quetzales, or you can drop me off at the next corner and I'll find another cab."

The driver made an abrupt left turn against traffic. The cab bounced across the gutter and over the sidewalk, narrowly missing several pedestrians, and sped into a narrow alley. "Actually," he muttered, "that Mercedes is old and shabby. No self-respecting policeman would be caught dead in such a vehicle."

Fifteen minutes later, after winding through a maze of back streets, the cab pulled up to the main entrance of the National Palace, an impressive-looking, gray granite building. Stony-faced soldiers wearing camouflage uniforms and maroon berets, with automatic weapons slung over their shoulders, were stationed at close intervals on the block occupied by the palace.

"Is this normal?" Melinda asked, eyeing the soldiers as she paid off the cab driver.

The driver smiled patiently. "In your country, señorita, you have your Secret Service to guard your president. In my country, the army does the guarding. Your Secret Service wears no uniforms—nothing to set them apart but those little lapel pins, I have read. Is it not better to wear uniforms and thus make it easier to recognize the players, eh?"

"I suppose," Melinda admitted, wondering if she'd ever be able to keep track of the players she'd encountered thus far.

Walking up the steps to the entrance of the palace, she looked back over her shoulder and caught a glimpse of a black sedan parked in front of the Metropolitan Cathedral on the east side of the Plaza. Was it the Mercedes? She couldn't be sure.

She was stopped twice before she got to the front door. The first time, a soldier stepped out into her path and stared at her questioningly, holding his automatic rifle across his chest.

Melinda reached slowly into her purse and brought out her diplomatic passport. She opened it so that the soldier could see her photo, then closed it and put it away and brushed past him.

At the doorway, another guard—this one wearing a light blue ceremonial uniform with golden chevrons and gleaming brass—held up his hand to stop her. He asked if she had business in the palace.

"Not exactly," Melinda replied in Spanish. "I am a consular officer of the United States, passing through Guatemala on my way to Washington. The people at our embassy told me how magnificent your National Palace is, and I wanted to see for myself."

The guard nodded somberly. "Would you please open your purse, señorita?"

Melinda did as she was told, and watched as the guard took it from her hands and carefully examined the contents. Satisfied she was not carrying a weapon, he handed back the purse and signaled to a subordinate.

"Corporal Echeverría will escort you, señorita," he informed Melinda. Turning, he signaled to another, younger man who had been standing just inside the entrance, admiring the trim gringa who stood at the door with his sergeant.

The corporal stepped out and saluted smartly.

"The señorita would like to see the public areas of the palace," the sergeant informed him.

"Particularly the grand ballroom," Melinda spoke up. "I've heard so much about it."

The sergeant consulted his watch. "Ah, you are just in time. There was a state luncheon in the ballroom and the guests are just now leaving. In fact—" he nodded his head toward the marbled hall inside the door "—there are two of them now, the Canadian ambassador and the noted anthropologist Lara Saavedra."

Melinda leaned in to get a better look. Lara, wearing the same rumpled suit he'd worn on the trip from Panajachel, was with a middle-aged man who bore the conservative, well-dressed stamp of the professional diplomat.

She couldn't let anyone else hear what she had to say to the professor. She'd have to try to get him away from the ambassador. She stepped forward quickly as the two men came out the entrance. "Hello again, Dr. Lara," she greeted him.

He stopped, blinked owlishly and then beamed. "Miss Harding! What a pleasant surprise!" He turned to the Canadian ambassador. "This is the young lady I was telling you about—Miss Melinda Harding."

"Ah," the ambassador nodded. "You were the one who had that run-in with the bandits up by Lake Atitlán—am I not right? Caused quite a stir here, you did—you and that chap you were with. What was his name? Young?"

Melinda nodded. "Chad Young." She wasn't sure, but she thought she saw a flicker of warning in the professor's eyes at the mention of Chad's name. "Mr. Young and I were very lucky to escape with our lives."

"Indeed you were, Miss Harding. What brings you here to the National Palace?"

"I was hoping to have a few words with the professor." She smiled to soften what was to follow. "In private, if possible."

The ambassador frowned in mock sternness. "You know, of course, the professor has agreed to be scholar in residence at McGill University in Canada next spring? You wouldn't be trying to get him to reconsider, would you? I'm well aware several of your American universities have tried to recruit him."

"Certainly not," Melinda insisted.

The professor brought out a small notebook and thumbed through it. "I shall be quite busy this afternoon, señorita, and I have a dinner engagement at eight, but if you would care to meet me before then—say, at seven—we could talk. Do you remember where you dropped me off?"

Melinda thought of her promise to attend the embassy reception, but decided she could risk being late and agreed to meet Dr. Lara that evening.

"Splendid. I live not far off campus. There's a quiet little café just a few doors from my building—the Corona de Alvarado. Any cab driver will know where it is." He smiled apologetically. "I would invite you to my home, but my maid has been ill and the place is rather a mess."

"The Corona de Alvarado will be fine," Melinda assured him. "I'll see you at seven."

THE CORONA DE ALVARADO was a neighborhood café at the corner of a block of well-kept apartment buildings less than a quarter mile from the main campus of the University of San Carlos. When Melinda arrived early for her appointment with the professor, all but a few of the red-and-white checkered tables were occupied, for the most part by well-dressed younger people who appeared to be either graduate students or else junior faculty members. There was only a sprinkling of the jeans and sweaters usually found in North American college hangouts.

Melinda could sense every man in the café eyeing her as she walked in and took a seat by the front window. Women's liberation had made a few inroads in Latin America, but unescorted females—especially attractive ones wearing clinging black sheaths such as the one she had bought specially for the embassy reception—still were something of a rarity in cafés.

Politely ignoring the looks and unspoken invitations she was getting, she ordered black coffee and rehearsed the questions she wanted to ask the anthropologist. It was a shot in the dark, she knew, but she was convinced she held the key to all that had happened two nights before in the mountains of Sololá. Everything pointed to it.

Why else had her room been searched? Why else had she been attacked while leaving the Patterson hacienda? There was no doubt in her mind that she was the target, and not Chad. She was also convinced that the reason for her visit to the highlands had something to do with it.

Dr. Juan Lara Saavedra could supply the answer. If only she could supply the questions . . . the right questions.

She couldn't tell the professor everything, of course. But she had to tell him enough so that the pieces fell into place. She had to be discreet. Very discreet.

The waiter came and refilled her cup with steaming black coffee and Melinda looked at her watch. Seven-twenty. She'd never make the reception. But it was just as well. She hadn't really been looking forward to it. She just hoped the professor hadn't forgotten their appointment.

The waiter hovered over her, his thin cheeks crinkled in a smile of professional solicitousness. "You are expecting someone to join you, señorita?"

Melinda looked up at him and nodded. "Yes...a Dr. Lara. Do you know him?"

The waiter's smile warmed. "Ah, *sí*! The professor frequently takes his meals here. He lives just down the street."

"You haven't seen him tonight?"

The waiter shook his head slowly. "I'm very sorry," he apologized. "He has not been in. I saw him at the university this afternoon—I am one of his students, you know—but I did not have the opportunity to talk to him. He was very busy. Some trouble with one of his projects, I understand." The waiter started to walk away, then stopped and turned back. "If you would like, I can call him for you."

Melinda started to decline the offer, then thought better of it. The professor did have a lot on his mind, and it was quite possible their appointment had slipped his mind. He was almost a half hour late now. It wouldn't hurt to jog his memory.

She followed the waiter to a phone at one end of the service bar and waited while he dialed the number. He said something into the receiver, then handed the instrument to her.

"*¿Bueno?*" she heard a scratchy voice say.

At a table a few feet away, two young men with guitars had begun to serenade the half-empty pitcher of beer that sat on the table in front of them. One of them was singing. Or howling. Melinda wasn't sure which.

She cupped her left hand to her left ear and pressed the receiver against her right ear. "Dr. Lara?"

"*Sí.*" It was a bad connection. She could barely hear him.

"This is Melinda Harding. I was hoping you'd still be able to make it."

Pause. "Make it? I do not understand."

"We had an appointment, if you'll recall. At the Corona de Alvarado. I'm here now."

"I am sorry, Miss Harding, but I—"

"I really have to talk to you, professor. If this is a bad time, perhaps we could meet after your dinner tonight."

"I am afraid that will be impossible."

"But—"

"Good night, Miss Harding."

And then *click*, he was gone. Just like that.

Damn it! Melinda thought. He had no right to brush her off that way. All she wanted to do was take a few minutes of his time in an attempt to get to the bottom of a mystery.

Melinda replaced the receiver on the hook and looked around for the waiter. He was standing at the far end of the bar, stacking beer mugs on a tray.

She walked over to him. "Can you tell me how to get to Dr. Lara's apartment?" she asked.

Leading her to the door of the café, the waiter pointed into the dusk toward the three-story apartment building at the far end of the block. "It is in that building. I don't remember if the professor has his name on the door, but he lives on the second floor, rear."

"*Muchas gracias.*"

The building he indicated was at least a half century old, with high ceilings and a broad, white-walled entry hall. It had a closed-up, musty air about it. There was no elevator, just an iron-railed staircase.

Melinda climbed the stairs to the second floor and looked around. There were four doors. One was at the front of the building, two at either side opposite the head of the stairs, and the fourth was at the rear. That one was standing ajar, and she went to it and knocked. "Professor? Professor Lara?"

No answer.

She looked around. There was no sign of life on the floor. She knocked again. And waited. Still no response.

"Professor Lara?" Melinda poked her head into the open doorway and squinted into the gloom. She was looking into a narrow hall that appeared to lead to a large room on the alley side of the building. "Professor?"

She stepped inside and groped around for a light switch. Finding none, she eased her way along the hall, reaching out in front of her to guard against running into obstructions.

There were several closed doors on either side of the hall, and at the end an open archway leading into a large study. Pausing as she entered this room, Melinda peered about, letting her eyes become accustomed to semidarkness that was relieved only by the yellowish glow cast by a streetlamp outside.

On either side of the room, floor-to-ceiling bookcases lined the walls. Tall file cabinets stood on each side of the hall door. "Professor?" she queried.

There was no sign of life.

She began to make out the shape of a desk in the center of the room. It was all but hidden in the shadows between two ornately barred windows. As she studied it in the darkness, she got the impression that it was strewn with papers. There was a high-backed chair behind it, a smaller one beside it. As she moved closer, she could see that both chairs were unoccupied.

"Professor Lara? Are you in here?"

Something white and bulky loomed from the corner of the desk, and she froze, startled. For an instant, she simply stared, then breathed a sigh of relief as she realized it was just a table lamp.

She groped out for the base and felt around for the switch. Finding it, she twisted it and then blinked at the sudden blaze of light from the high-wattage bulb behind the parchment shade.

Turning her head to avoid the full force of the blinding glare, she caught a glimpse of another chair in a corner of the room, against the bookcase to the right of the hallway.

Again, she froze, now truly terrified.

Professor Juan Lara Saavedra was seated in the chair, bound to it securely by heavy rope. He stared at her with wide eyes that were every bit as cold and lifeless as the blade of polished black obsidian that pierced his chest.

Chapter Seven

Chad watched from the shadows of the alley across the street as the police moved in. First, a small, black sedan circled the block, slowing as it passed in front of the apartment building. Then it picked up speed, turned the corner and disappeared. The men in the car would be covering the rear of the building, Chad knew from long experience.

Next, a gray sedan with blue and white emergency lights mounted on its roof cruised by, made a U-turn at the end of the block and parked in the middle of the street to his left. There were three uniformed men in the vehicle.

A few seconds later, another gray sedan with emergency lights drove by from the opposite direction and stopped in the intersection to his right.

Sloppy, sloppy, he thought. *You might as well pick up a bullhorn and tell the world what you're doing.*

He waited, and as he waited he peeked around the wall at the Corona de Alvarado, a half block away. The music and voices coming from it indicated the café was doing a brisk business. Maybe he should have slipped back to it and gotten lost in the crowd. There was no way he could run a one-man stakeout in a strange city. No way at all, not when he was dodging cops and worrying himself sick about a woman he was beginning to care for very deeply.

He glanced back over his shoulder, at the blackness at the other end of the alley. There was a six-foot wall at the far end, with trash cans lined up along its base. If he were spotted, he could dash back and scramble over the wall—no sweat.

But he didn't intend to be spotted. He intended to stay right here, in the shadows, and see who in the hell the cops pulled out of the building.

He squinted to read the faintly glowing dial of his wrist-watch. Seven-fifty.

Give 'em credit, he admitted grudgingly. The cops moved fast. But then this was a special case—a very special case.

A dark Mercedes came into view from the right, stopped briefly at the roadblock, then barreled down the street, coming to a halt in front of the apartment house. Two men jumped out of the back of the car and one from the passenger side of the front seat. All three ran into the house, pistols drawn.

In less than five minutes, two of them were coming back down the steps of the apartment house, leading, half carrying, a young woman wearing a black dress.

Lindy!

Instinctively, Chad started to move out of the shadows and onto the sidewalk.

What the hell was she doing here? He had to find out. Fast. This could ruin everything.

The two men bundled Melinda into the back seat of the Mercedes and got in, one on either side of her. The car sped away into the night, its siren wailing.

Increasingly edgy, Chad waited. There was still one man in the apartment, probably others on the way.

Moments passed and Chad finally grew tired of waiting. Stepping back into the alley, he turned and trotted to the far end. Bounding over the wall, he moved swiftly to the next street, and then, slowing his pace, turned left onto the sidewalk and walked to the corner and on to the Corona de Alvarado.

Ordering a glass of beer at the bar, he sought out the phone and called Ramirez.

"Sorry," a husky voice told him, "the major is unavailable. No, he did not say when he will return. Is there a message?"

"No," Chad said. "No message."

He hung up the phone and pocketed the handful of change he'd placed before him to use if the call had run into overtime. As he did so, he noticed a damp, dark streak on the side of his jacket.

Blood. Dr. Juan Lara Saavedra's blood.

"IT IS VERY CLEAR, señorita," said Oswaldo DeBeque, leaning back in his swivel chair and contemplating Melinda through heavily lidded dark-brown eyes. "You murdered Dr. Lara."

"For the hundredth time, I didn't!" Melinda protested, clenching her fists in her lap. Even though she was trying desperately to maintain her self-control, she could feel the hot tears of frustration on her cheeks. "I told you exactly what happened! I found the door open and I went into the apartment and discovered his body! I started to leave to summon help, but I was arrested before I could get to a phone!"

DeBeque brushed the knuckles of one hand against his mouth in a halfhearted attempt to conceal a yawn of disbelief. "Come, come, señorita—I am not talking about your second visit to the apartment. It is the *first* visit that concerns me. The pathologist tells us that Dr. Lara was killed sometime between four and five this afternoon. You were not at your hotel at that time, nor do you have witnesses to establish your whereabouts. I can only conclude that at the time in question you were..."

"Stop it!" Melinda interrupted him. "I already told you: I walked back to the Camino Real from the National Palace. I entered the lobby a little before four, and remained in the hotel until I went out again about six forty-five."

"From downtown to the Camino Real is a distance of several kilometers." DeBeque straightened up in his chair and leaned forward just enough to allow himself another glimpse of Melinda's feet, which were planted squarely on the floor in front of her straight-back chair. Instinctively, Melinda drew her feet back under the chair and smoothed out the skirt of her black sheath to conceal as much of herself as possible from her inquisitor's examination. "Rather a long walk in high heels, would you not say?"

"Who said I was wearing high heels?"

"The palace guards. They gave us a very thorough description of you. You are a young lady who invites close scrutiny." The last was spoken through lips curled in a sardonic smile.

Melinda was in no mood for backhanded compliments from a man who seemed bent on making her confess to a crime she hadn't committed. "As a matter of fact, I stopped at a store on Reforma and bought two pairs of shoes—these heels I'm wearing and a pair of flats. I also bought this dress. I was supposed to go to a reception tonight at the embassy."

"What was the name of the store?"

"I didn't pay all that much attention. I've got the receipt back in my room."

DeBeque glanced up at one of the two dark-blue uniformed police officers who were standing at either side of Melinda's chair. She was sitting in the middle of the room, several feet away from the desk, which was awash with the glow of a single bright overhead lamp that left all else in the room in shadows. DeBeque nodded, and the officer left the room.

"We will check your room and see," he announced. "Now tell me, Miss Harding: why did you murder Dr. Lara?"

"This is preposterous!" Melinda screamed, leaping to her feet and squirming out of the grasp of the officer who lunged forward to restrain her. She leaned over the desk and glared at DeBeque. "I want to call the embassy—now!"

DeBeque waggled a forefinger at the police officer who had seized Melinda by the shoulders and was wrestling her back to the chair. The man released his grasp and stepped aside, allowing her to sit down unassisted.

"Señorita, I am well aware you are an officer in the United States Foreign Service, but you are not attached to your country's diplomatic mission to Guatemala. In the eyes of our law you have no immunity whatsoever."

"I'm still a U.S. citizen!"

"True," DeBeque nodded. "You are a U.S. citizen who happens to be a suspect in the murder of one of Guatemala's foremost scholars. At the appropriate time, you will be permitted to contact your embassy and inform them of your situation. Until then, it would be to your advantage to cooperate in our investigation. Now, if you would be good enough to tell me again how you came to be involved with Dr. Lara."

Melinda closed her eyes. She knew DeBeque was trying to catch her in a lie. Well, he'd be sadly disappointed. She'd told him the truth, the whole truth—everything there was to tell. Everything except the real reason she'd sought out the professor.

Mechanically, she went through yet another recitation of her encounter with Dr. Lara. She told how she'd tried to call for help from the study, but the phone lines had been ripped out. Fearful that the killer might be hiding somewhere in the apartment, she'd run into the hall, headed for the stairs, and immediately was arrested.

As she repeated her story, the same old disturbing thoughts kept occurring to her. If she was the one who'd discovered the body, *who* had summoned the police? Surely not the real killer! *Who* had answered the phone and pretended to be the professor when she called? And *who* had ripped out the phone? It had to have been done in the few minutes between the time she'd called the professor and the time she arrived at the apartment.

The arresting officers hadn't even taken her back upstairs, hadn't even attempted to interrogate her. They'd simply loaded her into a police car and whisked her here to the National Palace to be questioned by this man DeBeque.

She opened her eyes and looked at her inquisitor. Throughout the interrogation DeBeque had remained in the shadows behind the desk. Nevertheless, the light was good enough for her to see that he was rail-thin and extraordinarily tall for a Central American—probably about six two or six three, she guessed—and he was on the graying side of middle age. But for his height, the most noticeable thing about him was the cool, almost offhanded manner in which he was handling the interrogation. Unlike many Latins she'd known, Oswaldo DeBeque didn't seem to have an excitable bone in his body. He had to be an important man, she realized—the deference with which the officers treated him told her that—and he had something to do with the Interior Ministry, judging from the gold-leaf insignia she'd seen stenciled on one of the doors in this particular suite of offices in the National Palace. But beyond that, she knew nothing and was told nothing.

She finished her account, but DeBeque still wasn't satisfied.

"Go over it one more time, if you please," he said, leafing through a notebook on which he'd earlier made several entries.

"I've told you everything I can." Melinda sighed.

"What was your interest in Dr. Lara?"

Melinda avoided looking at him. She had the distinct
feeling he was good at reading the slightest flicker in a fa-
cial expression. "Professor Lara is...was a highly regarded scholar. We'd met in Panajachel and he promised to
tell me more about his work." She hesitated, fishing about
for an explanation that would sound more reasonable. "I'm
something of an amateur anthropologist."

DeBeque seemed intrigued. "Are you now? I am told you
spent the morning researching anthropological tomes at the
National Library. What was it that so fascinated you? Surely
not Dr. Lara's dissertations on evolution of the Quiché language? Frankly, I found them quite boring."

"On the contrary," Melinda said, trying to sound
knowledgeable on the subject. "I always thought that Dr.
Lara wrote with a good deal of style and grace."

DeBeque shrugged. "Perhaps that was true with his other
work, but when it came to his main field of study—Mayan
linguistics—he was a very dull fellow. You *are* familiar with
his work in Mayan linguistics, aren't you?"

"Of course," Melinda replied quickly.

DeBeque's thin lips stretched out in a triumphant little
smile and he straightened up in his swivel chair. "Interesting, señorita. To my certain knowledge, Dr. Lara never did
any work in linguistics. Now, why do you persist in lying to
me?"

Melinda felt her cheeks flush as she realized the man had
trapped her. "I want to phone my embassy," she said res-
olutely.

"In due time," DeBeque said, settling back again in his
chair. "Tell me again about your encounters with Dr.
Lara...."

"WHERE THE HELL have you been?" Chad demanded angrily when he finally got through to Ramirez a few minutes
after ten. "I've been calling all over trying to get hold of
you!"

"Calm yourself, my friend. That highway episode last night has caused me no end of grief. The *Policía Nacional* are demanding that I assign army patrols to their hunt for the bandits. It puts me in a most difficult position."

Chad could hear the pop and sputter of static on the line. "Can you talk freely?" he asked.

"I am afraid not, my friend. I am returning your call via radio from my car and this is an open frequency. It will be some time before I can get to a phone. Do you have problems?"

"Big problems."

"Do they concern, ah, a certain individual to whom you introduced me last night?"

"They do."

"I see. May I assume that this individual has embarked upon an independent course of action that runs counter to ours?"

"You've got it."

"And this individual now is paying the price of rashness?"

"You might say that."

There was an audible sigh from the other end of the line. "I am afraid I shall have to take direct action."

"The hell you will!" Chad exploded. "You keep your hands off her!"

"The young lady won't be hurt. We're not savages."

"Damn it, I want to know what you have in mind!"

"Do not worry about it, my friend. And do not interfere. I would hate to have you pay the price of rashness, too."

MELINDA PUT DOWN her ballpoint pen and stared at the yellow legal pad on which she'd been writing. At De-Beque's insistence, she'd committed her story to paper— every last detail. Now, examining the seven pages she'd filled with her neat, blockish backhand, she was filled with misgivings. DeBeque was bound to realize she'd omitted much from her account.

The room in which she was being detained was perhaps twelve feet long and eight feet wide. There was a solid wood door in one of the narrower walls, a rectangular, built-in mirror covering the top half of the opposite wall. The only furnishings were a long, mahogany table and four straight-back chairs.

In the course of her work as a consular officer, Melinda had visited prisoners in a number of jails. She had no doubt that the mirror was in reality a one-way window, a window that allowed her captors to observe her every move while they themselves were concealed behind the reflective surface of the mirror.

Well, watch to your heart's content, she thought angrily. *I'm not going to slit my wrists or break down and cry or do anything that will give you the least satisfaction!*

She forced herself to reread the statement she had written, slowly and thoughtfully weighing every word, every phrase. When she was finished, she pushed the legal pad aside, folded her arms across her chest and waited.

It was almost midnight. She'd been arrested at seven forty-five, been questioned by DeBeque for two hours, and then brought to this room. What were they doing, she wondered. Checking out her story?

Probably—what there was of it to check. DeBeque and his people obviously had talked to the Canadian ambassador and to the guards at the palace. They'd also interviewed the waiter at the Corona de Alvarado. Before they were through, she suspected, they'd check the receipt for the shoes and dress she'd bought, and then touch base with the store and with other shopkeepers along Seventh Avenue and the Reforma to ask if any of them remembered seeing an auburn-haired gringa.

Fine. Let them. She had nothing to hide—nothing that they'd be able to find. Only the secretary at the embassy administration office knew about the parcel she'd received, and even if DeBeque did find out about it he'd have no reason to suspect it had any connection with his murder case.

At exactly midnight, the door opened and DeBeque stepped into the room. He closed the door behind him and took a chair across the table from Melinda.

"You have finished your statement, señorita?" he inquired, his thin lips scarcely moving as he spoke.

"I have."

He reached out and spun the legal pad around on the polished table. He read quickly, flipping the pages over with impatient flicks of one thumb. "You have covered everything?"

"Everything I can think of."

DeBeque slapped the ruled yellow pages shut against the pad. "Do you know a man named Young?"

Melinda nodded.

"Do you know him well?"

"We . . . we met in Panajachel. We stayed in the same hotel."

"What do you know of his background?"

A good question, Melinda reflected. "Not very much. He's a travel agent—from New York, I believe."

"I understand the two of you were involved in a bit of an adventure together."

"We were."

"Would you care to tell me about it?"

Melinda gave him a step-by-step account of what had happened after leaving the Patterson hacienda.

When she was finished, DeBeque cocked his head and studied her carefully. "Why didn't you mention this earlier?"

"I saw no reason to. It has nothing to do with Dr. Lara."

"Oh?" Before she had time to let the impact of that comment register on her, he continued. "Do you know a man named Ramirez—Gilberto Ramirez?"

"I know of him," Melinda admitted guardedly.

"Interesting, señorita. I see from your passport that you have been in Guatemala only a few days, and already you have become quite widely acquainted. However, I am not sure I fully approve of your choice of friends. The wrong friends can be nothing but trouble, you know." He picked up the legal pad, pushed back his chair and stood up. "I suggest you make new friends—in Washington—at the earliest opportunity."

Melinda looked up at him. "I'm free to go?"

"Not only are you free to go, I strongly encourage you to do so. As the chargé d'affaires at your embassy has told you, a seat has been booked for you on tomorrow morning's TACA flight to Houston, via San Salvador and Belize. One of my men will call for you at the Camino Real at six o'clock sharp."

"In other words, I'm being expelled from the country."

"Not at all. I merely think you would be happier in Washington. Happier, and most certainly healthier."

"Is that intended to be a threat of some sort?"

"Of course not, señorita. Do you think we are gangsters? I am merely looking out for your best interests."

"I'm no longer a murder suspect?"

DeBeque stared at her coolly, but did not reply.

"What if I don't wish to leave the country just yet?"

DeBeque turned away to reach for the doorknob. "Do whatever you like, señorita." He stepped out into the hall, leaving the door ajar.

"Wait!" Melinda called out, following him.

DeBeque whispered something to one of the uniformed police officers who had remained close at hand throughout most of the evening. Then he glanced at Melinda. "This man will take you back to the Camino Real. I suggest you go straight up to your room and lock your door."

Melinda had little choice but to obey. She accompanied the officer along the long corridor to a stairway leading down to the inner courtyard of the palace. He pointed out a black, unmarked Volvo and opened the passenger-side front door for her.

"Who is Señor DeBeque?" she inquired as her escort got behind the wheel and started the engine.

"An important man."

"I assume he's with the Interior Ministry?"

Without replying to the question, the police officer drove out the opening of the tall, iron gate at the front of the palace. He waved a two-finger acknowledgement to the two soldiers who stood on guard in full battle dress and with submachine guns slung across their chests.

When they were beyond the quiet, darkened downtown district and headed southward along Reforma, Melinda tried again. "Did Señor DeBeque come up through the ranks?"

The police officer glanced at her, obviously puzzled by the question. "I do not understand," he grumbled.

"I mean, did he used to be a patrol officer like you before he was promoted to his present position?"

"Señor DeBeque is not of the police."

"Isn't he? Then what is he?"

"He is an important man."

"He must be *very* important to be in command of so many fine police officers such as yourself."

"That is true," her escort admitted. "He is in the national government—very close to the president, in fact. They are distantly related, but this is not generally known."

"I see. Tell me, does he have a title?"

The police officer shrugged. "What does it matter?" He swung hard at the wheel and made a U-turn around the landscaped parkway separating the northbound and southbound lanes of the boulevard. "Here is your hotel, señorita. Shall I see you to your room?"

"That won't be necessary. About Señor DeBeque—"

"Buenas noches, señorita," the driver said, pulling up under the portico of the Camino Real. He reached across Melinda and opened the door for her, just as a uniformed doorman stepped up to the side of the Volvo. "Someone will be here at six in the morning to drive you to La Aurora Airport."

They never stop trying, do they, Melinda thought as she walked through the lobby to the front desk. Several couples were milling about the entrance to the main restaurant, and the hotel disco was doing a thumpingly brisk business. She had the feeling that everyone was staring at her.

Showing her hotel identification card to the desk clerk, she asked for her room key. The man smiled, took the key from her box, and handed it to her along with a plain, white envelope. As she walked toward the elevators, Melinda tore open the envelope and found a handwritten message, in perfectly constructed French.

When you get to the seventh floor, don't under any circumstances go to your room. Walk back down the stairs, then duck out the door to the parking lot. A block north of the hotel, on Thirteenth Street, you'll find an Argentinean restaurant named El Gaucho. Go there and ask for Señor Garibaldi. Tell him I sent you.

Your old swimming companion.

Chad Young! What was he doing in Guatemala City? How had he found her? And why had he written the note in French? Melinda wheeled about and marched back to the reception desk. She held up the opened envelope. "Do you remember when this arrived?" she asked the clerk.

"Sí, señorita," the man replied. "It was just after midnight. I had just come on duty."

"Did you see the person who delivered it?"

"Yes. It was a woman who runs a flower stall on Reforma. She said she was on her way home and that someone had asked her to drop off the note."

"I see," Melinda said.

She *didn't* see. Nothing that had happened to her that evening made sense.

She turned and walked to the elevator. She needed a shower and a good night's sleep, and perhaps things would start to make sense.

Getting off the elevator on the seventh floor, she looked again at the note in her hand. *Don't under any circumstances go to your room,* it said.

She frowned. She was in no mood for games. Nothing was going to happen to her, she told herself. DeBeque's men obviously had her under close surveillance. Stepping out of the elevator alcove, she turned left into the curving hallway leading to her room.

She hesitated. Whatever Chad was doing in Guatemala City, he obviously knew she was in trouble. She had no idea *how* he knew, but she sensed he was close... sensed he himself was very deeply involved in what was happening.

Her room was on the right side of the hallway, the second door from the end. A service cart was parked outside the open third door from the end, and Melinda guessed it was being used by a maid going from room to room providing turn-down service.

Melinda started forward again. Then, seeing a moving shadow in the open doorway of the third room, she turned and headed back to the elevator alcove. She decided to wait until the maid was finished with that end of the hall.

It was awfully late for a maid to come around turning down beds, she thought. Could DeBeque's men have bribed her to do some snooping? They were probably in that room with the open door, even now, giving her instructions.

She waited. No sign of the maid coming back down the hall.

Melinda reread the note. Maybe Chad had good reason to be afraid for her. Maybe she ought to follow his instructions and head for that Argentinean restaurant and find the man named Garibaldi.

Oh, make up your mind, she scolded herself. She started out from the alcove.

And as she entered the hallway, the entire floor was rocked by a thunderous explosion.

For a moment, she was deafened. The hallway, wispy with gray streaks of smoke, was wrapped in a hollow, ringing stillness, and all Melinda could hear was the panicked thumping of her own heart, the gasping breath being sucked into her lungs.

And then the stillness ended in a cacophony of screams and shouts and slamming doors.

Ahead, through the smoke, Melinda could see the gray-uniformed maid crouched against the wall opposite the door to her room. Her face was contorted in an expression of shock, and she was pressing the palms of her hands to her ears in an agonizingly futile attempt to dull the roar.

Melinda ran to her and, putting her arm around her shoulders, guided her away from the door. Suddenly, the woman began screaming and pulled herself free and ran toward the stairs, disappearing beyond the fire door.

Melinda looked back over her shoulder, saw that other people were now in the hall looking around, confused and frightened. She remembered Chad's note: *Don't under any circumstances go to your room.*

Why, she wondered. What did he know, and why couldn't he have been more direct? Why did he have to keep lying to her, keep hiding things from her?

She had to find him, had to get some answers. Ducking into the stairwell, she ran down the steps, hanging onto the railing to keep from falling in her haste. On the third-floor landing, the lights on the stairwell flickered. She tried to pull up short, and as she did so her right ankle turned under her, sending her pitching forward. Only the railing kept her from plunging forward the next full flight.

She kept going, more slowly now, favoring her aching ankle, and it wasn't until she paused before opening the heavy steel door on the ground floor that she realized she'd lost a shoe when she stumbled.

She couldn't go back. Not now. She had to get away from the hotel, find Chad, get some answers. She had to have some answers.

She shoved open the door to find men rushing about, looking every bit as confused as she felt. Some of them were carrying fire extinguishers and axes. At least two of them were yelling instructions.

She stepped out onto the ground floor, brushing past the men and looking around for the outside door. She saw it just ahead of her, ran up to it and shoved down the handle. It wouldn't budge. The door was locked.

Glancing about in desperation, she tried to remember the location of the ground-floor exits. It was no use. She hadn't paid that much attention, hadn't really had any reason to worry about such things.

Ahead, and around a corner of the ground-floor service hall, she heard loud voices. She ran forward.

Three men wearing the heavy, peaked helmets and yellow slickers of firefighters, were wrestling a dolly-load of breathing equipment through an open glass door, cursing as the pneumatic closure of the door kept butting the slab of thick glass against their load.

Melinda stepped up to the door and pulled it wide open. One of the firefighters looked at her and nodded his gratitude before he and his companions moved on down the hall, toward the service elevator.

Melinda ran out into the parking lot, past a single fire truck that was parked near the door, its engine running, its red and white lights flashing crazily.

She had to have answers. And she had to have them now.

Balancing herself precariously on her aching right foot, she raised her left foot and removed her surviving shoe, staring at it dumbly for several seconds.

The sound of other sirens stirred her to action. She had to get away from here, away from the hotel. Oswaldo DeBeque would try to blame her for this. She just *knew* it. Well, it wasn't going to happen, not if she could help it.

Favoring her right foot, she half limped, half ran out of the parking lot and onto the street, where she stopped for a moment to take her bearings. The hotel was to her left and behind her. The Argentinean restaurant Chad had mentioned was just around the corner and up a block or so, if she remembered correctly.

She had to find a man named Garibaldi.

There were several restaurants near the hotel and people had poured out of them, attracted by the explosion that had rocked the still night. The spectators were milling about, talking among themselves, pointing. Melinda slowed down, not wanting to be singled out for special attention.

A well-dressed young man standing alone on the sidewalk, a drink in his hand, grinned at her and held his glass aloft in an unspoken invitation for her to join him. She kept moving, eyes forward.

"You seem to have lost your shoes, pretty one," the young man called after her. "Perhaps I can give you a ride, eh?"

"My husband wouldn't like that," Melinda replied, smiling sweetly at him. "He wouldn't like that at all."

Ahead, on the corner, was the sign. El Gaucho.

A dozen men and women were standing in front of the restaurant, looking down the street at the towering arc of the Camino Real. More sirens were in the air, shrilling against the cool stillness of the October night.

She went up to a pair of white-jacketed waiters just outside the front entrance of the restaurant.

"I want to speak to Señor Garibaldi," she announced. "Where is he?"

"Over there," one of the waiters replied, nodding toward a portly, middle-aged man standing alone under the corner streetlamp. He seemed to be waiting for something. Or someone.

"Gracias."

Melinda walked over to the man and introduced herself. "I was told to get in touch with you," she said.

He seemed only mildly interested. "Were you, señorita? By whom, may I ask?"

"A friend."

"Does your friend have a name?"

"He does. His name is—" She stopped. What sort of a game was Chad playing, she wondered. What right had he to expect her to play it, too? She wasn't a spy, or a criminal. She was just a woman caught up in a situation over which she had no control. "Let's just say he's an old swimming companion," she said.

The man reached into a jacket pocket and brought out a thin leather key case. "You will find a light blue Mercedes parked at the curb a half block down Thirteenth Street. Get into it and sit behind the wheel." He handed her the key case. "The car is locked, so you will need this."

"But what am I supposed to—"

"Buenas noches, señorita," he said, walking away from her.

Melinda looked at the key case. Chad Young better have a damn good explanation, she thought irritably.

She turned onto Thirteenth Street, slinging her purse over her shoulder and holding her high-heeled pump in her right hand as if it were a weapon capable of protecting her from the unknown perils that lay ahead. The Mercedes was exactly where Garibaldi had said it would be, at the curb in the middle of the block. There were two other Mercedeses in the block, but both were dark colored and both were parked in the wrong location.

Melinda walked past the car, studying the shadows along the bushes at the base of the high rock wall that ran parallel to the sidewalk. No sign of movement.

At the end of the block, she crossed the street and came back on the opposite sidewalk, still studying the shadows. As nearly as she could tell, there was no one lurking in the shadows there, either. She couldn't stop now. Crossing the street in the middle of the block, she walked directly to the driver's side door and felt around for the lock under the handle. She found it and probed at it with the first of the two keys in the case.

Wrong one.

She tried again. This time she could feel the key turn, hear the clipped *thump* as the lock turned.

She hesitated. There was still time to back out. Still time to run back to the hotel and wait for Oswaldo DeBeque to show up. He'd have to believe her. Surely he wouldn't think she'd planted a bomb to explode in her own face—would he?

She'd even agree to take the first plane out of Guatemala. Anything. Anything at all.

Her left hand was sweating on the cold chrome of the door handle. She wasn't going to do it, she knew. No way. She wanted answers. She wanted answers most of all from Chad Young.

She threw open the door, slid behind the wheel and slammed and locked the door behind her. With fumbling fingers, she found the ignition key and slipped it into the switch.

Why hadn't the dome light come on, she wondered.

She suddenly felt trapped—had to get out of there. Now.

But she couldn't move. Strong hands had appeared from nowhere and were pressing against the top of her shoulders, near the base of her neck.

Chapter Eight

Melinda's head tilted sideways, her right cheek coming to rest on the back of Chad's hand as she struggled to gain control of her tattered emotions. A second before, she'd been terrified, certain she'd walked into a killer's snare. And then she'd caught a glimpse of his face in the rearview mirror and the tension drained from her body. For the first time in hours she relaxed, secure in the knowledge he was there in the car with her. "I don't know whether to laugh or scream," she whispered, tracing her fingertips along the edge of the hand that lay beneath her cheek. "I feel like I've just staggered off a roller coaster and can't even stand up straight."

He leaned forward and kissed her on the side of her neck. "It's probably the company you keep."

She straightened up and started to turn around, but the firm pressure of his hands on her shoulders prevented her from moving.

"Keep looking forward," he instructed her. "I don't want to attract any attention."

The tenseness began to return. "What are you doing here?"

"Just trying to keep an eye on you."

"Chad, who are you—really?"

"I'm whoever or whatever you want me to be. Does that answer your question?"

"What I want you to be is honest," she said sternly, looking straight ahead. "What are you doing in Guatemala? You're not a travel agent—I know that much. Travel agents don't go around getting shot at and hiding out in parked cars." Turning her head, she was able to get only the slightest glimpse of the outline of his. "Did you know that somebody planted a bomb in my room? One of the hotel maids was nearly killed."

The fingers on her shoulders became steely hard. "I warned you not to go up to your room!" he said gruffly. He removed his hands and opened the curb-side rear door. "Stay here. I'll be back in a couple of minutes."

Turning in her seat, Melinda saw him disappear around the corner. Had he turned into the Argentinean restaurant at the corner? She couldn't be sure.

He was back in less than five minutes. "I called the hotel and pretended to be a detective," he announced, motioning her to slide over to the passenger seat. He got behind the wheel and started the engine. "The maid's going to be all right. She was shaken up, nothing more. The bomb was just a concussion grenade, an oversize firecracker—a few ounces of black powder packed in some rolled-up paper attached to a trip fuse. Whoever planted it just wanted to scare hell out of you."

"I've got news for you, they succeeded. But why me?"

Chad drove around the block and pulled out onto Reforma, turning north toward the main business district. Passing the Camino Real they could see fire trucks parked in the circular drive leading to the entrance of the hotel.

"Somebody obviously wants you out of Guatemala," he said.

"Oswaldo DeBeque suggested I be on the next flight out."

"DeBeque," Chad mused. Melinda couldn't tell if the name registered.

"He has something to do with the Interior Ministry," she said. "Very high up, I gather."

"What did you tell him?"

"I told him I didn't plan to leave just yet."

Chad glanced at her. "Why not?"

"I have some things I want to do."

"What sort of things?"

"Personal business."

"Have it your way, Lindy. I'm just trying to be helpful."

Melinda looked around. They were downtown now, and not too far from the National Palace. She wondered what Chad had in mind.

Cutting across on a sidestreet, Chad swung the car onto a darkened thoroughfare and pulled into a parking lot between two buildings. "Home again," he said, cocking his thumb toward a blue and white oval sign across the street. "That's the Pan American Hotel. Doesn't look like much from here, but it's nice inside."

They got out of the car and Chad checked to make sure the doors had locked automatically. "Let me go in first and keep the night clerk busy. The stairs are to your right, just inside the lobby. Give me a minute, and then go on in and walk up to the third floor—room two-oh-four. Screwy numbering, I know, but that's the way they do it down here." He fished in his jacket pocket for a room key and handed it to her. "I'll be along in a minute."

He took her by the hand and started to cross the street. Suddenly he stopped and stared at her. "For some reason, you look different tonight." His gaze dropped. "Ah, no shoes. *That's* why you're so much shorter."

Melinda held up her surviving pump. "I lost the other one running from the hotel after the explosion. I'm going to have to see about my things in the morning. I can't go around like this."

"No need," he grinned, leading her across the street. "Your bags are up in two-oh-four."

"They're what?"

"I pulled a switch earlier in the evening. I had someone get your bags from the Camino Real."

Melinda shook her head in skepticism. "Did you know someone was booby-trapping my room?"

Ignoring the question, he stationed Melinda just outside the hotel entrance and went inside alone. A minute later, as he'd instructed her, she slipped into the lobby and walked to the stairs in her stocking feet. Chad was at the front desk with the night clerk, and both of them had their heads down over what appeared to be a map.

A porter was coming down the marble staircase as Melinda started up. He was a thin young man with the squat, bronzed features of an Indian. He smiled toothily at Melinda, showing not the least bit of surprise over the fact that she was carrying one shoe in her right hand. She smiled back.

He probably thinks I'm a streetwalker who's sneaking in to spend the night with a client, she thought crazily. *If the secretary of state could only see me now!*

Locating the room, she unlocked the door and slipped inside without turning on the lights. The room overlooked the street, not far from the corner, and the drapes were fluttering in the breeze blowing in through the open windows.

As her eyes became accustomed to the semidarkness, she could make out the familiar shape of her bags on one of the twin beds that filled most of one end of the room. At the foot of the other bed was a dark leather carryon.

I still need answers, she told herself.

She slipped the key into the lock on the inside and turned it, preventing anyone from opening the door from the hallway. Then she switched on the light and unzipped the dark leather carryon.

Her search came up with nothing unusual: just neatly folded shirts, underwear and socks, pajamas, a shaving kit and a pair of shoes in a plastic bag.

She looked around. There was a closet next to the hall door. She looked inside and found a leather garment bag hanging on the rod. The bag contained two jackets—a corduroy sports jacket and a dark-blue blazer—on hangers that also supported some slacks.

A search of the pockets yielded nothing, but as she zipped up the garment bag, her knuckles brushed across the breast pocket of the blazer and hesitated. She prodded at the area with her fingertips. There was something between the pocket and the lining of the blazer. A thick envelope of some sort?

Quickly unbuttoning the jacket, she felt around the lining back of the breast pocket. She could still feel the bulge, more pronounced now.

She looked inside the jacket. A heavy, embroidered manufacturer's label appeared to be sewn to the lining. She poked at it, and then, on impulse, pulled at it. It separated with a soft tearing sound, and she saw that it was actually a Velcro strip covering the opening of a concealed inside pocket.

Melinda glanced at the hall door, wondering how much time she had before Chad came up to the room. Well, there'd never be a better opportunity.

Reaching into the hidden pocket, she brought out a slim black leather case. Inside were three much-visaed passports, one in the name of an "Alan Whittaker," one issued to "Dan Todd," the third to "Chad Young." Also in the case were three separate sets of driver's licenses and credit cards, issued in the same names.

Melinda inspected the identification photos affixed to the passports and driver's licenses. The photos were identical. The face in each of them was that of the man she knew as Chad Young.

She was staring wide-eyed at the photos when she heard metal poke against metal. She glanced at the door, saw the key vibrate. Startled, she dropped the credit cards.

"Lindy?" she heard him say. "Come on, open the door. You've got it locked from the inside."

Melinda stooped down and gathered up the plastic cards. "Just a minute!" she called out. "I'm in the bathroom!"

She slipped the cards into the case and shoved the case back down into the hidden pocket, securing it with the Velcro strip. Then she closed the closet door, keeping the knob turned until the latch could clear the striker plate without making any noise.

"Come on, Lindy."

"On my way!" She spun around and stepped up into the tiled bathroom, turned on the water in the basin and splashed her face. Then, daubing at her face with a towel, she returned to the bedroom and unlocked the hall door.

Chad seemed amused when he entered the room. "Did you find what you were looking for?"

Melinda stared at him. "I . . . I don't understand."

"Sure you do. You had five minutes alone up here in the room. That's plenty of time to play detective."

Melinda could feel her cheeks flush. "If you're insinuating that I went through your things . . ."

"Under the circumstances, I'd be surprised if you didn't. That's what I would have done if I were in your position. I'll ask you again, did you find anything interesting?"

She shrugged. "It depends, Mr. Young. Or is it Mr. *Whittaker*? Or are you using the name *Dan Todd* this week?"

"You *are* thorough, aren't you?"

"It's time we had a talk." She sat on the bed on which her own luggage had been stacked. "It's time we had a *serious* talk."

"Suit yourself." He pushed aside his carry-on bag and sat down on his bed.

"Just who are you and what are you doing with those other passports?" Melinda began.

He didn't take his eyes off her. "It's like this: I'm always losing things so I always make it a point to keep extras on hand—extra passports, extra driver's licenses, extra credit cards. Satisfied?"

"You realize you're in violation of U.S. law."

"But we're not in the United States."

"That doesn't matter!" She threw aside the towel she'd been holding since she opened the door for him. "What matters is that I happen to be an officer of the United States Foreign Service, charged with specific responsibilities. Running around with you after all that's happened these past few days, I'll be lucky to stay out of prison, much less keep my job! Foreign Service people aren't *supposed* to get mixed up in things like this!"

Chad stood up and went to the window. He looked down at the street for a minute, then turned to her. "Lindy, I'm not what you think I am. I tried to tell you last night in your room at Del Lago, but I made a lousy job of it. I'm in a damned-if-I-do, and damned-if-I-don't situation. If I level with you, you could be in big trouble. And if I don't level with you, I'm in big trouble—with you, the one person whose respect and understanding I want. All I can do is ask you to bear with me. Will you—please?"

She looked at him long and hard. She wanted to believe in him—wanted to in the worst way. Damn! It was all so confusing.

Picking up the shoe she'd dumped on the bed with her purse, she examined it as if it were a crystal ball that would provide the answers she was seeking.

"I'll think about it," she said finally, pitching the shoe into the wastebasket by the dresser. She shoved her luggage off the foot of the bed and onto the floor, then pulled down the bedspread and plumped up the pillow. "What do we do now?"

"I can think of one thing I'd like to do," he said softly.

"That's not what I mean!" Melinda retorted. "Besides, I'm not in the mood."

"You were in the mood last night."

"That was different. Last night I was dealing with Chad Young. But three of you—I don't think I can handle it."

"There's only one of me here in this room right now." He drew the drapes and turned, his back to the window, and shrugged out of his coat, wincing as it slid off his wounded shoulder. Reaching behind him, he took something from his belt and put it in the pocket of his suit jacket. Melinda couldn't see what it was, but she suspected it was a pistol.

He hung up his jacket in the closet, then took his pajamas from his leather carryon. He tossed her the top half of the set. "Here, this will save you having to unpack tonight."

Turning, he went into the bathroom and closed the door.

Melinda got up from the bed and placed the pajama top on his pillow. Then, rummaging through her own luggage, she found her robe and shorty nightgown. She changed quickly and was again sitting on the bed when he came out of the bathroom, wearing the pajama bottoms. A white bandage contrasted starkly with the deeply tanned smooth flesh of his left shoulder.

"You haven't answered my question," she reminded him.

"What question?"

"What do we do now?"

He glanced at the pajama top she'd placed on his pillow. "Not what I'd like, that's obvious."

"You know what I mean," she said primly.

Chad removed his suitcase from the bed and sat down. "If you want my advice, Lindy, you'll be on that plane a few hours from now. Things are apt to get kind of nasty down here."

She stared at him. "Things are *already* nasty. I don't see how they can get much worse."

He reached across to turn out the lamp on the table between the two beds, then hesitated. "I'd better leave a call for five. That'll give you time to get to the airport." He picked up the phone next to the lamp.

"I have no intention of leaving just yet."

"We'll talk about it again in a few hours. Right now—" Suddenly he switched to fluent Spanish, and it took a few seconds for her to realize he was talking to the desk clerk, leaving word for him to ring the room at five.

When he hung up, she cocked her head and studied him. "The first time we met—that day you pulled me out of the lake—you said you didn't speak Spanish."

He switched off the light and lay down atop his bed, fingers laced behind his neck. "I lied," he admitted. "I speak fluent Spanish, Portuguese and Italian, and passable French and German. I lied because the people I work for want people like me to pass as an ordinary American, no better and no worse, and avoid attracting attention. Now that that's out of the way, you're going to want to know who I work for. And all I can tell you, my lovely Melinda Harding, is to go home—go home and give me a chance to start over again with you someday when the two of us aren't staring down gun barrels and hiding out in second-class hotels."

She looked at him across the semidarkness that pulsed with the neon of outside lights despite the drapes across the window. "I think I'd like that, Chad," she said softly. "Starting all over, I mean. I think I'd like that very much."

"Then be on the early-morning flight."

Melinda sat in the darkness for a while, bundled up in her robe, her legs tucked beneath her. Finally, she got up and opened the drapes. In the dull glow of the nearby streetlamp, she could see that Chad was stretched out on his side, gazing across at her.

"I can't leave Guatemala—not just yet," she said. "There's something I have to do first."

He sat up in bed. "Anything I can help you with?"

She shook her head. "Not really. It's . . . it's personal."

"In other words, none of my business, huh?"

"I didn't say that."

"Then why won't you tell me?"

Why not, she thought.

And so she told him the story. . . .

THE EARTH SHUDDERED and snorted fire on that crisp, golden February afternoon she first saw the jade jaguar.

She, Stefanie and Ellen Stuart had just finished a picnic lunch and were stretched out lazily on the mountainside, looking at the wind-rippled blue waters of the lake and at the slumbering volcanoes beyond. It had been a long, jouncing bus ride from the refugee camp in Chiapas, Mexico, across the Guatemalan frontier and along the twisting spine of the cloud-shrouded cordillera, and the girls were tired, dusty and more than a little homesick.

"I say we splurge and get a room in a *real* hotel tonight," Ellen spoke up. Ellen was a slender brunette who'd just turned twenty-two. "I've had enough camping to last a lifetime."

"Not so fast," Stefanie objected, raising herself up on her elbows. Stefanie, who like Melinda was twenty, was the poor little rich girl of the trio, a plump and perky blonde who forever seemed to be calculating the worth of something or someone. "We've got barely enough quetzales for bus fare into Guatemala City. If that money order isn't waiting for us at Eastern Airlines, we've all got big problems."

"Oh, the money order will be there all right," Melinda said confidently. "Tony told us not to worry."

Stefanie wagged a forefinger at her friend. "Correction. When I phoned Tony from Tuxtla Gutierrez, he said he'd pass the message along. But that doesn't mean my father's going to send the money. You know as well as I do he wasn't wild about your grand idea of spending the holidays doing volunteer work in Mexico. For all I know, he may have disinherited me.''

Ellen stretched languidly. "I still say we ought to get a hotel room. We all need baths. We're positively grubby!" She glanced at Melinda. "What do *you* say, Lindy?"

Melinda wasn't listening. She was staring in fascination at the massive rock formation that framed their view of the lake.

"Hey, Lindy! Don't you think we ought to rent a hotel room in Panajachel tonight?''

Melinda raised her head from the canvas knapsack that served as a makeshift pillow. "They moved," she murmured, brushing her windblown hair back off her forehead, then shaking her head in disbelief. "I swear, they actually moved."

"*What* moved?" Stefanie asked, looking around suspiciously.

"Those rocks down there—the ones that look like The Three Bears. See!" Melinda sat up and pointed as the smallest of the three boulders twenty yards farther down the slope teetered on its base, tipped precariously to one side, and then settled back against the two other rocks to one side of it.

"Oh, my God!" Ellen yelped. "It's an earthquake!"

She and Stefanie jumped to their feet, but Melinda stayed put, mesmerized by the rock formation.

Stefanie snatched up her backpack and denim jacket. "We've got to get out of here!"

"Wait!" Melinda cautioned. "I've read that the worst thing to do in an earthquake is to panic." She rose slowly and dusted off her faded jeans with swipes of her hands. "There's nothing up above us—nothing between here and the road that's apt to come tumbling down."

"But we can't just stay here!" Ellen protested. "We can't—look out, Lindy!" Ellen grabbed her friend's hands and dragged her out of the clearing as the first of several rounded stones, each the size of a bowling ball, came thumping down the hillside. One of them rolled over the spot where Melinda had been sitting.

Looking back over her shoulder, Melinda made a face that was half horror, half jest. "So much for what I've read about earthquakes." She peered at the heavy growth of stubby evergreens surrounding the clearing. "I wonder where those rocks came from."

"Up there in those bushes," Stefanie said. "There's a whole pile of them stacked there. I saw them when I was looking for the little girl's room. Somebody probably dumped them there to use to build a house. Who knows?"

Ellen marched across the clearing and poked her head into an opening in the thick clump of bushes. "Hey, guys! It's a cave."

The other two girls joined her to take a look. Sure enough, the earthquake had dislodged the rounded rocks blocking a dark opening in the mountainside.

"Let's have a look," Melinda suggested. She rummaged through her knapsack for a flashlight and tested it to see if it still worked. "Come on, there's nothing to be afraid of."

Wriggling through the opening, she flicked on the flashlight again and played its yellow beam along the walls of the cave, at the far end of which a man-made tunnel had been chipped and smoothed with some sort of bladed tool. It was obvious that, at one time, the walls had been daubed with chalky white inscriptions, but these had all but disappeared before the ravages of musty centuries.

"I'm not so sure this a good idea," Stefanie said, following Melinda and shining her own flashlight around the cave. "That earthquake could bring the whole tunnel down."

"Sure," said Melinda, moving forward into the tunnel. "And we could fall onto the BMT subway tracks next week when we get home, or get hit by a cab on Seventh Avenue." She hesitated. Maybe it *wasn't* such a good idea. There was no way of knowing how much damage the quake had done.

Perhaps just a few more feet and then they'd turn around and leave.

Suddenly, yellow eyes were glowering out at her from within almond slits, tracking her every move, unblinking in arrogant defiance of these intruders who'd ventured into this dank chamber where time had been frozen for a thousand years. They were a killer's eyes, hard and cruel, revealing a tortured spirit that was fiercely jealous of its eerie solitude.

Melinda halted in her tracks, spellbound by their glare in the harsh glow of her flashlight. *Go back,* they seemed to say. *This place is not for you, nor for any of the living. This is a place that belongs to the past, a place where only death is welcome. Go back.*

Melinda swept her flashlight beam across the musty blackness, illuminating a waist-high rock ledge upon which were perched a number of small, ghostly artifacts: a gold-crusted image of the god Quetzalcóatl, a dozen small statues of lesser Mayan deities, vessels of ground stone and fire-blackened clay from which ages-old morsels of food and dollops of drink had long since disappeared. The wall to the left was daubed with faded splotches of magenta, chalky white and ocher, arranged in a pattern she couldn't begin to understand. To the right of the ledge was a low, circular portal leading to another section of the tunnel.

Again directing the beam to the ledge—was it an altar of some sort—Melinda examined the square of black jade upon which had been carved a stalking jaguar. The eyes were not real, but tiny fire opals glistening in savage wariness.

She started forward again, more slowly now, picking her way through loose rock and bits of shale that were treacherous underfoot. If she and Stefanie should fall and break their flashlights, they might never leave this place of death.

Something thumped against Melinda's right shoulder and she cried out and jumped forward, spinning about and shining her light at whatever it was that had touched her in the darkness.

"Don't shoot!" Stefanie yelped, throwing up her hands in mock surrender. "I'll go quietly." She was grinning from ear to ear, trying her best not to appear nervous.

Melinda took a deep breath. "Damn it, Stuffy! You almost gave me a heart attack! Where's your flashlight?"

"I gave it to Ellie. She needed it more than I did." Lowering her hands, she edged forward until she was standing alongside her friend. "So what did you find?"

Melinda turned and shone the flashlight at the ledge. "I think we're in a Mayan tomb of some sort."

"No kidding! What's *that*?" Melinda sensed that Stefanie was staring at the jade jaguar.

"It's called a 'glyph,'" Melinda replied, moving in closer to study the jade carving, which measured about five inches square and an inch thick. "A lot of early cultures used them to record legends and historical information. My guess is that this one was owned by Mayan royalty." She reached forward to touch the polished surface of the carving. "It's positively exquisite! Just think of all the painstaking work that went into that piece!"

"It really turns you on, doesn't it, Lindy?"

"That's not quite the way I'd put it—but yes, it does."

Stefanie plucked the flashlight from Melinda's right hand. The beam danced about the cave, then returned once more to the ledge and lingered there. "Does it turn you on more than Tony Germaine?" she inquired, only half teasing now.

"*Especially* more than Tony Germaine," Melinda retorted, refusing to let herself think about the all-American football star from Princeton whose antics had nearly wrecked her junior year at Sarah Lawrence College. "At least this little fellow—" she gazed admiringly at the jade jaguar "—has the good manners to keep his paws to himself!" She stepped back from the ledge and glanced worriedly over her shoulder. "What do you suppose happened to Ellen?"

"Right behind you, Lindy," Ellen spoke up. "What do you say we get out of here?"

"You're not scared, are you?" Stefanie teased.

"As a matter of fact I am. If the Guatemalan authorities found out we were in here, they'd lock us up and throw away the key. They have laws about disturbing archaeological sites."

Stefanie brushed past Melinda for a closer inspection of the ledge. "I'm no expert on Mayan artifacts," she said, "but I'll bet there's a fortune in here. I wonder what it's all worth?"

"Probably five years of our lives in a Guatemalan prison," Ellen said. "I vote we get out of here—now."

Stefanie played the flashlight beam over the walls once more, first on the left side of the ledge and then on the right, settling in on a rounded opening barely four feet high. "As long as we're here, we might as well take a look." She moved to the opening, poked the flashlight inside, and froze. "Oh, my God! Come look!"

The other two girls hurried to the opening and peered into it. There, in the glow of their battery-powered lights, they saw a jumble of skeletons on the floor of the cave—a nightmarish ring of sentries around wicker cases that had rotted away and spilled their cargos of bits of yellow metal and chunks of jade.

"It *is* a tomb, isn't it?" Ellen said in a hushed tone.

Melinda studied the macabre scene. "I'm not so sure. A lot of these early Central American people were always on the move, what with wars and droughts and things like that. These are probably the skeletons of Mayan bearers who were getting ready to transfer the tribal treasures. I'll bet they'd just gotten things packed when they were trapped by an earthquake. My guess is they suffocated."

Melinda felt a tug at the sleeve of her khaki shirt, heard Ellen say, "Come on, let's go."

Still holding the flashlight, Stefanie stepped forward, then stopped and turned, her face pale and drawn in the glow of the artificial light. "I think that's a good idea," she whispered.

Turning back to the ledge, she snatched up the tiny statue of the god Quetzalcóatl. Slipping it into her jacket pocket, she then collected a second figurine—a six-inch jade image of something that was half man, half bird—and handed it to Ellen.

"How about you, Lindy?" Stefanie prompted. "Last chance, you know. We'll probably never ever see this place again."

Melinda shook her head silently.

"Come on, Lindy! You just said you liked that jade jaguar."

"I know what I said. But I can't steal it."

Stefanie grabbed the glyph and thrust it at her companion. "There! If they stop us leaving the country, we'll just say we bought them at one of the Indian markets. Okay?" Turning, she led the way up the sloping passageway to the entrance.

Once outside, they rolled the remaining boulders back over the entrance to the passageway, then stepped back and inspected the resealed opening. The rocks looked as if they'd been in place a thousand years, and would stay there another thousand.

"You know," Stefanie said, "I think Ellen has a point. Let's *do* stay in a hotel tonight. I think our luck is changing."

As she spoke, the mountainside shuddered again. Across the lake, the tallest of the volcanoes spat smoke and flame, and a terrifying stillness settled over the highlands....

CHAD WAS SITTING on her bed, his legs crossed under him, Melinda's head upon his lap. "And that was it, huh?" he said when she was finished. "That was the extent of your criminal career?"

Melinda smiled ruefully. "That was it, and it's bothered me for ten years. The funny thing was, I hardly ever looked at the jade jaguar after we got back to the States. It sat on my dresser for a while, but when I joined the Foreign Service I left it with my folks. I was always on the go and it would have been just so much excess baggage."

"Why didn't you just mail it back to Guatemala City with an anonymous note explaining the circumstances?"

She shook her head. "It wouldn't have been the same thing. I took the glyph from the cave, and it was up to me to return it to the cave. When I was reassigned from São Paulo to Washington, I saw my chance."

"What about the pieces your two friends took?"

"Stuffy brought hers with her this trip. It was on display in the Pattersons' salon the other night. As for Ellen's figurine—it was lost during one of her corporate moves."

"Where's the jade jaguar now?"

"At the embassy. I started to pick it up today, but I thought I'd better leave it there for safekeeping until I was ready to go back up to Panajachel."

Chad brushed the hair back from her forehead and bent down and kissed her lightly. "Don't do it, Lindy. Give it to me. I'll find the cave and put it back for you. You can fly out of here with peace of mind."

She twined her fingers through his and drew them to her cheek. It seemed so natural being here with him, touching him, believing in him on instinct alone. "Why is it everybody wants to do my penance for me? Stuffy tried to call me in São Paulo to tell me she'd take care of returning the glyph. Now you."

"Just trying to be helpful."

Melinda laughed. "No way. I've come this far, I'll do it myself. Besides, I think you just want to get rid of me."

She could feel those dark-blue eyes staring at her through the semidarkness. "That, lady, is the last thing in the world I want. Now get some sleep. It's late."

She closed her eyes, holding his fingers pressed to her cheek.

"Chad?" she said after a while.

"Uh-huh?"

"The non-hero you told me about last night—you said he talked out of turn, and as a result the woman he loved died. Remember?"

"I remember."

"Chad?"

"Uh-huh?"

"What happened to the killer?"

The fingers tensed, became as cold and hard as the voice that answered her question. "You don't want to know, Lindy. And I don't want to tell you—not now, not ever. Now go to sleep. Five o'clock comes awfully early."

IT WAS A DREAM, but not a dream. She was running after him through the narrow streets, dodging traffic, trying to keep him in sight. He was running, too, and every time she drew close to him he glanced back over his shoulder and winked at her and then ran all the faster.

"Wait!" she cried out, and the crowds on the sidewalk made way for her. "Please, Chad—wait!"

She was short of breath, and there were beads of perspiration on her forehead as she attempted to gain on him. Crazy thoughts raced through her head. *I've never ever chased a man before. Why am I chasing you this way?*

The street noises grew louder, punctuating the morning air with the blare of horns, the squeal of brakes, the babble of voices, unrecognizable snatches of rock music.

She was gaining on him. He was less then a half block
ahead, taunting her with his nearness.

"Wait!"

She'd lost her shoes, both shoes, somewhere, and other
pedestrians were pointing to her and laughing and saying
things she couldn't make out.

He stopped for a moment, and she ran up to him and
reached out to touch him and . . .

She was sitting up in bed, the warm sunlight of midmorning streaming in through the open windows, the
sounds of the city loud in the quietness of the room. She
looked around. He was nowhere in sight and his leather
carryon was gone.

Climbing out of bed, she checked the closet. His garment bag was gone, too.

What time is it, she thought fuzzily.

She'd left her wristwatch on the night table, alongside the
phone . . . the phone that was supposed to ring at five o'clock
so she could get to the airport on time. She wasn't going to
be on the early flight, of course. She'd told him so. She'd
told him, and she'd told that awful Oswaldo DeBeque.

She'd discuss it, she'd said. That was all. She'd have listened to Chad's renewed arguments, and then she would
have said no, she wasn't going to leave yet because she had
to return the jade jaguar to its temple in the mountainside.

Melinda picked up her watch and stared at it.

Ten o'clock. She'd slept almost eight hours. Slept . . . and
dreamed. She had to get going.

Shaking her head groggily, she drew the drapes and
stripped off her terry-cloth robe and shorty nightgown, then
went into the bathroom and turned on the cold water in the
tub shower. She stepped into the tub and the icily stinging
jet helped bring things into focus.

First things first. She was willing to bet that Chad had
gone back to Panajachel. Whatever business he had in
Guatemala was closely related to that part of the country.

Why? She couldn't begin to guess, didn't want to even try.
What she wanted to do was to see him again, make another
attempt to learn more about him.

Then there was the jade jaguar. Until Chad had come into
her life, the jade jaguar had been her number-one prior-
ity—her only reason for returning to Guatemala. She'd have
to go back to Panajachel, and she'd have to do it without
attracting the attention of Oswaldo DeBeque. But how?
Maybe the answer would come after coffee.

Stepping out of the shower, she toweled herself dry and
chose a green-and-blue plaid wool skirt, light blue nylon
blouse and green cardigan from her limited wardrobe. But
for a pair of dressy, high-heeled red sandals, the only shoes
she had left were the black loafers she'd bought the day before. They didn't go too well with the plaid skirt, but they'd
have to do.

She left her bags in the room and walked downstairs to the
coffee shop in the lobby. A waiter, wearing the bright crim-
son headscarf and black pantaloons of the Quichés, had just
poured coffee for her and was testing her willpower with a
tray of delicious looking sweet rolls, when a porter appeared at her side and placed a sealed envelope by her coffee cup.

Melinda tore open the envelope and found a set of car
keys, a note and a folded clipping from a newspaper.

Obviously, you didn't make the morning flight. In case
you'd like to get around town without attracting De-
Beque's attention, there's a red Datsun wagon in the lot
across the street. I'll meet you at the Corona de Alvarado at noon.

Johnny Weissmuller Jr.

She smiled when she read the signature. He might be public enemy number one, but at least he had a sense of humor.

The smile faded as she unfolded the clipping. It gave a graphic account of the Lara murder, stating that the professor apparently had surprised a burglar upon his return from luncheon at the National Palace. There'd been a struggle, and the professor had been stabbed to death. Several police officials were mentioned by name, but not Oswaldo DeBeque.

Neither was her name mentioned.

After finishing her coffee, she checked at the front desk and was told that Chad had paid the bill and had checked out a little before six. No, he hadn't left word as to where he could be reached.

She had a porter carry her bags across the street to the parking lot and load them into the wagon. She gave him a quetzal note, then slid behind the wheel. On impulse, she checked the packet of car-rental documents in the glove box, wondering what name he had chosen this time.

The car, she learned, was rented to a Scott Stearns. *Great,* she thought. Now she had yet another identity to contend with.

She reached for the ignition, then hesitated. Maybe modifying her *own* identity wouldn't be such a bad idea, she decided. DeBeque or other investigators probably would want to talk to her after the bombing incident of the previous night, and she wanted to avoid them if at all possible. Once she got the jade jaguar back to its cavern in the hills above the lake, they could question her to her heart's content and she'd have nothing more to hide. But now, first things first.

Climbing out of the car, she walked around the corner to the bustling Seventh Avenue commercial district. After buying oversize sunglasses and a dark red lipstick at one store and a green headscarf at another, she returned to the Datsun, applied the lipstick and put on the scarf.

She checked her reflection in the car mirror. She hardly recognized herself. And *that* was good.

She started the car, pulled out of the lot and headed toward the embassy to pick up the jade jaguar.

Had DeBeque told the embassy to notify him if she showed up? She had no way of knowing. But in any case, she suspected, DeBeque probably had someone staked out watching for her. She'd have to come up with another way to collect her package.

Fifteen minutes later, she was parked around the corner from the Corona de Alvarado, less than a block from Professor Lara's apartment building. Checking her reflection in the mirror once again, she tucked a stray wisp of auburn hair under her headscarf, then got out and locked the car and walked into the café, which already was doing a brisk lunchtime business.

She found a table in the corner, ordered a sandwich and coffee and then sought out the pay phone, which was at the opposite end of the service bar from the private phone she'd used the night before to talk to the professor. She dialed the embassy and asked for the administration office.

"This is Melinda Harding," she began. "I stopped in your office yesterday."

"Oh, yes, Miss Harding," the secretary greeted her. "Good to hear from you again. Are you enjoying yourself in Guatemala?"

Melinda gave a sigh of relief. Obviously, the chargé hadn't put out the word she was a no-show at the previous night's reception. A social gaffe like that would have touched off even more gossip than the murder of a university professor.

"I have a favor to ask. I left a package there at the embassy yesterday—a gift for a friend. I'd planned to stop by today to pick it up, but I won't be able to make it. Do you suppose it would be possible to have a messenger bring it to me? I'll pay him, of course."

"Where are you now, Miss Harding?"

"Out by the University of San Carlos. It's on the south-west side of the city, I believe."

"I know where it is. I'll tell you what: I was planning to send a driver out to La Aurora Airport at two o'clock to meet one of our people coming in from Mexico City. Let me get him started now and he can drop off your parcel before he goes to the airport. How does that sound?"

"Great. You don't know how much I appreciate it."

"Just tell me where you are now and..."

Melinda gave her the address of the Corona de Alvarado.

She could hear the secretary's gasp. "Miss Harding, I'd advise you to be careful in that neighborhood. Did you know that someone was murdered there last night? It's all over the newspapers!"

"I'll watch myself," Melinda said determinedly.

She returned to her table and, thirty minutes later as she was ordering a third cup of coffee, a black-uniformed driver delivered the parcel to her, waiting cap in hand while she signed a receipt. Melinda dropped the parcel into her purse and was about to ask for her check when she spotted a familiar face at the service bar. It was the waiter who'd called Professor Lara for her the night before. This time, he was wearing tan slacks and a faded denim jacket and had a canvas book bag slung over one shoulder.

Thinking he might be able to tell her something more, Melinda raised one hand and waved to him. He stared at her for a few seconds, then blinked recognition and walked over to her table, smiling broadly.

"Have you heard the terrible news about Professor Lara?" she began.

The smile became a frown. "*Sí, señorita*. It is a terrible thing, eh? And to think—the two of us, you and I, were among the last to talk to him before he died."

"Who could have done such a thing?"

The waiter hunched his shoulders in a dramatic shrug, and the frown turned into a dark scowl. "I do not know, but if I find him, he will wish he had not been born!"

"He?"

"The burglar, of course. He was here in the café, asking about the professor. Someone gave him directions to the apartment building." The waiter rubbed together his hands, as if warming them in anticipation of a much-sought-for encounter. "Ah, but it should not be difficult to find him. One does not see that many gringos with dark-blue eyes."

Melinda's pulse began to hammer. "Can you describe him?"

"For certain. He was not a big man—rather medium height, I would say, and quite fit looking. He had light, golden-brown hair, cut short, and a small scar by one eyebrow. He said he had come to Guatemala to study under the professor, but I knew that was a lie. I have worked with Dr. Lara for two whole years, and I know of no gringo students named Chad Young."

Chapter Nine

Melinda found it difficult to talk to Chad during the trip back to Panajachel, and he seemed to understand. He made a few attempts at conversation, but gave up before they were even out of the city, headed north on the Inter American Highway.

Just what do you say to a man who has done nothing but lie to you, a man who lives beyond the law, a man who's probably a cold-blooded killer at that, she asked herself. *It's a nice day, isn't it? Not much traffic. Were the people at the rental agency surprised when you told them that the last car you got from them is now at the bottom of a lake, riddled with bullet holes? Or were they more interested in what name you're using today?*

Pretending to read a roadside sign, she shifted about in her seat to steal a glance at him. He was the soul of innocence sitting there behind the wheel, the slouch brim of his soft khaki hat overlapping the tops of the dark glasses that masked those piercing blue eyes. He was wearing a navy-blue turtleneck, khaki slacks and loafers, and all he needed was a camera slung around his neck to pass for the typical tourist. Relaxed, easygoing, harmless. You bet, she thought. Two to one he had a pistol tucked away in his waistband.

Melinda faced forward again. She didn't want him to see her looking at him, although she wasn't at all sure why it should matter. Chad had to be aware there was a new wall between them. He wasn't insensitive. He wasn't at *all* insensitive.

The night before, she'd fallen asleep in his arms, feeling warm and secure and, yes, even loved. He could have possessed her then and there—he knew it, and she knew it. She would have welcomed it. But he hadn't. It was almost as if there were an unspoken bond between them, an agreement that everything was on hold until he could tear down the wall of mystery that separated them.

And then the awakening . . .

She tried to persuade herself the waiter had been wrong, that Chad couldn't possibly have killed the professor. Chad just wasn't that kind of person. He was thoughtful and caring, fun to be with much of the time, and she felt irresistibly attracted to him—more than she'd ever been attracted to any other man she'd met. She wanted desperately to believe in him. But facts were facts, and cold, hard reason told her to run from him and not look back.

Chad had lied to her from the minute they met. He'd lied about who he was and whatever it was he was doing. One thing, and one thing alone, seemed clear: he was on the wrong side of the law.

Why did he carry a gun? What possible use could he have for those forged passports? And why had her own friends told her to stay away from him, that he was "strictly bad news"?

Coolly and methodically, Melinda thought of every possible explanation she could. None of them made sense.

Coming into Chimaltenango, within sight of the open-air restaurant where she and the professor had stopped after dropping off Ybañez, Chad turned to her. "You hungry?"

Melinda shook her head.

"Well, I am. I missed both breakfast and lunch." He took his foot off the gas pedal and let the car slow. The restaurant was only a few hundred yards ahead now. "Mind if I pull in here? There's not much else till we get to Sololá."

"Suit yourself."

He shrugged, turned off the road and pulled up in front of the restaurant. "Lindy," he said softly, reaching for her hand.

"What?"

He quickly withdrew his hand. "Nothing—nothing at all. Come on."

"I'll wait in the car."

Chad removed the key from the ignition and pocketed it, then got out and started for the entrance of the restaurant.

I hope you choke, she thought angrily.

He wheeled around and marched back to the car and got in. "The hell with it," he muttered, backing out of the parking area and onto the highway.

Melinda looked at him. His jaw was set, and she could tell he was annoyed. "Turn around," she said. "I'll go in with you."

He didn't speak.

"Chad, I'm sorry."

"For what?"

"For...oh, never mind!" *Damn it!* she thought. Why should she have to apologize to him? He was the one at fault!

She settled back in her seat and closed her eyes. So what now? She already knew the answer. She'd do what she'd set out to do when she arrived in Guatemala six days before. She'd return the jade jaguar to the cave from which it had come, and she'd be on her way. Stefanie had already kept her part of the bargain, so that made it all that much easier.

When she was finished, instead of going back to the capital, maybe she'd take a bus to Huehuetenango, high in the mountains to the north. There were too many painful memories attached to Guatemala City. She could hire someone to drive her to La Mesilla on the Mexican border. She could get another bus to Tuxtla Gutierrez, the state capital of Chiapas, and from there she could fly on to Oaxaca, Mexico City and home.

End of adventure. And end of her brief and frustrating relationship with the mysterious Chad Young or whatever his name was.

But what if I don't want it to end—not now, not ever!

"Chad?"

"I'm listening."

"Chad, did you kill Dr. Lara?"

She couldn't bring herself to look at him when she asked the question, so she couldn't tell if his expression changed.

"What would you do if I said yes?" His tone of voice was deadly serious.

"I'd…" *What would I do? I'd leave an out for you—and hope that you'd take it, because I might not want to hear the truth.* "I suppose I'd ask you why."

"And then?"

"I . . . I don't know. I honestly don't know." She glanced at him. "Did you, Chad? Did you kill the professor?"

"No, Lindy, I didn't."

"You were seen in his neighborhood."

"Who told you that?"

"Someone who was able to describe you to a T."

"Did you tell the police?"

She shook her head.

"Why not?"

"I just found out about it—just before you picked me up at the café."

He glanced at her. "You were out there last night, too."

"*I* certainly didn't kill the professor. He was already dead when I got to his apartment. Even DeBeque told me that."

Chad grunted. "DeBeque's a real charmer, isn't he?"

"You know the man?"

"We've met."

"Who is he, Chad? What does he do?"

"You remember reading how Franklin Delano Roosevelt brought a bunch of big-business types into his administration during the Depression to help him save the country? They were known as dollar-a-year men because they donated their services to their country. That's what Oswaldo DeBeque is—an anonymous dollar-a-year man and a real power behind the presidency down here. His money comes from coffee, but he has a passion for archaeology and anthropology. He keeps a low profile, but take my word for it, he's important. When he talks, people listen. The *right* people."

Melinda shook her head slowly. "I still don't understand where he fits into this."

"Let me spell it out for you. Guatemala may be the largest of the Central American republics, but like its neighbors it's hardly very prosperous. With all the social upheaval of recent years, Guatemala has had too many problems with the here and now to worry much about preserving the past. As a result, a lot of hustlers have moved in to loot the country of its heritage. Antiquities such as that stuff you saw displayed at the Pattersons' the other night disappear before they can even be catalogued, and the next thing you know those pieces are fetching big prices at auctions in New York and London. DeBeque, who is a wealthy man with a lot of national pride, wants to put a stop to this, so he and some of his pals have declared war on the hustlers—a shooting war, I might add."

Melinda frowned her disapproval. "It sounds like Old-West vigilantism."

"Yes and no. The old-time vigilantes took the law into their own hands when the sheriff was unwilling or unable to do his job. DeBeque is working within the system. Early on, however, DeBeque realized that a few corrupt members of the *Policía Nacional* were taking payoffs from the hustlers.

He and his friends decided to fight fire with fire by bank-rolling an elite group of undercover investigators."

Suddenly, Melinda saw the straw she'd been searching for and she grabbed at it. "And you're one of those people. That's what you're telling me—isn't it?" *Please say yes!*

He gave a dry little laugh. "Sorry to disappoint you, but the answer is no, I'm not on DeBeque's payroll."

"But . . ."

"All of DeBeque's people are Guatemalans. I can tell you that much, Lindy. His pride has suffered enough without bringing in a bunch of gringos to do the job."

Melinda was silent for a moment as she turned this new information over in her mind.

"What about Major Ramirez?" she asked after a while. "Is he one of DeBeque's undercover investigators?"

"You'll have to ask him."

"I'm asking you."

"All I can . . ."

Without finishing what he was about to say, he braked hard, then swung the rented station wagon around in a tight, skidding U-turn. "Hang on!"

They were approaching the junction at Los Encuentros, and in the distance they could see a line of trucks, buses and cars backed up at a roadblock. Melinda had a fleeting glimpse of blue-uniformed police officers standing on the highway directing traffic as the station wagon spun about.

"What was *that* all about?" she demanded as she glanced back at the roadblock.

"Problems," Chad muttered between his teeth, keeping a close eye on the rearview mirror. "And we've got enough of our own right now. We sure as hell don't need any more."

Melinda saw that two motorcyclists had taken off after them, red lights flashing. "Look," said Chad, "next chance I get I'm going to bail out. I want you to slide behind the wheel and pretend you were driving."

"I'll do no such thing!" Melinda protested. "I don't know what you're up to, Chad, but I absolutely refuse to be an accessory to a crime."

Chad gave a throaty little laugh and stepped on the gas. "When you get through moralizing, shut up and listen. You know the military barracks on the road to Sololá? When you get finished with the cops, I'll meet you just on the other side of the barracks. Got it?"

Without waiting for an answer, he swerved onto the shoulder of the road and jammed on the brakes. Leaning over, he gave her a quick kiss on the ear. "Boy, are you cute when you sputter!"

And then he was out of the car, sprinting into the trees at the side of the road as the sirens drew closer.

NOW LET'S SEE WHAT HAPPENS, Chad thought as he watched from his hiding place on the mountainside. He'd found a stack of logs no more than twenty yards from the highway, and it gave him an ideal vantage point.

The two white-helmeted motorcycle officers, wearing black uniforms with matching submachine guns slung around their necks, didn't even bother to lower their kick-stands when they pulled up behind the station wagon. They simply dropped the bikes on the gravel and closed in on Melinda as if she were a one-woman crime wave. One of them went to the passenger side of the car, the other to the driver's side.

"Out of the car with your hands up!" Chad heard one of the officers shout in Spanish as he brought his submachine gun to bear on the driver's-side door.

The door opened and Melinda stepped out, her arms held high. "Thank heaven!" she cried, peering purposefully at their badges. "You're not bandits after all!"

The two officers looked at each other across the roof of the station wagon. "Is that why you sped away from the roadblock, señorita?" one of them inquired in a dubious tone. "You thought we were bandits?"

Chad could see Melinda dab at her eyes with a tissue. "Yes, of course. I've had trouble before and when I saw all those men with guns..." She let her voice trail off in a choking sob.

"What do you mean by trouble, señorita?"

Another dab at the eyes. "On a road near Panajachel. You must have heard about it. I made a full report to the police."

"I believe I recall hearing something about that," said the officer closest to her. "You were with a man, were you not?"

Melinda nodded.

"Was this a man of thirty-five or so, with flaxen hair and blue eyes and a tiny scar on one brow?"

"Why, yes," Melinda said quickly. "That was Mr. Young. Do you know him?"

"I can tell you only that he is wanted for questioning in connection with a police matter. How well do you know this fellow?"

"Not well at all, officer. We just happened to be staying at the same hotel and he offered to give me a ride to a party. If you want to know the truth, I'm sorry I accepted. I never should have gone with him. Mr. Young is a terrible man!"

"Ah, how is this, señorita?"

Melinda gave a sigh that Chad had no trouble hearing even from a distance. "Well, for one thing he drank much too much. What's more, he told off-color jokes and he even had the nerve to make indecent advances."

Oh, come on, Chad groaned, noticing Melinda gave a dark little frown in his direction. *Don't overdo it, huh?*

"Tell me," said the other officer, "have you seen this Mr. Young lately?"

Another glance in his direction, then, "I'm afraid not— not since that awful night. May I put my hands down now?"

What a woman, Chad thought admiringly as he backed away from the woodpile and began working his way up the hillside. When he was out of sight of the highway, he started north, moving along at a steady trot.

A half hour later, he was beyond the roadblock. He had to get to a phone, had to call Ramirez.

From the hillside, he saw two Indian men trudging along the shoulder of the road, carrying bundles of serapes for the market at Sololá. They were headed north, away from the roadblock. Keeping an eye out for the police, Chad moved quickly down to intercept the pair.

Five minutes later, wearing a black-and-gray striped serape and a battered straw hat one of the peddlers had thrown in as a bonus, Chad was on the phone at the gas station in Los Encuentros.

"I thought you were going to arrange to call off the law?" he began.

"I have to apologize, my friend. You know how it is. It takes time for word to filter down through channels. Until it does, you had better plan on staying out of sight. The police would like nothing better than to get their hands on the fair-haired gringo who led the attack on the convoy."

Chad lightly touched the bandage on his upper left arm. The pain had subsided to a dull, burning ache. "That reminds me: you said there wasn't supposed to be any shooting."

"A breakdown in communication," the major apologized. "The fellow who fired at you has been transferred out of the district."

"Keen."

"Any other problems? How is Miss Harding behaving?"

"She's not stupid. She's got a handle on the situation."

"That could be an irritant," Ramirez allowed. "It would be so much simpler if only she'd leave the country. We can't have her running around, tipping our hand. There is too much at stake, my friend." He paused, then added, "Perhaps I should arrange another—how shall we say...'incident'?''

"No way!'' Chad exclaimed. "That concussion grenade at the hotel was bad enough. You people like to play too rough.''

"We have no choice, my friend. It is a rough game. You have only to consider what happened to Professor Lara and Señor Cronin to appreciate that.''

"YOU'RE NOT REALLY a prisoner,'' Chad assured her, drawing the thick drapes on the barred window overlooking the walled garden. "All I'm asking you to do is stay here tonight, and then tomorrow I'll take you up into the hills and you can drop your jade jaguar at the cave and get the hell out of here. I'll even drive you up to Huehuetenango myself so you can get a bus to the frontier.''

Melinda looked around the sparsely furnished room, which had all the warmth and charm of a dentist's office. It had a red tile floor and there was a cheap, plastic-covered couch along one bare, whitewashed wall. Across the room from the couch were a pair of mismatched chairs and a scarred coffee table, on top of which sat a stack of dog-eared, Spanish-language magazines. The dark-red drapes were shutting out the waning sunlight of early evening, and the sickly yellow flame in the tiled fireplace was giving out more light than the single, low-wattage overhead bulb.

"I have no intention of spending the night here,'' she said determinedly. "I think I'd be just as safe in the hotel—safer even.'' She glanced at the scowling figure in the hallway, by the front door. He was wearing unpressed khakis and a wide-brimmed sombrero, and he had a revolver holstered on one hip. "At least, the people at the hotel don't wear guns.''

Chad glanced back at the man in the hall. "He's here for your protection, Lindy.''

Melinda sniffed. "You and your friends are the ones I need protection from. Things happen when you're around.

I don't know what I was thinking when I waited for you in the car.''

Chad hadn't said a word about the escapade at the road-block. An hour before, he'd rejoined her as promised, on the side of the road near the barracks at Sololá, motioning her to slide over and slipping behind the wheel as if nothing had happened. He'd driven straight to this walled cottage near the beach at Panajachel, making her crouch down in her seat to avoid being seen as they drove through the village business district.

Chad motioned to the guard, and the latter went out through the front door. "Lindy," he said softly, "there's a lot about this business you don't understand. In fact, there's a lot *I* don't understand. But it's almost over, I promise you. Just bear with me for one more day."

Melinda looked straight at him. "In other words, I'm just supposed to trust you. Right?"

"Something like that."

"Trust is a two-way street, Chad."

"So I've heard."

"If you want me to trust you, then I think you ought to level with me. Let me ask you again, who are you and what are you doing in Guatemala?"

He came across the room and put his arms around her waist, drawing her close. "Later, Lindy."

"But, I don't—" Her words were lost under the soft warmth of a kiss. She made a feeble attempt at resisting him, then surrendered, slowly, reluctantly, closing her eyes and losing herself in him. Her fingers pressed against the back of his neck, holding him tight.

"I've got to go," he murmured finally, his lips hovering over hers. "There are two bedrooms down the hall. Take your pick. I should be back by midnight, but if I'm not, don't worry about it. Get some sleep. You've got a full day tomorrow."

He turned and left the house, and as he went out the front door, the guard came back inside. "There is food in the kitchen, señorita," the man announced, stationing himself in the hallway by the door.

"I'm not hungry," Melinda said, settling down on one of the plastic chairs and picking up one of the magazines from the coffee table. She thumbed through it, wishing the guard would go away. He made her nervous.

She stared at the magazine, but couldn't concentrate. Too many thoughts were racing through her mind.

The whole thing was a picture puzzle, and the puzzle finally was beginning to take shape. But several key pieces still were missing. She had no doubt that Major Ramirez was one of DeBeque's undercover people, but where did that leave Chad? She wasn't sure just why, but she believed him when he told her he wasn't working for DeBeque. Whose side was he on then? And why was he running from the police?

It seemed clear the Pattersons were mixed up in the smuggling of antiquities. But what about her old friend Stefanie? Stefanie had said she'd never met the Pattersons before, never had done business with them, and Melinda had no reason to doubt her. Were Joel and Nicole Patterson trying to recruit her and the other art dealers to act as outlets for stolen antiquities?

That had to be it.

If Stefanie wasn't too deeply involved with the Pattersons, it might be possible for her to come out of this unscathed. Melinda decided she had to try to get in touch with her friend, tell her what was happening. Maybe Stefanie would want to go with her to Huehuetenango to catch a bus for the Mexican frontier.

Melinda looked up from the magazine. "Perhaps I will have something to eat. A sandwich or a bowl of soup, if it's not too much trouble."

The guard shrugged. "I let you fix your own, señorita. Come."

She didn't budge. "I'm really not very good in the kitchen. Why don't *you* fix the food?"

Grumbling, the guard shuffled off down the hall.

Melinda waited until she heard pans clattering, and then, carrying her shoes and slinging her purse over her shoulder, she hurried to the front door, eased it open, and slipped outside into the gray twilight. Closing the door, she slipped her feet back into her loafers and ran to the front gate and out onto the cobblestone road.

She headed straight for the main business district and found a pay phone at a bar. She tried Del Lago. Stefanie didn't answer. She had her paged. No response. She looked up the Pattersons' number and phoned the hacienda. A servant told her Joel and Nicole Patterson were still at their gallery in town.

Melinda left the bar and headed for the gallery, looking back over her shoulder from time to time to make sure the guard wasn't about to catch up with her. It was almost dark when she reached the gallery, and from the road she could see people milling about inside. She recognized several of them as art dealers she'd met at the hacienda earlier in the week.

No sign of Stefanie.

Two barefoot Indian girls balancing heavy bundles on their heads approached, and Melinda offered them a quetzal each if one of them would carry a message into the gallery—a message to be delivered personally to Señora Germaine. The older girl nodded gravely and said she would carry out the assignment.

Melinda and the second Indian girl stepped across the road to wait in the shadows.

A minute later, Stefanie came out of the gallery, following the messenger. A tall, heavy figure was silhouetted in the open door, watching them. Melinda couldn't be sure, but she thought it was Joel Patterson.

Staying in the shadows, Melinda moved down the road, toward town, with Stefanie and the two girls following. When they were well clear of the gallery, Melinda gave the girls another quetzal each and sent them on their way.

"Why all the skulking about, Lindy?" Stefanie asked, a faint smile on her lips. "Joel and Nicole would have been delighted to see you."

"I'm not so sure about that," Melinda said, taking her friend by the arm and leading her toward town. "And I think you'll agree after you hear what I have to tell you." She gave a quick account of the investigation being conducted by DeBeque's undercover agents.

When she was through, Stefanie laughed. "And you think I'm involved—is that it, Lindy?"

"The thought had crossed my mind."

"Then why did you warn me? Aren't you afraid I'd go running back and tip off my partners in crime?"

Melinda shook her head quickly. "I don't care about the Pattersons, Stuffy. I *do* care about you. We've known each other a long time and I'd hate to see you hauled in with the rest of them. It's not too late to back out of whatever arrangement you've got with the Pattersons. Look, I'm leaving tomorrow. Why don't you come back to the States with me?"

Stefanie reached out and put her hand on Melinda's shoulder. "I thought the accused was innocent until proved guilty."

"It's just the other way around, Stuffy. The Napoleonic Code is the basis of law in most of these Latin American nations, and suspects are presumed guilty, not innocent. You could end up in jail for months before you even came to trial."

"You're awfully quick to assume I've done something wrong. Don't you think you could at least *ask* me?"

Melinda hesitated. "I'm not sure I'd want to hear the answer, Stuffy."

Her friend leaned forward and gave her a hug. "Thanks for the vote of confidence, Lindy. But I have business here in Guatemala and I'm not going anywhere. And no, my business doesn't involve fencing smuggled goods for the Pattersons."

Melinda sighed. "That's good enough for me." She glanced along the road. "Come on, I'll walk you back."

"Whoa, girl!" Stefanie tightened her grip on Melinda's shoulder. "Since this is the time for giving advice, I think you'd better take some from me. *You're* the one who's sticking her neck out—not me. I've been worrying about you ever since that business on the road the other night."

"I was in the wrong place at the wrong time."

Stefanie shook her head slowly. "You were with the wrong man at the wrong time—that was your problem. Nicole told me about Chad. She said he was trouble. She has a lot of friends in Panajachel, and they've seen Chad hanging out with the wrong crowd. If *he* gets arrested, he could drag you down with him."

Melinda said nothing.

Stefanie lowered her voice. "Do me a favor, Lindy. The tour people are sending a private bus for my group first thing in the morning. We're going to Antigua for a few days, then back to Guatemala City. Why don't you be there at the hotel at six and go with us?"

"I can't, Stuffy. I have to go up to the cave and return the jaguar. I probably won't be ready to leave until noon."

"I'll take care of it. I'll rent a car in Antigua and come back here. It's not all that far. You can go on into the capital and get the next flight out to the States. How does that sound?"

Melinda considered it. "You'd have trouble finding the cave. I know I did. The road has been moved, and I had to hire a guide and..."

"Don't worry," Stefanie said confidently. "I'll find it. Just bring me your glyph and I'll see that it's put back."

"Thanks anyway, but it's something I have to do myself. Now come on, I'd better get you back to the gallery before the Pattersons send out a search party."

Maybe it wasn't such a bad idea, Melinda thought as she left her friend and headed alone down the road toward the cottage. She was already walking a tightrope as far as her State Department career was concerned. If Chad *was* arrested and she was found to be involved with him, she'd face at least a reprimand if not outright dismissal. The Foreign Service was understandably sensitive about its employees' private lives.

The lights of an oncoming car blinded her, and she lowered her eyes. The vehicle stopped a few feet in front of her and she heard the front door open.

"Grab her!" someone shouted in Spanish.

Startled, she turned to run but strong arms seized her around the waist and carried her, kicking and squirming, back to the car. She started to scream, but a hand closed over her mouth, stifling her cries.

"Put her in back," she heard a second man say. "I'll sit on her if need be."

The second man got into the back seat and the first man shoved Melinda inside.

"I advise you to be quiet, señorita. I don't wish to use force, but I will do so if necessary."

Melinda lunged toward the door as it started to close behind her, but the man alongside her seized her by the shoulders and forced her back. "You leave me no choice, señorita." The man forced her wrists behind her and clamped manacles on them. Then, reaching into a pocket of his jacket, he brought out a dark kerchief and gagged her.

"I suggest you blindfold the lady as well," the first man said as he got behind the wheel and closed his door.

"If you think so."

A dark hood was dropped over her head, and she was rudely shoved down onto the floor between the front and rear seats.

The next hour was a nightmare of the unknown. She felt the car sway, bounce, speed up, slow down, but she had no idea of what was happening or where they were going. Neither of the men who had taken her prisoner said another word.

Until, "I will go in and ask," she heard the driver say as the car came to a halt.

"I will accompany you," the second man said. "Trussed up as she is, the lady is going nowhere."

Front and rear doors opened and closed, and Melinda could hear the springs creak as the two men got out of the car.

More silence.

I've got to get out of here, she thought. *Now, before they return.*

She struggled up into a sitting position, wincing as a thousand hot needles jabbed into the wrists and hands that had been pressed under her back against the floor mat. Taking a deep breath in an attempt to wash away the pain, she rolled up onto the back seat.

First things first, she thought. She had to get the hood off so she could see where she was.

But how?

She shifted about on the seat, probing the impenetrable blackness with either knee. Her right knee bumped into something angular and metallic. The door handle. Or was it the window crank? It didn't matter. Whatever it was, it might serve the purpose.

She bent down from the waist, nudging her head against the protrusion she'd felt. If only she could hook the handle, or whatever it was, under the drawstring of the hood.

It took several minutes of nudging and maneuvering, but finally she could feel the tip of the metal catch under the drawstring of the hood, just below her right ear. Carefully, she forced her head down lower against the rear door, holding her breath as the pressure on the drawstring increased.

Now...

She pushed down hard. The hood slid up over her forehead, and she could see!

She looked around. All she could make out was a faint light in the distance. A house? Possibly. She wasn't in town. She was sure of that much. There were stars overhead, but no moon. The darkness around her had to be trees.

She squirmed about on her seat, trying to work her wrists under her hips so that she'd have the manacles in front of her. But it was no use, she just didn't bend that way.

She stopped wriggling, and listened. Had she heard voices?

She had to get out of the car. Now!

Swiveling about so that her back was to the nearest door, she felt for the handle. She found it, pressed it, shoved down and pushed back. The door flew open and she tumbled backwards, landing on her neck and shoulders in the dirt.

Dazed by the impact, she slowly drew her hips and legs out of the car and rolled over on her side. She had to get up, run, get help.

Forcing herself to her feet, she lurched away from the car, moving toward what she could now see was a stand of pine trees. She could hear snatches of voices at a distance. One of the voices sounded familiar. Did it belong to Major Ramirez? She couldn't be sure.

"You have your orders. If she gives you trouble..." The voice faded.

"Silence her," somebody else said.

"Do what you have to do."

"And the gringo?"

"I will handle him."

They were going to kill Chad, too! She had to warn him! She stumbled over a rock and gave an involuntary little cry that was only partially muffled by the gag still in place over her mouth.

"She's loose!" a man yelled.

"After her!" someone else shouted.

Melinda plunged forward, dodging through the trees. She had gotten no more than ten yards when she was seized from behind and lifted off her feet. Kicking and squirming, she was hauled to the car and dumped into the back seat.

"She is a spirited one—I will say that," one of the men admitted grudgingly.

"Put the hood back over her head," another man said. "If she tries to escape again, you know what to do."

Blackness.

Then someone got into the front seat and started the car. Again, the vehicle swayed, bounced, sped up, slowed down. And finally stopped.

The rear door nearest her opened and someone reached in and pulled her outside. She spun around to escape his grasp and kicked out blindly. She wanted to scream, but her rage blunted itself against the tightly stretched cotton of her gag.

The man holding her gave a little laugh and slung her over his shoulder like a sack of flour.

"Her purse is on the seat," he said. "Bring it."

She could hear footsteps crunch on gravel. Then another door, a wooden door, opened and she knew she was inside a house.

"Straight back," another voice said. This voice, too, was familiar. It was the guard from whom she'd escaped earlier, she realized.

Suddenly, she was dumped onto a bed.

"Don't turn on the light," said the man who'd been carrying her.

He reached down and removed the hood from her head, untied the gag and unshackled her hands.

And then he was gone and she was alone in a dark room.

She got up and groped at the bare walls, finding a window hidden behind heavy drapes. Drawing them back, she looked out. She had a faint impression of thick shrubbery, and between her and the shrubbery were heavy, ornamental iron bars.

Continuing her circuit of the room, she found a light switch by the door and flipped it, blinking instinctively against the anticipated glare of light.

But there was no light. There was nothing but darkness that pressed in upon her from all sides.

"Let me out of here, damn you!" she shouted, pounding at the locked door.

No response. Nothing but stillness. And darkness.

She pounded at the door again and again, shouting until she was hoarse. It did no good. They were ignoring her.

Think, she told herself, feeling her way across the room and sitting down on the edge of the bed. *That was the guard's voice you heard, so you're probably back in the bungalow. And if that's the case, Chad knows what's happened.*

Chad. Where is he, and what right does he have to hold you prisoner like this?

After a while—it could have been ten minutes, or it could have been an hour—she heard the door open and she looked up to see a shadowy figure standing in the portal.

"Who's there?" she demanded, her every muscle tense as she readied herself to spring at the figure.

"I thought you agreed to stay put," she heard Chad say. He stepped into the room and closed the door behind him, shutting out what little bit of light had come in from the hallway.

Melinda jumped to her feet. "You mind telling me just what's going on, *Mr.* Young?"

He came closer, stood silently in front of her for a few seconds, then said, "I'm trying to save your neck—that's what's going on, *Miss* Harding. There are some people who'd like nothing better than to get their hands on you."

"I don't believe you."

"Believe what you like. The word is that the smugglers know you spent a long time with DeBeque last night. They're convinced you blew the whistle on them, and they don't much like that."

Melinda thought of her conversation earlier in the evening with her college roommate. "Is Stefanie Germaine one of them?" she asked in a tone that suggested she'd refuse to accept his answer.

Chad sat down on the edge of the bed and looked up at her. Even in the darkness, she could feel those blue eyes burning into her. "It doesn't look that way. My sources tell me your friend is just one of several art dealers the Pattersons are trying to recruit. They figured she was a likely candidate because she's been dealing in Mayan art for several years and has developed quite a clientele. But DeBeque's people can't tie her to any of the Patterson operations, so she appears to be in the clear."

A sigh of relief escaped Melinda's lips. "I guess that's something. But how come you know so much about it?"

"I have big ears."

"Great." Melinda turned and yanked back the thick drapes even further to let in what light she could. She wheeled about, hands on her hips and confronted him. "That makes it all the better to hear what I'm going to tell you. You're a lying, conniving, double-crossing bastard and I'm—" She bit off the words, trying to keep her temper under control. "It's all a one-way street with you, Chad Young. I put my reputation on the line to keep you from getting arrested at that roadblock this afternoon, and what thanks do I get? I get kidnapped, roughed up and flung into this damn cell!"

"You're still alive, Lindy," he said softly.

"You better believe it, mister. And I—"

"You probably wouldn't be alive if I'd let you come back up here to Panajachel alone. There are hired killers out looking for you. That's why I wanted you to stay put. That's why I had Ramirez's people hunt you down and bring you back here."

"Just what is your connection with Ramirez?"

"Let's just say we have mutual interests, Lindy."

"What sort of mutual interests?"

He reached out and took her wrists and pulled her to him. "We'll talk about it tomorrow."

She tried to draw back, but he wouldn't let go. "I don't want to talk about it tomorrow! I want to talk about it now! And, damn it, turn on the light so I can see you!"

"Can't. There's no bulb in the fixture."

"That's stupid! What sort of a room is this anyway?"

"It's a room designed to keep people like you out of mischief."

Again, she tried unsuccessfully to pull free of his grasp. "How many people like me do you have to deal with, *Mr.* Young?"

He laughed. "You're one of a kind, *Miss* Harding." His hands left her wrists and his arms encircled her waist. He looked up at her. "Look, it's almost over. Bear with me, huh? I can't let you out of here because Ramirez can't afford to tie up any more of his people keeping an eye on you."

All at once, Melinda was exhausted. The events of the day were beginning to catch up with her. She pushed away his arms and he made no attempt to prevent her from slipping free.

"I want to go home," she said in a weak voice, shivering with the realization he was no longer holding her, protecting her. "I want to get out of here and do what I have to do and go home." She sat down next to him on the bed, and before she realized what was happening her head was resting on his chest and tears were streaming down her cheeks. "Why did we have to meet like this, Chad?"

He kissed her lightly on the forehead and brushed away her tears with a gentle stroke of one finger. "There are some things no one can explain, Lindy. There are some things that probably shouldn't be explained. I guess that's just the way love is."

Melinda tilted back her head and looked up at him. In the darkness, she could barely make out the outline of his head. "Love?" she echoed in a hollow, little voice.

He reached up and brushed back a tangle of hair, and his lips brushed her forehead. "Love," he said softly.

She buried her face in the hollow of his neck. "This is an impossible situation, you know. We hardly know each other."

"Nothing's impossible," Chad said reassuringly. "And I think we've gotten to know each other better in a few days than some people do in a lifetime together." He rose up from the bed, then turned and pushed her down gently until her head was on the pillow. She kicked off her shoes and stretched out full length, and he knelt beside the bed and rested his face against her chest, gazing up at her. "Get some rest now, lady mine. Big day tomorrow."

Her eyelids were heavy and she felt as if she were drifting on a cloud. "Chad," she murmured sleepily, pulling his head toward hers, "stay with me tonight—won't you, please?"

His head moved up and his lips grazed the velvety softness of her neck and chin and searched out her lips, tentatively at first, then hungrily as his tongue probed against hers. Her fingers ran through his hair, then settled on the back of his neck and held him tight, feeling the stepped-up thumping of his heart beneath the lean, hard bands of muscles on his chest. Her sleepiness was gone, replaced by a hot, breathless yearning that cried out for fulfillment.

His left hand fumbled at the topmost buttons of her blouse, and she reached down and helped him. Then the hand slipped inside the open blouse and lightly came to rest on one breast.

Suddenly, his head pulled back and he withdrew his hand. "I can't, Lindy," he said in a barely audible voice. "I don't know that it's right—I mean here, under these circumstances."

Melinda reached behind her and unhooked her bra, then pulled his face into the cleft of her freed breasts. "It *is* right," she corrected him as his head shifted and his darting tongue licked at a nipple, stroking it into a hard nub of almost unbearable passion. She pulled his left hand to the other breast and traced his fingertips against it. "It's right because it's real. It's the only real thing that's happening to us. Everything else is a dream, a bad dream."

Chad got up from his knees and lay down beside her on the bed, cradling her in his arms, his left hand cupping her bosom, the right hand coming to rest up under her skirt on the softness of her inner thigh. "I've told you a lot of lies," he confessed.

"I know," she said, unzipping her skirt and arching her hips to push it down. She took his right hand and hooked his fingers around the lacy waistband of her bikini as she snuggled in close.

"I had to. For your own good."

"I don't want to hear about it, Chad. Not now."

"One thing I have to tell you isn't a lie. I love you, Lindy."

Raising up again, she pushed at his right hand and the bikini slid down along her thighs. She kicked the wispy fabric free of her knees and ankles and slipped her hand inside his slacks, feeling him swell with need for her.

"Show me," she murmured, using her other hand to unbuckle his belt and force down his waistband.

"Lindy..."

"Don't talk. Just show me." She rolled over on top of him, straddling his hips and leaning forward to silence him under the gently insistent pressure of her open mouth.

Words have come between us from the moment we met, she thought as she eased herself against him, guiding him into a pulsing unison with her very soul. *This is no longer a time for words....*

His hands closed over her hips, drawing her closer as the tempo of their mutual passion grew into a pulsing fury. Without missing a beat, he rolled over until he was on top of her, her legs locking around him, her hips arching to meet his every thrust. She buried her face against the hollow of his neck, her cheek brushing the bandage on his left shoulder, the tip of her tongue teasing and tormenting him into repeated spasms of mounting ecstasy.

Then, moaning softly, she drew herself more tightly against him as her every fiber went limp. They lay together, without moving, for a long time.

Finally, he said, softly, his words a mere whisper in her ear, "Lindy, there's never been anyone like you."

"What about our non-hero—the one who talked too much? I seem to recall that our non-hero once loved another woman."

He tensed for a second, then relaxed. "That was a lifetime ago."

"A lot can happen in a lifetime, darling. Who were you in your other lifetime?"

He kissed her lightly on the lips. "It isn't time for explanations—not yet."

"When *will* it be time for explanations?"

"Soon. Very soon."

Chapter Ten

"The time for games is over," Ramirez said as he clambered down from the driver's side of the Jeep and surveyed the steep drop at the edge of the abandoned highway. He had a submachine gun slung over one shoulder, a military-issue musette bag over the other. Squaring his maroon beret, he looked over his shoulder at Melinda, who was in the back of the open vehicle. "I ask you, señorita, why is it so important that you find this cave?"

"It just is," Melinda replied as she got out of the Jeep and slung her leather purse over her shoulder. She'd changed to the same bush jacket, jeans and chukka boots she'd worn on her last expedition to the mountainside, and she wished she'd remembered to bring along a baseball cap to keep the midmorning glare of the sun out of her eyes.

"Maybe she lost something there," Chad said lightly, winking at Melinda as he joined the major at the edge of the road. He held his hands above his forehead to shield his eyes from the sun as he studied the slope and the rippled waters of the lake.

Maybe I did, Melinda thought. *Maybe I lost a kind of innocence in that cave ten years ago.* The fingers of her right hand strayed down the shoulder strap of her purse and touched the bulge of leather behind which rested the jade jaguar.

The major snorted. "There is much that has to be done this morning. Our inquiries have attracted a good deal of attention and time is running out. If we find this cave of yours, all well and good. But I can't spare any men to help you search for it." Glancing back along the road, where a dozen soldiers wearing camouflage outfits and floppy-brimmed field hats were lining up beside an olive-drab military truck parked behind the Jeep, he twirled one hand above his head and then pointed down the slope.

The sergeant in charge of the detail saluted and promptly led the men over the side of the road in single file.

Chad pulled Melinda aside. "Do me a favor, Lindy?"

She looked at him silently.

"Tell Ramirez about the cave. He's ticked off because he figures we're holding out on him, and I need his cooperation."

Melinda shook her head slowly. "I can't take a chance."

"Look, nobody's going to give you a bad time because of some college stunt that happened ten years ago. Besides, all you want to do is return the damn glyph."

"I don't know, Chad. I . . ."

"I promise you: Ramirez won't say a word about it to anyone. He still needs me."

"Ramirez works for DeBeque, doesn't he?"

"He does."

Melinda took a deep breath, held it for a few seconds, then let it out in a sigh. "I don't know why you couldn't have told me that from the beginning—that and a lot of other things. All right, if it'll help you . . ."

Chad walked over to the major, spoke to him in Spanish, and then the two men came over to her. "You've got a deal," Chad said.

"Very well," Melinda agreed. She brought out the jade jaguar from her purse and set it on the hood of the Jeep, where the fire-opal eyes glittered in the sunlight. And for the second time in less than two days, she told her story.

When she was through, Ramirez picked up the glyph and examined it thoughtfully. "So this is what brought you back to Guatemala, eh?"

Melinda nodded.

Ramirez handed the jade jaguar back to her. "I suggest you keep it as a memento."

"I can't do that, major. I think it may be part of a set— you know, those nine glyphs that Joel Patterson has on display. Professor Lara thought the glyphs might provide a key to the hiding place of some Mayan treasure."

"Oh?" The major dropped the carving into her purse. "We shall have a look when we get to the hacienda. First though, I intend to have my men make a thorough sweep of this area. This is our last chance." He patted his web belt, and Melinda noticed the walkie-talkie clipped to it. "If we get separated," he told Chad, "give me a call on the radio. All right, my friend?"

"All right," Chad said, pushing aside his jacket to reveal a matching walkie-talkie.

Picking his way carefully, Ramirez stepped off the road and started down the slope, with Melinda following and Chad bringing up the rear. At a switchback in the rocky trail, Melinda halted and waited for Chad. "What does he mean 'last chance'?"

"He's got orders from DeBeque to move in on the Pattersons. The word is that the smugglers are going to arrange to ship one more load out of the country and then close up shop. DeBeque wants to nail them before they can do it."

Melinda lowered her voice. "Are you sure Stefanie's in the clear?"

Chad nodded. "All of the art dealers in her group are, Ramirez tells me. Apparently, the Pattersons got wind of the investigation and backed off their recruiting efforts a couple of days ago."

"I see. Tell me, Chad, did Joel Patterson kill the professor?"

"Personally? No. He didn't leave Panajachel the afternoon Dr. Lara was murdered—I've checked. But that doesn't mean he couldn't have ordered someone to do the job." As Chad spoke, the question-mark scar over his right eyebrow twitched, and he rubbed it thoughtfully with the knuckle of one finger. "Now that you mention it, I've got bad vibes about the whole thing. The professor was killed with a rather distinctive Mayan ceremonial knife. Patterson has a whole bunch of them in his collection, and I'd be willing to bet that when we get up to the hacienda we'll find one of those knives is missing. Why would he have given the knife to someone to use? Hell, it would only lead back to him."

Melinda thought about it. "I assume you heard about the knife from Ramirez or one of DeBeque's people. I read the newspaper story about the murder, and it didn't mention a thing about ceremonial knives."

"I was there, Lindy."

"There?"

"In Dr. Lara's apartment just after he was killed. I had an appointment with him at five-thirty, and I must have shown up just after he was stabbed. I went into the apartment, and it occurred to me I probably scared off his killer. The killer must have recognized me and figured I was in no position to go running off to the police. I left and staked out the place, and next thing I knew the cops were hauling you out the front door. You must have slipped in when I was checking my escape route."

Melinda shuddered at the recollection. "I phoned to see if Dr. Lara had forgotten our appointment, and the man I talked to must have been his killer. It certainly couldn't have been the professor. He'd already been dead a couple of hours. Do you have *any* idea who it could have been and why he would have returned to the apartment after you scared him off?''

Chad shook his head. ''My guesswork doesn't extend that far, Lindy, but whoever it was, he must have had a darn good reason for going back to take that sort of risk. I'm going to have to let Ramirez and DeBeque figure that one out.''

''And you?''

''What about me?''

''Why did you have an appointment with Dr. Lara? How do you figure in this?''

He motioned her to keep walking down the trail. ''This isn't the time nor the place to talk about that. Now where's this cave of yours?''

Ahead, on a line with the level of the abandoned highway, Melinda could see the stone hut of Don Felipe. ''That way,'' she said, pointing beyond the hut.

''We covered that area the other day, but we didn't find anything.''

''You didn't know what to look for. Come on.'' She moved on, and after a few paces looked back at him. ''That reminds me, what *are* you and Ramirez and his soldiers looking for?''

''I'm not sure. I can only tell you that I'll know it when I see it.''

Ten minutes later, they were standing at the base of The Three Bears, peering up into the trees.

''The entrance is up here,'' Melinda said, working her way up the mountainside.

But the clearing wasn't where she remembered it.

''You're sure you're in the right spot?'' Chad prompted her.

She turned around. ''Of course I'm sure. The three of us—Stuffy, Ellen and I—stopped here for a picnic lunch, and that was when I noticed The Three Bears down there.

It was during that big earthquake, and the ground shook so much the little bear actually moved."

Chad looked at the rock formation, squinting into the bright glare of the sun's reflection off the surface of the lake. "They don't look like bears to me," he said.

"Darling, that's because you have no imagination," she laughed. "Hold up your hands alongside your eyes, just like blinders on a horse." She showed him what she meant. "You can't help but see the outlines of bears."

"First bears, then horses. You're a great girl, Lindy, but what is this fixation you have about animals?"

"Just shut up and—oh, my God!"

"What is it?"

"Look!"

He sighed. "I *am* looking. But as you say, I have no imagination. Rocks are rocks."

"No, not the rocks—the lake!" She stabbed the index finger of her right hand straight out, toward the water. "Look! You can see the outline of a big glass bubble of some sort at the bottom of the lake!"

Chad squinted harder. "Where, Lindy?"

"There—stand here and look right between the baby bear and the mother bear. See? What do you suppose it is?"

Chad cupped his hands around his eyes and studied the lake. "Son of a gun!" he muttered. He grabbed the walkie-talkie from his belt. "Ramirez—what's your location?"

The reply came crackling back within five seconds. "About fifty yards above the edge of the water, straight down from the hut that sits alongside the old highway. Did you find anything, my friend?"

"The lady did. You'd better come have a look."

"What is your location?"

Melinda took the radio out of Chad's hand and spoke into it. "Can you see a rock formation that looks like three bears?"

Pause. "Affirmative."

"We're just up the slope from those rocks."

"I am on my way, señorita."

Melinda gave Chad a smug smile. "It's nice to see that *some* men can use their imagination."

He didn't hear a word she said. He just stood there, staring straight at the water for the full five minutes it took for Ramirez to reach them. There was a hard cast to his eyes, an angry squaring of his jaw. He was a man bracing himself to face an unwelcome truth.

"All right, what did you find?" the major demanded, breathing hard after his climb.

"Look straight out there—about one hundred feet offshore," Chad said, pointing. "There's a big chunk of rounded plexiglass maybe fifteen or twenty feet under the surface, probably resting on the bottom. It's got to be a chopper."

Ramirez held his hands to his eyes, looked, then nodded gravely. "I think we have found the evidence we need, my friend." He reached for his walkie-talkie.

Within an hour, a Guatemalan Army helicopter was hovering a few feet above the water where Melinda and the two men had seen the giant bubble. A pair of divers wearing black wetsuits and air tanks crawled out onto the pontoons of the chopper and tumbled backwards into the lake.

"I suggest we get down to the shore," Ramirez said. "I want to be on hand when they come up."

He led the way down the slope, over the rocks and through the brush, moving swiftly, keeping one eye on the hovering helicopter.

The first diver had just surfaced when the major stepped up to the water's edge. Ramirez signaled to him, and the diver struck out for the shore. As he got near, the man pushed back his face mask and removed the air tube from his mouth. "It's a civilian Alouette II!" he yelled in Spanish, shaking his head to clear the water from his eyes. "It appears to have been on the bottom for some months."

"Is the cockpit intact?" Ramirez asked.

The diver swam closer and stood up in the water. "More or less, sir. There are two men inside, and a number of heavy cases strapped to the floorboards. We managed to squeeze into the cockpit and we pried open one of the cases and found this."

He reached for the rubberized canvas bag hanging from his weight belt and held out a dull gold figurine of a Mayan god.

Ramirez waded into the water to take the figurine. He examined it carefully. "There are more of these?"

"That particular crate is filled with pieces like this, sir. The crate was stamped Caution: Delicate Seismic Instruments, just as were all the others. However, we have opened only the one crate."

"What about the two men in the cockpit?" Chad demanded. "Any indication of what happened to them?"

The diver glanced at Ramirez, who nodded permission for the man to answer the question.

"Both bodies are badly decomposed, of course, but it would appear the pilot was shot in the head. The second man was pinned by one of the crates. If I had to speculate, I would say that the crate came loose when the helicopter crashed, and trapped the second man in the cockpit."

Chad's face clouded further in an angry frown. "You mind if I borrow your scuba outfit for a few minutes?" he asked the diver. "I'd like to see for myself."

Again, the man looked at Ramirez. And again, Ramirez nodded his approval.

Chad stripped off his jacket and shirt and struggled into the underwater-breathing rig. He washed out the face mask and slipped it over his head, adjusted the oxygen flow, then waded into the cold water and disappeared beneath the surface.

"What's he looking for?" Melinda asked Ramirez.

The major looked at her with sad, dark eyes, then took her arm and led her back from the shore, out of earshot of the diver. "He is looking for something he never wanted to find: the body of a good friend at the bottom of a lake in a land far from home."

"Was Chad's friend named Cronin—Mark Cronin?"

Ramirez seemed surprised. "Where did you hear that name?"

Melinda told him of her phone calls to Washington. When she was finished, Ramirez smiled. "You missed your calling, señorita. You should have been a detective."

"You're wrong, major. I'm really not very good at riddles. It's taken me much too long to put the pieces together, and I'm still in the dark about some things." She looked out at the lake, and at the air bubbles breaking on the surface over the submerged helicopter. "Chad Young's role in all this, for one thing."

Ramirez glanced at her. "I shall defer to him on that score, but there are some things I *can* tell you. When this investigation began, my superiors at the Interior Ministry suspected that a good deal of the smuggled antiquities were being funneled through intermediaries in New York, and thus it would be essential to have the cooperation of the New York police. Arrangements were made through your State Department and Mark Cronin was assigned to work undercover with us. The Interior Ministry needed an American helicopter pilot to infiltrate the smugglers' organization, and Cronin was perfect for the role. He had flown hundreds of missions in Vietnam, had kept up his helicopter ratings in the U.S. Army Reserve and had risen to the rank of captain in the New York Police Department. He—"

"You said that he and Chad were good friends," Melinda interrupted him. "Is Chad also a New York police detective?"

Ramirez frowned. "If you will permit me to finish, señorita? Nine months ago, Cronin accepted employment with a charter company partially owned by our friend Joel Patterson. The company was under contract to provide service to geologists working in Petén. Cronin won the trust of his employers and was given the opportunity to make additional money by flying sidetrips to Panajachel on his way to and from Guatemala City and Petén. All the while, of course, he was gathering evidence for us." The major paused. "This was to have been his final trip. He was to have flown directly to the barracks at Sololá, and we would have impounded the cargo and arrested the Pattersons and their helpers. But Cronin disappeared off the face of the earth and we were left with no case. This gave the smugglers sufficient time to cover their tracks and devise new ways of smuggling artifacts out of the country."

Melinda tried again. "But what about Chad? Where does he fit into the picture?"

"As I told you, señorita, I will have to let him answer that question. There are others involved and I do not wish to jeopardize their position." He peered out at the lake. "Ah, here he is now...."

Melinda turned to see Chad rise to his feet in hip-deep water. He pulled off his face mask, spat out his breathing tube and began unbuckling his air tank harness. The anger had left his face and been replaced by a grim resignation.

"I can't tell for sure," he announced, stepping up onto the shore. "But it's probably him." Blinking, he turned away from them and stared out over the water. "Fifteen years a cop, four years in Vietnam—more medals than you can shake a stick at. Damn it, it's not right! Mark Cronin deserved one hell of a lot better than this!"

Melinda sensed the anguish he was feeling. She stepped up and put her arms around him as he dropped his air tanks. "Darling, I'm sorry."

"He had three kids, Lindy. His wife had died, and he'd raised them himself. Now they've got nobody."

"Was Mark Cronin another one of your non-heroes?"

"We're all non-heroes, Lindy. Each and every one of us."
He turned and held out a thick, clear plastic packet to Ramirez. "We've got what you need, major. This is his logbook. I haven't had a chance to go through it yet, but the
entries should be more than enough to nail Patterson and his
pals."

Ramirez took the plastic packet and dropped it into his
musette bag. "Can you tell what happened?"

Chad shrugged out of his harness and handed the air tank
and face mask to their rightful owner. "Your man here—"
he nodded his head in the direction of the diver "—had it
pegged. Mark was shot and the chopper went down. The
passenger apparently tried to climb out when the chopper
struck the water, but he was trapped and drowned. The hacienda isn't far from here. My guess is that they'd loaded up
at the hacienda, and Patterson sent along a man to ride
shotgun. The passenger probably got spooked when Mark
headed for Sololá instead of Guatemala City, and he pulled
a gun and tried to force him to change course. You'll have
to wait for the autopsy to make it official, but I don't think
I'm far off."

Ramirez turned aside to talk to the diver, who had put
back on his equipment. The man headed out into the lake
once more, and the major raised his walkie-talkie to his lips
and gave instructions to the helicopter.

"The divers will bring up the bodies and the crates, but
we shall have to bring in a heavy-duty helicopter from the
capital to raise the wreckage itself," he announced.
"Meantime, I think it is time to pay a call on the Pattersons."

"You don't need me," Chad said, pulling on his shirt.
"My job is done. If you can have somebody pick me up and
take me back to Panajachel, I can drive into Guatemala City
and catch a late flight from La Aurora." He held out his
hand. "If you wouldn't mind, major, I'd like to take a look
at the logbook before I leave. I'd like to know just what

Mark wrote.'' He paused. ''I'd like to know what to tell his kids.''

The major frowned. ''It would be best if the packet were opened by one of our laboratory people. In all likelihood there has been some water damage to the contents, and we must be careful not to damage the evidence. After the laboratory people are finished...''

Melinda wasn't listening. She was staring at Chad. He couldn't leave—not yet. She still had too many unanswered questions. ''You promised to help me find the cave,'' she reminded him.

Chad's scarred eyebrow rose. ''You mind, major? It should only take a few minutes.''

Ramirez shrugged. ''Why not? If you show me where the cave is, I can bring some people back to it later and inventory the things that are hidden there.'' He nodded to Melinda. ''Lead on, señorita.''

On the way up the mountainside, Melinda reached back for Chad's hand and brought him alongside her. ''You know, the major told me about Mark Cronin and the work he was doing for the Guatemalan government,'' she said in a low voice, not wanting to be overheard by Ramirez, who was several feet in back of them. ''But he won't tell me about you.''

''The major is very discreet,'' Chad allowed.

''All right, then,'' Melinda persisted, ''*you* tell me.''

''Tell you what?''

''Who you are, of course.''

''Sorry, but I'm very discreet, too.''

Melinda snatched away her hand. ''Damn it! This isn't fair. I've cooperated with you, and the investigation is over—you said so yourself. Why can't you level with me, Chad?''

''Steep hill,'' he said, exhaling loudly. ''Either that, or I'm getting old.''

''You're the most exasperating man I've ever met!''

"Several young ladies have said that. Several not-so-young ladies, too. It's one of my many personality flaws."

"What do I call you? Detective? Sergeant? Lieutenant? Or were you a captain like your friend Mark?"

"Chad will do nicely."

"Are you an inspector of some sort?"

"'Fraid not."

"You *are* with the New York Police Department, aren't you?"

"Nope."

"I give up," Melinda sighed.

He turned and winked at her. "The last woman who said that to me pulled a knife and tried to carve out my right eye for a souvenir. Now where's this cave of yours, Lindy?"

They'd come to the place on the mountainside where the clearing had once been. Melinda looked around. "I'm not exactly sure. It's around here somewhere, I know. Why don't we split up and look?"

"Look for what?" the major asked, huffing and puffing after the steep climb.

"There's a pile of round stones blocking the entrance. It's a pile four or five feet high, as I recall."

The major glanced at his watch. "Very well, but I want to make this fast. My men are already gathering at the truck."

In less than ten minutes, Chad stumbled upon the pile of stones, all but invisible under a clump of scrub brush. He shouted, and the others pushed through the bushes to join him.

"It was pure accident," he explained as they tugged the clump out by its roots. "I was moving uphill and one of the stones gave way underfoot. I doubt if this place has been disturbed for years."

"Ten years, to be exact," Melinda said, starting to roll aside the stones covering the entrance. Something moved in the brush and she sucked in her breath sharply and jumped back.

"Watch out for snakes," Ramirez warned.

Melinda stared at the remaining rocks. "I'm not so sure this is a good idea, after all."

"We're here," Chad reminded her. "We might as well have at it."

Carefully, they removed the pile, stone by stone. When they had an opening large enough to squeeze through, the major brought out a flashlight from a deep pocket of his camouflage coveralls. "If you permit me, I will lead the way," he said, switching on the flashlight.

"I've got a flashlight, too," Melinda said, taking it from her purse. "I picked it up the other day in the village."

"It looks like I'm the only one who came unprepared," Chad said. "That being the case, I'll bring up the rear."

The major maneuvered his way through the opening, followed by Melinda and then by Chad.

The white inscriptions on the tunnel walls were just as Melinda remembered them, ghostlike and forbidding in the yellow light of the flashlight beam.

"Our archaeologists will have a field day," Ramirez observed, pausing to study the markings. "Caves much like this were found near Quiché, and they proved tremendously valuable."

"The altar is straight ahead twenty feet or so," Melinda said, patting her purse to make sure she hadn't lost the jade jaguar.

"Stay close," the major cautioned, moving forward along the tunnel.

His flashlight beam stabbed through the darkness ahead.

"That's it!" Melinda cried. "Straight ahead—that altar or ledge or whatever it is. That's where I got the jade jaguar."

Ramirez trained his light on the ledge. It was bare.

Melinda's thoughts raced back through the years, to the day she'd first entered the tunnel. So much had happened in her life, so many things had changed since she saw those yellow eyes staring out at her. She reached into her purse, took out the jade jaguar and stepped forward, past Ramirez, and set the glyph on the altar.

"You're home," she whispered.

The major pointed his flashlight beam at the glyph. The opal eyes glistened in snarling rage.

"You are a sentimentalist, señorita," he said softly. "And I think that speaks well of you."

"I've been meaning to do this for years," Melinda explained. "This is the first opportunity I've had."

"The jade jaguar will remain our secret." He removed it from the altar and dropped it into his musette bag. "You say it may be part of a set. We shall see about that when we get to the Pattersons. Now, what about that treasure trove you mentioned?"

Melinda ran the beam of her flashlight to the right. "In there—through that rounded portal."

Ramirez moved to the portal, hunched over and shone his light inside. Melinda and Chad could hear his gasp.

"Let's have a look," Chad said, crouching down beside him and looking along the beam of the flashlight. He stared, but said nothing.

Melinda pressed in behind the two men and looked over Chad's shoulder. The ring of skeletons was just as she remembered: deathly white against the powdery gray of the cavern floor. And inside the ring . . .

Nothing.

The major crawled through the opening and motioned for his companions to follow him. "Are you sure you did not imagine the treasure, señorita?" he asked, shining his light around the cavern.

"Certainly not!" Melinda exclaimed. "It was right there in the center in some rotted baskets."

"Just what sort of treasure was it?"

"A lot of gold jewelry and jade carvings—some silver, too, I believe."

"Nothing here now," Chad said, kicking at the dust on the cavern floor. "Just a mass tomb."

"There seems to be another portal over there," the major said. "Perhaps the treasure is in there."

"No," Melinda said adamantly. "It was right here in this cavern. I remember we didn't go any farther than this."

Ramirez and Chad moved to the second portal and Melinda shone her light around the floor. Bones. Nothing but bones. Deathly white and crumbling. The palace guard of a long-gone empire.

The moving beam continued to pass over the floor, and something flickered briefly in the light. Melinda moved the beam back, searching for the source of the flicker.

And then she found it.

It was a thick gold ring with a black stone, and it encircled the third finger of the right hand of the skeleton nearest her feet.

Gritting her teeth, Melinda bent down and slipped the ring off the finger and studied it under the beam of her flashlight. She stood up slowly, taking one last, long look at the ring as a chill went down her spine. Then she dropped it into the pocket of her bush jacket.

The jade jaguar had been right all along. She never should have come to this place of death.

Chapter Eleven

"I still don't understand," Melinda said as they bounced along in Major Ramirez's Jeep, headed for the hacienda, leaving the army patrol to assist in the search of the crash site. "How'd you manage to get yourself shot the other night?"

"It was the major's idea," Chad said. "Ask him."

Ramirez gave a throaty little laugh. "I needed a talented gringo to play Jesse James, and our friend here just happened to be handy. He gave a masterful performance, I must say."

"What do you mean?" Melinda demanded.

Ramirez geared down for a switchback and Melinda's knuckles whitened around the grab bar mounted on the dashboard. "My esteemed superior Oswaldo DeBeque suspected that Joel Patterson was making clever reproductions of some of the more valuable relics recovered from our Huehuetenango archaeological site. Patterson made no secret of this—it was his 'fee' for helping the Interior Ministry in the project. Ah, but he had a trick up his sleeve the ministry did not know about. Patterson and his confederates planned to place the *reproductions* in the government collection being assembled by Professor Lara, and then sell the *originals* to collectors in the United States and Europe. I can only assume that Dr. Lara discovered the scheme, but was killed by one of Patterson's henchmen before he could expose it.''

Melinda wasn't satisfied. ''That still doesn't answer my question. How did Chad get shot?''

''You need not worry your pretty little head about technical details,'' replied Ramirez with a shrug.

Melinda glowered at him. ''Look, major, whether you realize it or not there happens to be a brain buried inside what you so glibly refer to as my 'pretty little head.' That brain demands answers. How did Chad get shot?''

Ramirez glanced at Chad, who was sitting in the passenger seat of the Jeep. ''She is a stubborn one, eh?''

''I thought so the minute I set eyes on her,'' Chad agreed. ''You might as well tell her. She's not about to back off.''

''Very well,'' the major sighed. ''We needed what the law refers to as 'a chain of evidence,' so we daubed a bit of radioactive compound on the contents of some of the key crates sent down from Huehuetenango earlier this week. The compound was such that it would have enabled us to electronically detect the originals if any attempt were made to smuggle them out of the country.''

''Couldn't you have applied that compound at the site?'' Melinda persisted. ''Why did you have to risk Chad's life?''

''Drop it, huh?'' Chad spoke up.

Melinda turned about in the front passenger seat and directed a glance of rebuke at Chad, who was seated alone in the back seat of the Jeep. ''I don't want to drop it. The whole thing has been one big mess from the word go, and I for one would like to know why!''

Again, Ramirez gave a sigh of exasperation. ''We could not take a chance of doing it at the site itself, señorita. There was no way of knowing whom we could trust. So we chose to stage a mock hijacking. Unfortunately, one of the officers assigned to the *Policía Nacional* guard detail got off a shot at our friend here before our other men could disarm him.''

Chad gave a dry little laugh. "The hell of it is, the hijacking was a wasted effort. Patterson had already gotten wise and was about to close up shop anyway."

Melinda looked over her shoulder at Chad. "You like to live dangerously, don't you?"

"All in a day's work." He grinned good-naturedly.

"Oh? You still haven't told me: just what *is* your line of work?"

Ignoring the question, Chad rose up in his seat and looked straight ahead. "Pull up, major!" he said crisply. "Now!"

Ramirez jammed on the brakes. He studied the road ahead, but there was nothing to see but the single-lane trail of gravel as it topped a rise on the side of the mountain and then disappeared. "What is the matter?" he demanded.

"I heard shots," Chad said.

"Nonsense," Ramirez said. "They wouldn't dare shoot at us." He patted the walkie-talkie radio clipped to his web belt. "I could have a battalion of men on this mountainside in fifteen minutes."

"Turn off the engine."

"Come now, my friend. I don't think that is necessary...."

"Turn off the damn engine!"

"Better do as he says," Melinda advised. "He's stubborn, too."

Ramirez switched off the ignition.

Cocking his head, Chad listened. "That's small-arms fire," he announced. "Come on, major—let's have a look." He vaulted over the open side of the jeep and reached for the pistol tucked into his belt. "You stay here," he instructed Melinda, "and keep your head down."

"Not on your life!" Melinda objected, climbing out of the Jeep and standing close to him. "I'm not going to be a sitting duck in that open Jeep!"

Chad frowned, and she frowned right back. His frown melted first. "Will you at least stay out of the way and keep your head down?"

"I'll think about it."

"Do that, huh?" Grinning, he chucked her under the chin. "Did I ever tell you that you're cute when you're mad?"

"I don't get 'mad'—I get angry. Now if you're through playing the big macho hero, do whatever it is you're going to do and I'll tag along."

Chad started to say something more, but changed his mind. He turned and started for the rise at a jog, his revolver in his hand. Ramirez, a submachine gun slung around his neck and his musette bag bouncing on his hip, was a half dozen steps behind him, with Melinda following. They crouched behind the crest of the rise and cautiously raised their heads to peer over it.

Fifty yards ahead, nestled against the side of the mountain, lay the white-plastered Patterson hacienda, its red-tile roof standing out vividly under the early afternoon sun. There was a dark Mercedes limousine parked in the walled courtyard, and two men were hunched down on the near side of the vehicle, with pistols in their hands.

Ramirez brought a small set of binoculars from one baggy pocket of his camouflage coveralls and raised them to his eyes. "My God!" he muttered as the scene came into focus. "Oswaldo DeBeque and his driver are pinned down behind their car!"

"You'd better bring in some reinforcements, major," Chad said under his breath.

Ramirez reached for his walkie-talkie. He raised it to his lips, thumbed the transmit switch and spoke into it. "Cobra One to Cobra Two," he intoned in Spanish.

No answer.

The major stared at the radio for a second, shook it, then tried again. "Cobra One to Cobra Two."

Still no answer.

"The power cell must be dead," he said. He looked at Chad. "Perhaps your unit will work."

Chad shook his head. "I left my radio on the shore so the divers could use it to keep in voice contact with the helicopter."

Ramirez pulled back from the crest. "Then one of us will have to go back for help. What do you say, my friend?"

"It'd take too long," Chad replied. "DeBeque and his driver are pinned down. There's no way of telling how long they can hold out."

The major glanced at Melinda and framed an unspoken question.

"Don't look at me," she said quickly. "I'm staying right here. Besides, I agree with Chad, there isn't time. We've got to do something now."

Ramirez looked dubious. *"We?"*

"We," Melinda assured him. "In my business, you help people who need help."

"Not so fast," Chad said, keeping a watch on the scene in the courtyard. "What you're looking at is no tea party for the striped-pants crowd. It's a shoot-out at the OK Corral."

A puff of dust rose from the gravel a few feet from where Melinda was crouched, and it took her several seconds to realize someone was shooting at her. She pressed face down into the roadbed, beneath the crest.

"We've got to do *something*!" she exclaimed.

"Yeah," said Chad, with all the enthusiasm of a veteran firefighter about to go back into a raging inferno for the tenth time. He glanced at Ramirez. "Major, you work your way along the brush on the downhill side of the road. Lindy—" he grabbed her hand and pulled her after him as he moved down from the crest "—you come with me."

"What are you going to do, my friend?" Ramirez demanded.

"My Rambo number, what else?" Chad fired back.

Breaking into a trot, he led Melinda back to the Jeep and pointed her south, toward the main road. "Start hiking," he ordered her. "When you get back to the main road, hitch a ride into Panajachel and bring back help."

"There isn't time!" Melinda protested.

"I said move it!" he barked.

"I'm going with you."

"The hell you are!"

Angrily, she spun about. "Don't you try to give me orders, Chad Young! You're treating me like some damn schoolgirl and I don't much care for it!"

Chad grabbed her by the shoulders and pulled her so close she could see her twin reflections in his dark-blue eyes. "How do you want me to treat you, Lindy?"

How indeed, she wondered. Like a friend, an equal partner, a lover—how? So many questions, so few answers. But somehow, answers no longer seemed important. Just being with him, touching him, knowing he was there was enough.

The twin reflections in his eyes blurred as he leaned over her, and his parted lips touched hers, tentatively at first, then pressing down and laying claim to her very soul. Then, abruptly, he pulled away, turned her around and again pointed her down the road. "Later, Lindy," he murmured.

He jumped into the Jeep, switched on the ignition and moved out, up over the crest and toward the hacienda beyond.

"Chad!" she yelled, running after him. "Chad—wait!"

The Jeep bounced up over the crest, and she could hear the sound of gunfire.

Damn him, she thought. *He's out of his mind!*

She returned to their original vantage point and sprawled below the crest, peering over the top to see what he was doing.

The Jeep was barreling straight for the open gate of the courtyard, and Chad was crouched low behind the steering wheel, barely visible above the level of the hood. She could see puffs of dust in the roadway in front of him as someone in the hacienda sprayed the onrushing vehicle with machine-gun fire.

As the Jeep came up to the gate, Chad yanked sharply at the wheel and pointed it straight into the courtyard, on a track that would take it in front of the Mercedes limousine. And at that instant he jumped clear and tumbled into the gully at the side of the road, at the base of the white stuccoed wall.

She winced as she watched him hit the ground, rolling head over heels, his body doubled up. He obviously knew what he was doing, but just as obviously he was going to need all the help he could get.

Keeping low, Melinda moved down from the roadbed to the lake side of the slope, the way the major had gone. She had no definite plan in mind. All she knew was that she had to help Chad.

She could still hear gunfire, but the shots were less frequent now. She thought of the revolutions and riots she'd observed, how it had always struck her that shots never really sounded like shots, but like the popping of corks from champagne bottles, so innocent, yet so terrifying.

There was a heavy cover of brush on the mountainside. It made the going slow, but also safer, as she crept forward, parallel to the roadway.

When all this is over, Chad, you're going to sit down and tell me everything I want to know or else!

But, then, will it ever be over?

Ahead lay the stone steps that led down from the hacienda to the wooden dock that poked out into the lake. Two boats were tied up at the dock. One was a small rowboat, the other a speedboat with two large outboard motors mounted on its stern.

Did she hear a throaty rumble coming from the motors? She couldn't tell for sure, but there was no time to check.

She had to slip up to the hacienda, see what was happening.

She reached the steps, ducked under the waist-high pipe handrail and started climbing the stairs, keeping close to the rail and pausing every few steps to listen. She heard a burst of machine-gun fire, followed by a single shot. And then silence from the hacienda.

All at once someone shouted, and footsteps crunched against pavement. Melinda hesitated. There was no way of telling what was happening up above.

"Chad?" she called out, crouching down, prepared to duck under the rail and dart into the brush of the mountainside if someone she didn't want to see should show up at the top of the stairs.

There were two more shots, and then silence once more.

"Chad—I'm coming up the stairs! Don't shoot!"

She started climbing again, more rapidly now, but warily. *This is insane,* she thought. *I have no idea what I'm getting myself into. I have no gun...wouldn't know what to do with it if I did have one. Why am I doing this?*

She knew the answer before she even framed the question in her mind. *Because of him. Because I want to help him...because I have to help him. Because I'm in love with the man, damn it!*

"Chad!"

Silence from the top of the stairs.

Another half dozen steps and she was on the level of the main patio, outside the salon in which the reception had been held four nights before.

Slung over the top railing of the stairs, where they opened out onto the patio, was an olive-drab musette bag. It occurred to her that it might belong to one of the people who'd ambushed DeBeque and his driver. Perhaps there were additional weapons in it.

She grabbed it and raised her arm to fling it out into the brush of the mountainside. But it was too light to contain weapons, she realized.

She looked around and listened. There were no signs of movement in the hacienda, and she heard nothing more.

She glanced down at the bag, hesitated, then opened it.

Inside was the jade jaguar, along with a sealed, clear plastic folder, clammy and discolored, with beads of sweat clinging to its contents. It was the logbook the diver had recovered from the wreckage of the helicopter. Mark Cronin's logbook.

The musette bag belonged to Ramirez, she realized. He must have left it there intentionally so it wouldn't encumber him when he moved in to outflank the ambushers.

She slipped the logbook back into the case and slung the strap over her shoulder, alongside her purse.

Now she could hear voices beyond the door of the salon, no more than twenty feet from where she stood.

"...didn't have to kill all of them!" she heard Chad saying. "They were just about to give up!"

Melinda peered cautiously around the edge of the patio door. Ramirez was standing just inside it, his back to her, his submachine gun resting on his right shoulder. Chad was on the far side of the salon, standing alongside Oswaldo De-Beque and a man she'd never seen. Midway between Chad and Ramirez, the bodies of two men were sprawled on the polished brown tile floor.

"They did not leave me a lot of choice, my friend," the major said. "They were turning around as if about to open fire."

"We can discuss all this later." DeBeque spoke up, trying to take command of the situation. His gray suit was rumpled and blood-splattered, and his patrician face was ashen. "Since the phones seemed to have been ripped out from the walls, I suggest you get on that radio of yours and broadcast orders to arrest our fugitives."

"Yes, sir." Ramirez nodded compliantly. Keeping his right hand on the grip of his submachine gun, he used his left hand to detach his walkie-talkie from his belt and raised it to his lips.

He spoke quickly into the radio, in a low voice.

Melinda barely suppressed a gasp of surprise, and a horrible suspicion began to form in her mind. She risked a quick glance at Chad to see his eyes narrow fractionally as Ramirez continued to talk into his radio. So he, too, had realized something was terribly wrong.

Able to restrain herself no longer, Melinda stepped into the salon, brushed past Ramirez and ran to Chad. Jamming his revolver into his waistband, Chad threw his arms around her protectively.

"You're not very good at following orders, are you?" he scolded her. "I told you to get the hell away from here."

"I must have taken a wrong turn somewhere," she murmured, her face against his chest.

Ramirez hadn't moved when she barged into the room. He'd stayed in position at the door, his submachine gun at the ready. "You startled me, señorita," she heard him say. "It is not healthy to run up unannounced behind a man with a weapon."

Melinda turned slowly and stood alongside Chad. "Were you going to shoot me, too, major?" she asked defiantly.

"What nonsense! You are—" He stopped talking as he noticed the waterproof case hanging from her shoulder. "I believe you have something of mine, señorita. May I have it?"

Melinda stepped away from Chad and started across the floor of the salon, stopping when she was halfway between Chad and Ramirez. She slipped the web strap of the waterproof case from her shoulder. "Is this what you want?"

Ramirez stared at her coldly.

She half turned and looked at DeBeque. "Perhaps I'd better hand the case over to—"

"You had better give it to me!" the major said in an icy tone, pointing at the case with the barrel of his submachine gun.

Frowning, Chad started forward, but Ramirez held up his left hand to signal him to stay where he was. The man's right hand remained closed around the grip of his submachine gun, and his attention was riveted on Melinda. "Well, señorita?"

She took a deep breath and wondered how far she dared push her luck. "As I was about to say, I think I'd better hand this case over to Mr. DeBeque. I'm sure he'll be interested in Mark Cronin's logbook." She paused, then added, "I know I found it quite fascinating."

Chad moved close to her and put his left arm around her shoulder. His right hand strayed toward the butt of the revolver tucked into his waistband.

"You are making a mistake, my friend," Ramirez advised him, training his submachine gun on Melinda. "Admittedly, I would not want to have to face you one on one. You have too many tricks up your sleeve. But with the young lady in the line of fire..."

Chad lowered his right hand.

"Much better," the major sighed. "Now, señorita, I believe you have something more to tell us?"

Melinda wondered if she hadn't made a mistake. For the moment, Ramirez clearly had the upper hand. But it was too late now to turn back. It had been too late the minute she realized Chad's life was in danger.

"That's right, major...I do," she said, struggling to keep her voice under control. She didn't want Ramirez to see how nervous she was. "First, though, I want to ask Señor De-Beque a question." She glanced around at the man who had been her inquisitor in Guatemala City. "What happened to you, señor?"

DeBeque's tone suggested he was not at all happy to be on the answering end of things. "I drove up from the capital to be here when the Pattersons were arrested, if you must know."

"And who said they were going to be arrested?"

"Major Ramirez, of course."

"But the Pattersons were gone, weren't they?"

"Yes, Miss Harding, they were gone."

"Do you know when they left?"

"We talked to the maid. She said they never came back to the hacienda from their gallery in Panajachel last night. They must have fled."

Melinda smiled knowingly. "It looks very much as though they knew what would happen today, doesn't it?"

DeBeque scowled at the major. He said nothing.

"When were you attacked?"

"Just as we were leaving. Five men with guns appeared as if out of nowhere and chased us to the car. I can only assume they were smugglers who meant to kill us. We held them off until these two rescued us. Mr. Young shot it out with two of the attackers, and Major Ramirez dispatched the others."

"In other words," Melinda said, "there's no one left alive to testify against the Pattersons. Doesn't that strike you as rather convenient?"

"Much *too* convenient," Chad agreed. Melinda could feel a coiled tenseness in the muscles of the arm around her shoulder, and she knew he was about to make a move. She had to stop him. He wouldn't have a chance against Ramirez's submachine gun.

She pushed aside Chad's arm and stepped forward, toward the major. "I suggest you put down your gun and surrender," she announced. "I've already sent for help."

The man smiled and shook his head slowly. The muzzle of his weapon didn't waver. "Come now, señorita. Do you really expect me to believe that? There is no traffic on that road out there, and no one lives nearby."

Melinda sensed DeBeque moving forward. "Would someone be good enough to tell me just what is going on here?"

Chad glanced back at DeBeque. "The lady here has just solved a mystery for you, amigo. You wondered how the smugglers were able to operate for so long without being caught. Simple—they had the major's protection. He was playing both ends against the middle, and making a lot of money doing it."

Ramirez's gaze wandered from Chad to DeBeque, then to Melinda. "I am sorry, señorita. I tried to keep you out of it, you know. Give me credit for that."

Melinda's eyebrows arched in disbelief. "Oh? How was that, major? By having me killed last Thursday night on the road?"

"You were not going to be killed, señorita. That little incident was staged merely to frighten you—to send you packing to Washington. You see, I had your room searched and discovered that you were with the U.S. State Department. Since a number of your countrymen were involved, I concluded that you were sent to Guatemala to investigate. I was wrong, wasn't I?"

"Quite wrong, major. You know why I came to Guatemala."

Ramirez nodded. "Ah, yes—the jade jaguar. Be good enough to remove those other glyphs from the display case and put them into my musette bag. Carefully now. I may be able to turn a profit out of this yet."

Melinda moved to the display of nine glyphs and studied them. Reaching into the musette bag, she brought out the jade jaguar and placed it in the tenth, vacant slot.

What was the story they were intended to tell, she wondered.

The jade jaguar's eyes flashed an angry yellow, almost as if the beast were trying to speak.

"Hurry, please, señorita," the major said. "Time is short."

One by one, Melinda removed the glyphs from their case and placed them carefully in the musette bag.

"It all fits together now," she said as she strapped down the flap of the case. "All the little things add up. I should have seen it before." She wrinkled her nose at Chad. "You're some detective! You should have seen it, too."

"What little things?" the major inquired.

"For one thing, that business on the road after we left the reception. You were the only one who knew for sure when we'd be leaving. You knew because it was you who phoned Chad to tell him to meet you at the hotel—right, Chad?"

Chad nodded.

"Another thing: you sent him out to hold up that police convoy hoping that he'd be killed. And he almost was. What's more, you knew every step I took in Guatemala City because you were having me followed." She bit her lower lip. "You also killed Dr. Lara, didn't you?"

"Nonsense. I was here at the lake all day. Ask your friend. He called me on the telephone."

"I talked to you on a radio telephone," Chad corrected him. "You could have been anywhere, a few blocks away in Guatemala City even."

Ramirez stared at Melinda, and she sensed that Chad had hit upon the truth.

"It was you who answered the phone when I called Dr. Lara, wasn't it? You were scared off by Chad, but you went back to search the professor's apartment for any evidence he might have had against you. You knew Chad couldn't risk calling the police to report the crime.

"Then," she went on, "there's the business of the walkie-talkie. You said it was broken, so we couldn't call in help from your troops when we saw what was happening here at the hacienda. But a few minutes ago, you pretended to use it when Señor DeBeque told you to put out a bulletin on the Pattersons.''

"If you are through, señorita, I suggest you hand me that case.''

Melinda walked toward him, slowly, holding the straining strap of the now-heavy case with both hands. "The logbook is what really did it, major. You haven't looked at it yet, have you?''

Ramirez snorted. "I am afraid I have not. I have had a few other things to keep me busy.''

"Well, *I* opened it up and looked at it,'' Melinda lied. It was all bluff, but she had to chance it. "Mark Cronin was a very skillful undercover agent. In the back of his logbook he wrote down a complete chronicle of his investigation. He knew about you and how you were protecting the smugglers. He was going to turn over his logbook to Señor DeBeque as soon as he got back to Guatemala City after that last flight. He never made it, because you had one of your men with him—and your man killed him, sending the helicopter crashing into the lake after it had made a pickup right here at the hacienda.''

DeBeque pointed an accusing finger at his subordinate. "Put down that gun and consider yourself under arrest, Ramirez.''

The major snatched the strap of the waterproof case from Melinda's outstretched hands and slung it around his neck, keeping his submachine gun trained straight ahead. "Like many rich men, you live in a fool's paradise, DeBeque. You think you can get what you want simply by snapping your fingers. Hah! Think again.'' Ramirez's left hand came down atop the barrel of his weapon to steady it. "And keep thinking until the last breath leaves your body. Stand aside, señorita!''

"No!'' she screamed.

"Stand aside or I swear I shall kill you, too!''

She returned Ramirez's icy stare, knowing she had to keep talking or else risk losing her nerve. "You shoot me and you've got the United States government to worry about the rest of your life! They'll find you no matter where you try to hide. Is that what you want?"

She was so close to Ramirez she could feel his warm breath on her face.

"The lady makes a good point, major," Chad spoke up. "Uncle Sam's got a long memory."

Ramirez blinked and lowered the muzzle of his gun a fraction of an inch. "Your Uncle Sam is also a businessman," he said. "Perhaps we can strike a deal...."

Before she realized what he was doing, he grabbed Melinda and spun her around, holding her in front of him, the crook of his left arm locked around her throat.

"The deal is this," he announced, his voice a growling hiss in her ear. "I have a boat at the dock and a car waiting across the lake. My late, lamented associates were to have used the boat and car after they had taken care of the esteemed Oswaldo DeBeque. Unfortunately, they botched the job and I had to terminate them. Miss Harding will accompany me to the boat, and I will set her free on the other side of the lake. If you attempt to pursue us, I shall put a bullet in her brain and dump her into the water. Is that clear?"

"I also have a long memory," DeBeque said in a menacing tone. He took a step forward, but stopped when he saw Ramirez tighten his grip around Melinda's throat. "If the United States government does not track you down, I will. And that, sir, is a promise."

Ramirez began inching back toward the salon door. "I shall take my chances on that, Señor DeBeque. *¡Adiós!*"

Half dragging Melinda, he moved through the open door and onto the patio. Gasping for breath, she clawed at his arm, trying to break his stranglehold, but he was too powerful.

Chad, DeBeque and DeBeque's chauffeur started after him.

"Stay back!" Ramirez shouted.

Reaching the head of the steps, he lowered his gun to his side and felt for the railing. Seeing her chance, Melinda grabbed at his right wrist and threw herself toward the staircase, landing on her hands and knees on the first few steps.

Ramirez lost his balance momentarily and, releasing his grip around her neck, grabbed for the rail to steady himself. Keeping his eye on Chad and DeBeque, who were now on the patio, he leaped over Melinda and reached down with his left hand to seize her.

"Drop it!" Chad called out.

Melinda saw Chad move forward, his revolver in his hand.

The major spun around and leveled his submachine gun at Chad. As he moved, Melinda grabbed him around the waist from behind and wrestled him off balance again just as the muzzle of the gun spat out a burst of shots.

Ramirez slammed the barrel against her shoulders and she crumpled to the steps.

Chad's first shot caught Ramirez in the shoulder, and the major's dark eyes opened wide in astonishment and pain. He shook his head to clear his trauma-numbed brain and again leveled his weapon at his pursuers.

Chad's next shot missed.

Ramirez vaulted over the fallen Melinda and began running down the steps, hanging onto the rail with his free hand.

"Ramirez!" Chad shouted as the major reached the last landing before the steps opened onto the wooden dock.

The man wheeled about, pointed his gun up at Chad and fired another burst. Then, spinning around, he jumped for the waiting speedboat, which was bobbing on the water a few feet from the dock.

Perhaps the shoulder wound had thrown off his timing. Or perhaps the jade glyphs in the case strapped around his neck weighed him down more than he realized. He missed the deck and splashed into the water, his forehead grazing the edge of the boat, knocking him unconscious.

The jade jaguar did the rest. The jade jaguar and its nine silent companions in the musette bag strapped to Major Gil Ramirez's neck.

The weight of the glyphs carried him down into the cold water at the edge of the dock.

Melinda ran to the top of the steps and stood there with Chad's arm around her waist, watching the bubbles rise and pop on the surface of the water where the major had sunk.

The jade jaguar had found a new place of death.

CHAD HAD CHANGED into gray wool slacks and a loose black pullover. As he leaned against the bedroom doorway in the safe house watching Melinda repack her carry-on bag, he seemed strangely ill at ease.

He hadn't said much since leaving the Patterson hacienda, where DeBeque had lost no time sending his driver into Panajachel to arrange for an archaeological team to fly up from Guatemala City to inventory the relics in the salon and the adjacent workroom. DeBeque had taken Chad aside for a few minutes of whispered conversation. Then and only then had he called Melinda over to thank her for her help.

"I am sure you will wish to file a report with your own State Department, Miss Harding," he said as they shook hands. "Perhaps it would be best for all concerned if you neglected to mention Mr. Young's role in this business."

Melinda had looked to Chad for some sort of explanation, but none was forthcoming. He'd simply winked at her, then put his arm around her waist to steer her toward the door.

And so the adventure was over, and it was time to get on with her life.

But questions remained, and it troubled her that even now Chad was unwilling to tell her who he really was. It wasn't mere curiosity, but the thought she might never see him again.

She zipped up the carryon and started to sling it over her shoulder, but he stepped up and silently took it from her.

She looked at him and saw a sadness in his eyes. "What are you going to do now?" she asked.

He shrugged. "I have a couple of things to take care of in the capital, then I'm heading home."

"And where is home? Or am I permitted to ask?"

"You can ask me anything you want, Lindy."

Sure, she thought. *Anything at all. But whether I get an answer is something else again.*

"Will I ever see you again?"

He put an arm around her waist and drew her close, pressing his cheek against hers. "You'd better believe it. I'll show up one day when you least expect it and we'll go from there."

"Why can't we go from here?" she murmured, nestling her head against his shoulder. "I have some vacation time left, and you still owe me an explanation."

His lips brushed her cheek, and she turned her head to look at him. As she moved, his mouth closed on hers, and for one throbbing moment time stood still as they lost themselves in the warmth and closeness of each other.

Don't let go, Melinda thought, closing her eyes. *Stay with me and answer all my questions so that I can really know you. I love you, Chad Young. I love you and I don't want to lose you.*

"We'd better be going," he said softly. "We keep this up, I may decide to chuck everything and carry you off into the sunset."

"Chad . . ."

He went to the closet and got her garment bag, then headed for the door.

"Chad, I'm in love with you."

"That goes both ways, Lindy."

"Then why can't you tell me about yourself? Two people in love shouldn't have secrets from each other."

"Maybe," he said, still not looking at her, "this is a case where two people in love *have* to have secrets. Someday soon you'll understand. Now, come on."

"Chad, I . . ." She gave up. *What is the use,* she thought. *He's not going to tell me what I want to know. Not now, probably not ever. There are 'somedays' that never come.* "Would you mind taking me by the hotel?"

He led the way to the rental car parked in the driveway, just inside the gate. "You want to drop in on your friend?"

"That's right. I want to talk to her before I leave."

They drove to Del Lago in silence and left the car in the circle drive outside the lobby door.

"I'll only be a few minutes," Melinda said, starting for the elevator.

"Lindy?"

She looked back at him.

"Lindy, you want me to come along?"

She shook her head. "I think not."

"It might be a good idea," he persisted.

She studied his expression. The sadness was still there in his eyes, but mixed with the sadness was a hard, calculating coldness that sent a chill down her spine. "You know, don't you?" she said in a low voice.

"Let's just say I've had a hunch. I did some checking and what I found out supported that hunch."

"You haven't told anyone? Anyone like DeBeque, I mean?"

He shook his head. "That wasn't part of the deal."

Melinda saw her opening. She had to make one last try. "What deal, Chad?"

He smiled. "Yell if you need me."

Melinda took the elevator to the fourth floor and found Stefanie's door ajar. She started to push it fully open and step into the room, then decided it would be better to knock first.

"Come in!" she heard Stefanie call out in Spanish. "I'm all ready."

Melinda entered the room. Stefanie, wearing a bulky, cowl-necked red sweater and gray slacks, was seated on the edge of the bed, the telephone receiver propped up to her ear, an airline ticket in her hand. A half dozen pieces of expensive tan leather luggage were lined up just inside the door.

Stefanie quickly cupped the mouthpiece with the hand holding the ticket. "I thought you were the porter, Lindy. Sit down. I'll just be a minute."

Melinda remained standing, suddenly wishing she hadn't come up to her friend's room.

A minute later, Stefanie was finished with her call, and she jumped up and rushed to the door and embraced Melinda. "I'm so glad you caught me!" she exclaimed. "I wanted to get word to you that I've got to rush back to New York and I won't be able to get to the cave this trip."

"It's all taken care of," Melinda said. She stepped back and studied her friend. "You told me last night you were supposed to leave at six this morning with the other dealers."

Stefanie laughed. "I was, but I had to change plans at the last minute. Problems in New York."

"We all have problems, Stuffy. And we all have different ways of dealing with them."

Stefanie cocked her head quizzically. "What's that—"

She was interrupted by a rapping at the door and a porter poked his head into the room. Stefanie pointed to the row of luggage, and said she'd be along in just a moment.

When the man was gone with the bags, Stefanie sat down at the foot of the bed and looked up at Melinda. "You were saying something about problems, Lindy?"

Melinda took a deep breath. "Did the insurance company ever pay off on Tony's death?"

Stefanie frowned. "I don't understand."

"Don't you, Stuffy? I asked you a simple question: did the insurance company ever pay off?"

"Of course it did. I had to take them to court, but they finally came through with a check for the full amount."

"What was the full amount, Stuffy?"

The frown darkened. "I don't think that's any business of yours, Melinda Harding!"

Melinda reached behind her and closed the door to the outer hall. Then she sat down on the edge of the second bed and looked straight at her former roommate.

"Neither of us has much time," she said, "so I'll make this short, Stuffy. You married Tony Germaine nine years ago, and two years later he disappeared while diving off the coast of Belize. Your father had gone bankrupt and killed himself, Tony's business was on the rocks, and you didn't have a dime. And yet, you were able to establish a very prosperous gallery in New York."

Stefanie stared at her. "What are you driving at, Lindy?"

"I don't like loose ends," Melinda replied, returning the stare. "Tell me, how long did it take for the insurance company to pay off?"

"I don't see that that's any of your business!"

"Two years? Three years? I know a little bit about the law, Stuffy. How long did it take?"

"A little more than four years, if you must know!"

"And how much did the insurance company pay?"

Stefanie rose to her feet and walked to the sliding door leading to the balcony. She stood there, her back to Melinda, and looked out at the lake. "I don't like what you're insinuating."

"I don't either," Melinda said. "I don't like it one bit. So I'll come straight out and say it. Stuffy, I think you and Tony faked his death in Belize so the two of you could collect on his insurance. And it wasn't just the insurance, either. You'd told Tony about the cave, about all the treasure that was there, and he helped you clean it out—bit by bit, over a period of time. You obviously liquidated some of the artifacts for cash, but used the others to set yourself up in business long before you could collect on his insurance. And everybody lived happily ever after—everybody except poor Tony." Melinda paused, then asked softly, "Why'd you kill him, Stuffy?"

Stefanie spun around, her eyes flashing. "This is absurd!"

Melinda shook her head slowly and reached into her purse and brought out the ring she had found in the cave less than six hours before. She tossed it on the bed. "It's not absurd, Stuffy. It's the truth. I found Tony's class ring in the cave. I took it from the finger of a skeleton—Tony's skeleton."

Stefanie picked up the ring. She turned it over and over, examining it. "Who else have you told about this, Lindy?"

"No one. But the Guatemalan authorities know about the cave now, and when they start poking around they'll see that Tony's remains don't belong with those of the Mayan warriors guarding the treasure. Pathologists can be quite thorough. Things like dental work will help identify him—and that will lead the authorities straight to you because you're the one who reported him drowned, you're the one who collected on his insurance." Melinda stood up. "What I don't understand, Stuffy, is why you and Tony weren't satisfied with what you stole from the cave. Why try to cheat the insurance company?"

One minute her ex-roommate had been the soul of righteous indignation. Now, though, she looked tired and considerably older than her thirty years. "Tony's ad agency had a lot of debts—a half million in unpaid media bills," she said in a voice so low that Melinda could barely hear her. "If his creditors found out he'd come into money, they would have been all over him. Not having to pay those debts, coupled with a half million dollars from a double indemnity life insurance policy, meant a net profit of one million."

"I see," Melinda nodded. "But why did you kill him, Stuffy?"

Stefanie's face was a mask of cool indifference. "You can't prove that I did."

"When I walked in here a few minutes ago, Stuffy, I couldn't prove anything—except that Tony's ring was in the cave. And now I can't even prove that, because I'm handing over to you my one bit of evidence." She paused. "I know now why you were so anxious to return the jade jaguar yourself. You didn't want me anywhere near that cave. You didn't want me to find out you'd looted it. I'll ask you one more time, Stuffy: why'd you kill Tony Germaine?"

Stefanie turned back to the balcony door and looked out. "It was an accident."

"What do you mean 'an accident'?"

"Just beyond that chamber where the treasure was stored is a steep drop. Tony went into it, exploring, on our last trip to the cave. He fell and broke his leg. I managed to drag him back up to the chamber, but I just wasn't able to move him any farther than that." She turned, and her eyes pleaded for understanding. "I *couldn't* go for help, Lindy. The police would have found out what we were doing."

"So you took the last of the treasure, then sealed up the cave and left him to die?"

Stefanie nodded.

Suddenly, Melinda was angry. She felt used, betrayed. The rage took shape on her lips, but nothing came forth.

She went to the hall door and opened it.

"Lindy! Wait!"

Melinda turned, saw Stefanie moving toward her.

"Lindy, I know it sounds awful, but there was nothing else I could do—nothing at all. Try to understand, won't you?"

"I do understand, Stefanie."

Stefanie reached out for her hands, but Melinda drew back. "You're not going to say anything about this to anyone—are you?"

"No, Stefanie, I'm not going to say anything. I don't have to say anything. The…the other evidence from the cave will speak for itself."

Stefanie looked at her imploringly. "You're still upset, Lindy. We'll get together in the States. You can fly up from Washington some weekend and we'll have a real visit. Maybe Ellen could come in from Chicago and—"

Melinda shook her head slowly. "We don't have anything more to talk about, Stefanie—not now, not ever. Goodbye, and God help you. You're absolutely pathetic!" She turned and ran from the room, not wanting Stefanie to see the tears in her eyes.

When she got down to the lobby, Chad was nowhere in sight, nor was the car in the driveway. The clerk on duty at the desk waved her over. Mr. Young, he said, had left just a minute before she came down and had arranged for a car to take her to Guatemala City. The driver was waiting outside.

"Did he say anything else?" Melinda asked, her heart heavy.

"He said to give you this," the clerk said, handing over a folded note on hotel stationery.

Melinda looked at the note. It was brief, very brief: two short words in Spanish that did the work of three in English.

But they were words that chased the tears from her eyes. Words that made her smile.

"Te quiero."

I love you.

Chapter Twelve

It had been a cold, bleak December, but the month had two redeeming qualities for Melinda. Christmas had come early that year—had come early twice, in fact.

On the fifteenth, just as she was about to leave the office for the day, a messenger brought her a sealed envelope from the Guatemalan Embassy. It was a Monday, a dreary Monday, and she was looking forward to six o'clock when she had a date to meet Peg Hodgson for a drink in Georgetown. Peg had been on extended leave ever since Melinda had returned to Washington, and Melinda wanted to sit down with her and find out more about her inquiries into Chad Young's background. To whom had she spoken? Would Peg's contacts talk to her? She had to find out more about Chad. She hadn't heard a word from him since he'd left the hotel in Panajachel. He'd simply disappeared after leaving that note.

Te quiero.

Did he mean it? Did he really mean it? Or was it just his way of saying goodbye, his way of saying that no, sorry, Melinda, I can't give you the explanations you want?

She tried to stop thinking about him. It was impossible.

She had other things to think about . . . a career, Christmas, the coming new year.

Where are you, Chad? Why haven't I heard from you?

She glanced at the embossed return address on the heavy, pale-gray vellum envelope. Guatemala. Memories. Terrible memories, and wonderful memories.

If only Chad hadn't left so abruptly. If only she'd had a chance to talk further with him, get to know him better...

She opened the envelope.

Inside was a check for fifty thousand dollars, drawn on the account of the Guatemalan Interior Ministry. The check was made out to her. There was a letter too.

My Dear Miss Harding:

You have experienced a great deal of inconvenience and personal trauma in assisting the government of Guatemala in an affair of considerable delicacy. I know that as a member of the Foreign Service, you probably are barred from accepting any sort of honorarium for your service. However, I am sure that you can find some ethical way to put the enclosed to good use.

My best personal regards, and my thanks for a job well done.

Oswaldo DeBeque

Melinda stared at the letter and at the check for a full ten minutes. Then she reached for her desk pen and endorsed the back of the check, and buzzed for her secretary.

"Make a Xerox of these—" she handed over the check and the letter to the secretary "—and send them to the deputy undersecretary. Then first thing tomorrow, go to the bank and get a money order for fifty thousand dollars. Send it to the children of a Captain Mark Cronin of the New York City Police Department. I'm sure the New York police can give you their names and address. All right?"

The secretary looked up from her notepad. "Do you want a letter to go with the money order?"

Melinda shook her head. "No, no letter. I don't think I'd quite know what to say."

That had been on Monday, the fifteenth.

Eight days later, on Tuesday, the twenty-third, Christmas came again.

It didn't start off as a special day. It started as a very ordinary day. Until she saw the newspaper.

The story was at the bottom of page one of the *Washington Post* Melinda had picked up at the bus stop, and she didn't even notice it at first. There was standing room only on the bus that snowy, blustery morning, and she wasn't even able to open the newspaper until the crowd thinned out a few blocks from her destination on C Street.

She scanned the headlines above the fold first and was pleased to see that not a single new international crisis had developed overnight. Maybe it would be a slow day at the State Department. Maybe she could even slip away from the office early and finish her last-minute shopping.

And then she saw the headline. Priceless Mayan treasures uncovered in Guatemala. Eagerly, she read the story beneath.

Armed with newly discovered evidence, archaeologists had found an immense cache of gold and jade and other antiquities near the foot of the Tolimán volcano in the Guatemalan Highlands. The riches had been hidden there almost five hundred years before by a Mayan king fleeing from his enemies in what is now northeastern Guatemala. Archaeologists had been led to the cache by information contained on a collection of glyphs, the tenth and final piece having turned up mysteriously after being missing for five centuries.

On either side of the story were two photos. The photo on the right was a group shot of government officials making the announcement. Flanking the president of Guatemala were the interior minister and Oswaldo DeBeque. The photo on the right was that of the jade jaguar, eyes gleaming, fierce as ever.

Melinda was so engrossed in the story she missed her stop and had to walk back a block to the State Department building. Showing her pass to the guard on duty in the lobby, she rode the elevator upstairs and breezed through the reception area, reading the story a second time.

"Good morning," her secretary greeted her cheerfully.

"Morning," Melinda murmured, not looking up from the paper.

She entered her office and laid the *Post* out on her desk and, eyes still glued to the front page, shrugged out of her heavy gray tweed overcoat and tossed it onto the couch against one wall. Leaning against the desk, still reading intently, she balanced herself on first one leg and then the other as she zipped off her snowboots and reached for the plastic bag in which she carried her midheeled black pumps.

She'd just finished changing her shoes when her secretary came to the door. "You've got someone waiting to see you, Miss Harding," the woman announced.

Melinda looked at the door, and beyond. There were three people in the outer office—two of them early-arriving coworkers, the third a man seated on a couch, his face hidden behind the newspaper he was reading.

"I didn't think I had any appointments until nine."

"You don't. This gentleman was in the hall, waiting, when I opened up a few minutes ago."

"Who is he?" Melinda asked, taking another look. Her visitor was still hidden behind the newspaper.

"He didn't give me his name."

Melinda frowned. "What does he want?"

"All he said was that it was time for explanations."

Her heart pounding, Melinda hurried to the outer office and stood in front of her visitor. "Chad?"

The newspaper came down, and Chad grinned up at her. "I told you I'd drop by when you least expected me."

The secretary was standing behind her desk, watching them. Melinda pointed to her private office. "Inside," she said crisply.

"Yes, ma'am," Chad said meekly, putting aside his newspaper. He draped his trench coat across his shoulder and followed her into her office.

Melinda closed the door behind them, and he took her into his arms.

"Not so fast," she said, mustering every bit of willpower she could. "You told Miss Laurentz it was time for explanations—so start explaining. Maybe you ought to start by telling me how you got into this building. You aren't supposed to be here unless you have a pass, and you can't get a pass without an appointment."

Chad reached into his jacket pocket and brought out a small black case. He opened it and displayed a State Department identity card. "Will this do?"

Melinda eyed the card dubiously. "You mean you work for this department?"

"'Fraid so, Lindy. I'm one of those faceless peons in the security office. They're always sending us out to work with other governments on investigative matters. Central America happens to be my specialty."

"I'd just about decided you were a New York City policeman!"

"I was for several years, until I switched jobs. I used to work with Mark Cronin, in fact."

Melinda leaned against her desk, arms folded against her chest. "I don't believe this. Why couldn't you have told me before?"

"I had strict orders to maintain my cover. When I left you in Panajachel, I still had some loose ends to tie up." He motioned to the open newspaper on the desk. "That was one of them. Another thing, I had to help the Guatemalans track down the Pattersons—and they led us quite a chase. I finally found them in Costa Rica. DeBeque is handling the extradition even now.''

"Were they the ones who had Dr. Lara killed?"

"No, you were right. That was Ramirez's doing. He was afraid the professor was learning too much, and was about to blow the whistle on him. In fact, it now looks like Ramirez planned all along to get rid of anybody he viewed as a threat—you, me, DeBeque, even Joel and Nicole Patterson. Then, when you confronted him there at the hacienda, he figured he'd better cut his losses and get the hell out of there. I suppose he figured he could take the glyphs and have them deciphered, then slip back into the country a few years later and recover the treasure himself.''

She looked at him admonishingly. "Couldn't you have written me—told me what you were doing? I've been worried sick.''

He shook his head. "I wanted you out of this, Lindy. The Pattersons were still running around loose, and there might have been others—buddies of Ramirez—who might have wanted to get at me through you. I just couldn't take a chance.''

"I don't believe this," Melinda sighed. "I simply don't believe this.''

He moved in close and again put his arms around her, and this time she made no attempt to push him away. "Aren't you glad to see me?''

She took a deep breath. "After all the lies you told me in Guatemala, I wasn't sure I ever wanted to see you again.'' She almost smiled when she said it. *So who's a liar now?*

Chad leaned in and kissed her softly on the side of the neck. "Never?''

"Never. At least not until I stop being annoyed with you, Chad Young.''

"And how long will that be?''

Her hands were on the back of his neck, and she raised her left wrist and squinted at her watch. "Take a deep breath and count to ten, and then—" she smiled and kissed him on the chin "—we'll discuss it."

ABOUT THE AUTHOR

Fran Earley, who comes from a newspaper family, had her first article printed at age eighteen and since then has been nominated twice for the Pulitzer Prize in journalism. Fran first developed an interest in Latin America when she was sent to Mexico on an investigative assignment for the *Denver Post*. That trip has led to a continuing interest in the area, and Fran has now traveled extensively throughout Central America. Following the completion of her second Intrigue *Ransom in Jade*, Fran visited the Guatemalan National Museum of Anthropology and saw for the first time a display that was almost identical to the treasure cave described in this book.

Books by Fran Earley
HARLEQUIN INTRIGUE
52–CANDIDATE FOR MURDER

Don't miss any of our special offers. Write to us at the following address for information on our newest releases.

Harlequin Reader Service
901 Fuhrmann Blvd., P.O. Box 1397, Buffalo, NY 14240
Canadian address: P.O. Box 603,
Fort Erie, Ont. L2A 5X3

Sarah

MAURA SEGER

Sarah wanted desperately to escape the clutches of her cruel father.
Philip needed a mother for his son, a mistress for his plantation.
It was a marriage of convenience.
Then it happened. The love they had tried to deny suddenly became a
blissful reality... only to be challenged by life's hardships and brutal
misfortunes.

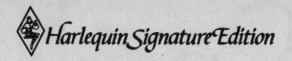
Harlequin Signature Edition

Carole Mortimer

Merlyn's Magic

She came to him from out of the storm and was drawn into his yearning arms—the tempestuous night held a magic all its own.

You've enjoyed Carole Mortimer's Harlequin Presents stories, and her previous bestseller, *Gypsy.*

Now, don't miss her latest, most exciting bestseller, *Merlyn's Magic!*

IN JULY

MERMG